EXPOSURE

ERIN VANCE

Published in Canada by Engen Books, St. John's, NL.

Library and Archives Canada Cataloguing in Publication

Title: Exposure / Erin Vance.
Names: Vance, Erin, 1992- author.
Identifiers: Canadiana (print) 20200333461 | Canadiana (ebook) 20200333496 | ISBN 9781989473825
(softcover) | ISBN 9781989473832 (PDF)
Classification: LCC PS8643.A6875 E97 2020 | DDC C813/.6—dc23

Distributed by:
Engen Books
www.engenbooks.com
submissions@engenbooks.com

First mass market paperback printing: October 2020

Cover Image: Ellen Curtis

EXPOSURE

ERIN VANCE

CONTENTS

"A photograph is a secret about a secret. The more it tells you, the less you know."

-Diane Arbus

For Miles and Michael – you may be men now, but you'll always be "the boys" to me – and for Jessica, who is far more patient with me than I deserve.

PROLOGUE: FRAMING THE SHOT

On Josh's fourteenth birthday, his dad bought him a camera – a really fancy, Nikon camera with about a dozen different options and settings and a durable strap and carrying case, which was necessary because Josh was a clumsy creature. His dad said it was for doing so well in school, but Josh thought at the time it was more of an incentive for Josh to go outside and get some fresh air.

(Now, five years later, Josh kind of suspected it was also a small bribe in preparation for him meeting his dad's new girlfriend.)

The thing was, Josh loved that camera. He discovered a new reality behind the lens, a way to see his life as if he were outside it. He could tell stories about himself without actually being present; he could shape a world to only include what he wanted; he could show people the way he saw this particular moment in time.

Photographers, after all, are trying to convey a message. They use light, shadow, angles, and framing the same way an author might use semi-colons, dialogue, metaphors, and adjectives. They want their audience to understand a truth as they see it. A good photograph can contain multitudes.

Sometimes Josh's mouth didn't work the way he wanted it to; maybe that was true of most young adults. Sometimes his brain thought and his mouth tried to catch up, and instead of a clean race, he ended up with a giant stumble and a sprained ankle. But he still had a story to tell – and this was a very important story. Adrian's story was important. Their friends' stories were important. And getting them right might make the difference between life and death.

He was responsible, then, to tell this story to the best of his ability. He would set the stage, introduce the characters, capture the way the shadows played in the background, frame the shot as perfectly as he could to ensure that the story was accurate.

...and maybe he'd add some director's commentary as well. People paid extra for the bonus features, didn't they?

Chapter One:
Introductions, Inspiration, and Off-Screen Italian

Josh lowered his camera, rested it on his knee, and sighed to himself. It was time he admitted it: he had lost his inspiration. He hadn't been able to snap a single photograph for days; not a decent one anyways. Everything was bland and unremarkable and unoriginal and all the other dozens of synonyms he could think of for boring. He might as well dump his camera in the river for all the good it was doing him.

"Not that we even have a river for me to dump you in," he grumbled, tapping the camera with his finger. "And you're too big to flush down the toilet."

The camera sat there like an uninterested cat. You won't dump me, it seemed to say. I own you. I am the reason you exist.

"Okay, now you're being creepy," Josh said, squinting at it. "And although creepy is better than boring, I still can't use you for my project." He threw his head back, resting it against the back of the bench he sat on. "I'm doooooooomed," he moaned to the sky.

The late November sun glinted back at him as a cloud slipped past it and decided to blind him – probably because he was a waste of human space. He closed his eyes against the glare and groaned, "Whyyyyyyyy…"

He sat there, waiting for the sun's glare to lessen, for a wind to blow past, for a hot chick to pass by and take pity on him, or for lightning to strike. Bam! Crash right down on his crappy head and kill him dead because what use was he if couldn't even take a damn photo.

He was going to fail his class. And then that was it: he'd be stuck in Business for the rest of his miserable, uninspired days. He'd probably turn into a zombie. Except instead of eating brains, he'd be eating numbers because he'd probably become an accountant and all he'd ever see would be purchases and accounts that didn't even belong to him.

"You aren't seriously wearing that to supper, are you?"

He sighed and raised his head, opening his eyes. Tori stood in front of him, her dark hair brushing her shoulders and an unimpressed frown turning down her lips. She wore a dark red, fall jacket that almost matched the shade of red she'd done her lips in.

Honestly, when he'd asked for a hot chick, Tori wasn't exactly the girl he had in mind. Physically attractive? Sure. But not exactly comforting in his time of need.

Josh knew that he was basically a ball made of rubber bands stretched to their limit and ready to snap. He was sulky and desperate and frayed at the edges, and he wanted to throw something, or sing some ridiculous rock ballad, or chug a too-sugary drink. None of these were activities that his ex-girlfriend-turned-English-tutor would approve of. Especially when he was supposed to be taking her out to her favourite Italian place to thank her for all the time she'd put in to ensure he went into their final exam with a low A.

He bit down what he wanted to say (You aren't seriously nagging at me already, are you?) and decided to look down at his outfit instead. Yesterday's jeans, a hoodie he'd gotten for his birthday last year, his favourite pair of runners. Typical clothes, really. He looked back up at Tori. "Uh… yes?"

She closed her eyes and took a long, deep breath. "Please tell me the hoodie is clean at least."

Of course it was. Mostly. "Yup. Sure is."

She opened her eyes just enough to glare at him. "I am buying the most expensive dessert on the menu."

He shrugged before grabbing the camera case nestled into his side. He took his time setting his camera in its proper place, making sure it wouldn't shake around, then zipped it up tight and pulled the strap over his shoulder. He stood up, looked down the couple of inches into Tori's eyes, and announced, "I'm going to fail my final project."

She didn't blink. "You're such a drama queen."

What happened next was her own doing (after all, he had been in the mood for a rock song):

"She's a killer queen, gunpowder, gelatin-"

"Drama, Josh, drama," Tori snapped, turning on her heel and marching down the path.

"-laser beam; guaranteed to blow your mind," he continued over her. He jogged to catch up to her, looked her in the eye, wagged his eyebrows once, and whispered, "Anytiiiiiime!"

She didn't look impressed, which was weird because Josh's singing voice was definitely at least halfway decent.

Was he Freddie Mercury? No, but no one was. But he was at least as good as, like, John Goodman or Billy Crystal, and they got to sing Monsters Inc.'s end-credit song.

They started walking to the bus stop – one nice thing about the University of Illinois was that it wasn't in the middle of nowhere. Admittedly it was mostly churches and parks surrounding it, but normally that appealed to Josh's artistic sensibilities. Not recently, however. Currently, nothing appealed to Josh's photo-senses.

Tori, for all that she was usually his harshest critic, was also one of the most analytical people he knew. She also liked fixing things; it was why they had started dating in the first place, and why she was still tutoring him in English even though they'd been broken up since the start of the semester. As they walked, she pointed out various places that she thought might give him some inspiration:

"How about the Arboretum?"

"You could always try the art museum."

"Sadie said there was this really cool exhibit at Spurlock Museum..."

"Well, what about horses?"

"Look, there's like a dozen churches around; there's gotta be one that has a cool structure or something—"

"Oh look. It's a tree. Why don't you take a picture of that?"

Admittedly, he could maybe have been more receptive of her ideas. But the thing was, he had tried most of those places already—

(Except for the horses. He made the mistake of mentioning the horses once to Alden, and she had gushed about them for literally an hour and that was fifty-seven minutes more than he needed.)

--and nothing had worked. There had been no spark, no sudden connection, no itch underneath his skin waiting to work its way out into the world (God, that was a gross metaphor, but it was pretty accurate). Sure, the places and buildings and people and trees had been beautiful, but nothing had been inspiring.

It was a good, long walk to the bus stop since Josh had decided to live in residence at the University of Illinois. This was partially because once you're out of Rockford, you might as well move into something as opposed to commuting, but mostly it was to get away from his family. Not that there was anything wrong with them, but, well… Josh and his dad had never really understood each other, and while Lilly was perfect, she was also twelve. Josh, however, was nineteen and he couldn't stay in that house just for her. Besides, she and Jennifer – their stepmom – got along just fine, so it wasn't a big deal for her to be there. It was a bigger deal for Josh, though. He actually remembered his mom, and as nice as Jennifer was, there was something in him that balked at the idea that she was (in a way) taking his mom's place.

So it probably wasn't completely Tori's fault that by the time they got off the bus and walked the ten minutes to the restaurant, she had thrown her arms into the air and shouted, "Oh my God! Just go to the damn cemetery for all I care!"

And Josh… paused. He stopped in the middle of the sidewalk and thought about it for a second. Something twitched inside of him, rather like a dog tilting its head to the side in interest. That was… not a terrible idea, actually.

"That's kinda creepy though, Tori," is what he said out loud.

She sighed a heavy sigh, still facing away from him. "Yeah, but you like creepy."

He shrugged. He could give her that one. "Yeah, there's that." He looked down the street; from where he stood, Tori was surrounded by the setting sun and the recently illuminated streetlights. She was a dark silhouette amongst a yellowy-orange sky and local businesses with funky writing on their windows. Last year, he would have taken a picture of her. But she had gotten sick of being in so many photos ("I'm not going to be your muse, Josh.") – and consent was sexy, even for something as simple as a picture.

Instead of dwelling on the past, he returned to the present. That brought him back to his current issue: "Tori, I'll die if I don't pass this class."

She was quiet for a few seconds before she sighed again. This time it sounded like surrender. "C'mon, drama queen. You still owe me a meal."

Mount Hope Cemetery was basically right around the corner from the University of Illinois, which was incredibly useful for Josh because all he had was a crappy Toyota Corolla if he didn't want to use the metro system. It was gray, had driven over 120,000 miles, the air conditioning didn't work, it didn't have automatic windows, and Josh pretty much hated the damn thing. This was an odd situation for Josh because generally he strove to love

– or at least politely tolerate – everything and everybody. But Cory wasn't even his; she was his friend Alden's car that he sometimes got a loan of when emergencies came up. Thankfully, although Josh could admit that he was sometimes, on occasion, more dramatic than the situation really called for, he rarely felt the urge to call something an emergency.

Especially when doing so might cause him to associate with Cory the Corolla.

Which, he was aware, was a very long, roundabout way of saying that he walked to the graveyard. It was getting rather cold now, which made sense as it was the last week of November, and there was a light dusting of snow on the ground. If Josh was feeling romantic or hell, even inspired, he might have thought something about the world being covered in sugar, but as it was Josh just huddled into his coat and tugged his hat farther over his ears. Then he shoved his hands deeper into his coat pockets and headed for the gate at the entrance of Mount Hope.

It was the kind of gate he had assumed most cemeteries would choose (was there a gate catalogue that landowners could page through, because that would be cool). It stood a good foot taller than him with twisted vertical bars roughly as thick as a quarter's circumference. There wasn't any lock that he could see, but there wasn't any handle or latch, either.

He stopped there and glared at its closed nature. Okay, so it was about 8:00pm; that didn't mean that people didn't want to visit their dearly departed! What if someone didn't get off until now, and this was their only time to visit their dead wife on their anniversary? What then?!

"Crap," he said, frowning at the gate. He kicked it – not hard but more in a way that demonstrated that he was resigned to his fate, wanting to feel the resistance of the metal vibrate through his leg and up into his spine.

But he wasn't met with resistance; instead, the gate quietly creaked open, inviting him inside.

He stood for a moment, feeling a mixture of satisfaction and disappointment that basically sunk down into his gut and made him feel kind of queasy with embarrassment. He huffed out another breath, reached out with one hand to grab the gate, and swung it gently back and forth. It creaked slightly with the motion, like an old rocking chair, and he kept it up until his stomach finally settled. He gave it a final push, making it swing wide and loud, and then crossed the threshold.

He squatted down and swung his bookbag off his shoulder, resting it on the stone path before him. He unzipped it and pulled out his flashlight and camera, then he set the former on the ground beside him and pulled the strap of the latter over his head and settled it against his chest. He closed the bag and swung it back over his shoulder, picked up the flashlight in his right hand, clicked it on, and then straightened to his full height.

He took a moment, wondering… This gate was pretty creepy, in that elegant, sinister way that villains sometimes were; like Jafar from Disney's Aladdin. Maybe it would turn out nice. Maybe this would be enough…

But no. The camera rested heavy on his chest, like a deadweight dragging him down into the depths of mediocracy, and he couldn't even bring himself to touch it.

Not yet. But maybe soon.

"Alright, inspiration," he muttered. "Come out, come out, wherever you are."

He followed the path – there was no reason not to. There were graves on either side of the path: some tall tombstones with names like Franklin Bauer and Elizabeth Mackenzie, Wife of Jonathan; some small ones with decorations like May Fitzgerald, May You Fly with Angels; Paul Cruiz, gone too soon; and some with names so faded he couldn't read them without leaving the path. While Josh wasn't the kind of person who was afraid of cemeteries – after all, everyone in them was either dead or grieving – he still didn't feel like tromping around in the dark. The very idea of it made him feel uncomfortable, like when someone says something that they obviously expect you to laugh at, but you don't think is an appropriate joke and so you stand there awkwardly wishing you could go home.

Still, although there were lights off the street nearby, the soft crescent moonlight, and the beam of his flashlight; although there were the soft thuds of his boots against the stone path, the huffs of his breath, and the soft zoom of cars; although there was the smell of dying grass and far-off gasoline, Josh didn't feel inspired. He mostly felt alone.

He came to a stop right where the path forked off in two different directions. One to the right, one to the left. "Oh boy," he said aloud. "A crossroads. A decision. Should I flip a coin?"

He shone the flashlight's beam down to the right – back towards the road. Then he shone it to the left, where he saw a string of trees all stretching their skinny arms towards the sky. He blinked and said, "Well, at least that's aesthetically pleasing, right?" He turned that way and let the light dance off the tombstones on the right and the trees on the left.

And then he swung his flashlight back, because there was someone kneeling at a grave twenty feet away.

It wasn't like he had night vision, so all he could see was a figure in dark clothes with dark hair reaching out with a hand to touch a tombstone. Josh paused, suddenly feeling super awkward because, hell, there really was someone who didn't get off work until 8:00 and came here to visit his dead wife's grave on their anniversary. What was he supposed to do now?

"You do know that light is shining right in my eyes, right?" a deep male voice said. Then the figure turned his head to face Josh. And yes, the light did shine right in his eyes.

"Shit!" Josh blurted, dropping the light down a foot, so it shone on the man's lower body. "I mean, shoot, or, hell, or, uh, oops?"

The man was still looking at him, but with the light where it was, Josh couldn't really read his facial expressions. "Did you need something?" the man said. He put one hand on his knee and used it to push himself up to his feet. He pulled his hands into his coat pockets, and only then Josh dared to raise the light up to the man's chest.

"You mean besides inspiration?" Josh answered, and then made a face at himself.

"Inspiration?" the man echoed. "In a graveyard?"

"I like creepy things," Josh said with a shrug. He took a step forward, and when the man didn't move, made another one. And then a third. "And, y'know, desperation makes a man do crazy stupid things, right?"

As he neared, he could read the man's expression, and right now, his eyebrows were raised above a deep frown. "I don't think you have any idea what real desperation is," he said.

Josh swung the flashlight in a loose circle, getting a better look at the man's face and the long stretch of the cemetery behind him. The man was younger than Josh originally thought, only about Josh's own age. He had pale skin, the kind that typically came out of winter; straight, dark hair trimmed neatly around his ears and the curve of his jaw; a sharp chin; and a thin, pointy nose.

Josh shrugged a shoulder, returning the light to the centre of the man's chest. "What is real?" he joked, grinning. When the man didn't return his grin, Josh let the (admittedly slightly manic because, c'mon, no one actually expects to meet someone in a cemetery!) grin slip off his face. He tilted his head and narrowed his eyes at the man for a moment before shrugging that same shoulder again. "But honestly, I don't think that's really fair. Is it my fault that my life has been so secure that my definition of desperation is rather tame compared to others? What is real but what you decide for yourself based on your own experiences?"

The man blinked, and his frown lessened a fraction. He lifted his chin and said, "And I suppose you want me to feel sorry for you and your tame life?"

"Uh, no." Josh swung the flashlight again; the man wasn't wearing a hat, the moron. "I want you to feel sorry for me because I have no inspiration for my final photography project. Duh," he added because sometimes he was kind of an asshole.

The man scoffed and looked away, towards the grave again. "I think I'll pass," he said dryly.

Josh rolled his eyes and shone the light on the grave. It illuminated the words Irene Burne, 1929-2004. There was a little dove between her name and her dates. Josh blinked at them and said, "I guess that's not your dead wife, huh."

There was silence, but Josh wasn't really expecting a response to that. Instead, he turned in a circle, letting the flashlight shine around the cemetery. "So, uh, what'cha doing here?"

"Walking," the man said, his voice curt. Josh turned back to face him, and the man was standing tall and taut, shoulders pulled back and face tense. "Is that a problem?"

Josh blinked and said, "Well, it's kinda creepy, but whatever floats your boat, dude."

The man relaxed slightly, but his frown stayed. "Right. Well, if you'll excuse me." And he passed by Josh, heading back the way Josh had come. As he passed, his shoulder brushed Josh's, and a shiver went down Josh's arm, making the flashlight beam waver slightly.

Josh turned, letting the light shine on the man's back as he walked rather briskly down the path. He tilted his head to one side as he watched and pursed his lips.

"Creepy," he repeated. But he lowered the beam towards the path, creating a long shadow before the man. He waited until the man turned right, back down the main path, before he turned back to the grave.

"Well, Irene, I don't know about you, but that was weird," he said. He placed the centre of the beam right on the dove, and for the first time in weeks, the camera felt like part of him again. "Kinda inspirational, though."

Chapter Two:
Alden, Advice, and Pumpkin Spice

Dr. March looked sympathetic. She really did. From what Josh knew about her, she was a sincere person, so maybe she really did feel badly for him. It would be nice for someone to pity him. Dylan had just patted him on the shoulder, Tori had punched him in the shoulder, and that creepy man had just brushed his shoulder.

Josh frowned. There was a common theme there. With so much attention on his right shoulder, he should have felt off-balanced. Maybe he actually was off-balanced and that was why he had lost his inspiration.

No, wait. That didn't fly. Alden had kicked his left leg the other night, and she had walked into his left side just yesterday. It all probably evened out in the great cosmic balance sheet.

"You know I'd like to help you," Dr. March said. She had her hands folded on the desk between them, and her eyebrows were scrunched over her glasses. "But inspiration isn't something I can really teach you. Everyone is inspired by something different."

He nodded, crossing his arms and slumping slightly in his chair. "I just. I need to do well in this course."

"You have an A- average, Josh," she said, smiling at

him. "As long as you pass either the final exam or the project, you'll pass the course. You don't even need both of them."

He shook his head and glared at the woodgrain of the desk. "I gotta do more than pass, Dr. March. If I don't get an A, my dad won't let me stay in the program."

He watched as her hands flexed before her fingers held each other – like her hands were giving each other a hug. "Oh. I didn't realize..."

Josh shrugged a shoulder, suddenly feeling that heavy weight of embarrassment on his chest, making it hard to breathe. "He makes too much to let me get student loans," he explained shortly. "He never wanted me to take Photography, but we made a deal." He swallowed. "I've, uh. If I don't ace this semester, it's Business for me."

There was quiet for a long moment, and then Dr. March said, "That would not be a good fit for you."

Josh raised his eyes. They felt hot, but his cheeks were still dry. "You're telling me."

Dr. March nodded slightly, then rubbed her forehead with a long, slender hand. "Well, you're going to have to give me something. I'll do what I can for you, but I can't just pass you without you earning it." She looked him in the eye and said, "I have to be fair to everyone, you know."

He nodded. "Yeah. Yeah, I know." He exhaled a long breath, and rolled his shoulders, forcing himself to sit up straight in his chair. "So, uh. I should just... take pictures of everything?"

Dr. March huffed out a breath. "I didn't say that. But I would take your camera with you everywhere. You never know when inspiration will strike." She shrugged her shoulders. "And don't worry about how weird it might look, or commonplace it might seem at second-glance. If it made you feel something, it will come across in the photo. I promise." Then she smiled at him, and something in his chest loosened slightly.

📷

Alden squinted at him over her mug of pumpkin spice latte.

"Your nose piercing is super noticeable when you do that," Josh said.

She lowered her mug enough to stick her tongue out at him, and then raised it again to take a sip. She laid it back onto the table with a soft, pleased sigh, and then said, "Mount Hope Cemetery."

"That's what I said." Josh drummed his fingers on his own mug of coffee. "So, uh. What do ya' think?"

She looked back at him and said, "Joshua. You're interrupting my experience."

"Right, sorry." He leaned back in his chair and looked down at his mug. He lifted it to his mouth to take a sip, placed it back on the table, then looked out the window. He watched a couple of students ride their bikes past, and then looked to his right to watch three people with caffeine addictions spend their money.

He took another sip of coffee, and listened as the girl in the next table with obvious blonde highlights told some person on the other end of the phone that, "No, I didn't kiss him; gawd, it was just a peck, baby; it didn't mean anything!"

(A peck where? What kind of affection didn't mean anything? How much money had she paid for that dye job? Josh had so many questions.)

He forced himself to stop listening to her and focused back on Alden. She had her eyes closed and seemed totally at peace with the world. It was a nice change, because Alden was a Music student and was usually running around doing a dozen things at once. She was tiny and full of life and wore the brightest clothes he'd ever seen, and over the summer she'd gotten her nose pierced and he was pretty sure she changed the stud every week.

"So. What do ya' think?"

She sighed, set her mug back onto the table and said, "He sounds interesting."

"He sounds like a creep, Alden," Josh corrected, raising his eyebrows.

Alden rocked her head back and forth, and her multitude of tiny braids waved like little snakes. Medusa herself couldn't have asked for a more hypnotizing hairstyle. "Interesting, creepy; potato, potahto."

Josh frowned at her. "Now you're being creepy."

She waved a hand. "You're the one who went to a graveyard for inspiration, man."

"Because Tori suggested it," Josh said, hearing his voice rise slightly.

Alden rolled her eyes. "Right, because we should all listen to our ex-girlfriends, right? No," she added, leaning forward. She took up most of the table when she did. "That was a no."

"I know," he said, frowning at her. "I'm not stupid."

She slapped his hand with a quick movement. "Don't

be an asshole. I was only saying that maybe Tori isn't the best person to get advice from."

Josh exhaled a grumpy breath and then rubbed at his head. Alden and Tori had never really gotten along. Probably because they both loved to boss Josh around and he could only listen to one person at a time. "Except she was totally right. He's the only interesting thing I've seen in weeks."

She sighed and curled her hands around her mug again. "Listen, Josh. You know I want to help, but this pity party has gone on long enough. I think you should find the creep-a-zoid. I mean, you were in a cemetery at night too; that makes you just as creepy as him. And creeps of a feather should flock together."

Josh paused for a moment and thought about that. "Is creep losing its meaning for you too, because it doesn't even sound like a real word to me now."

She raised her head to the ceiling and frowned in thought. "Yeah, you're right. We need a more varied vocabulary." She paused for a moment, obviously thinking some more, then shrugged. "Right, well, we can do that tomorrow. Today we find your inspirational creep."

"We?" he repeated, his lips quirking at the corners.

She shrugged her shoulders. "Well, it's either this or I actually start studying for my Psych exam. Like, yeah right, right?" She grinned at him, her teeth bright white in her lovely face, then lifted her mug and chugged the rest of her latte. She practically slammed it back onto the table, pushed herself up, grabbed her bookbag, and shouted, "We're coming for you, creep!"

Almost everyone in the small café turned to face their

small table. Alden merely faced Josh and planted her fists on her hips. Josh looked up at her – who cared if people were staring at them; Alden was cute, and he was pretty used to whispering behind his back – and held up his coffee.

"One second," he said, and then proceeded to follow Alden's example and chugged the coffee… except, halfway through, he had to stop and catch his breath. "Hot!" he gasped, choking slightly.

She sighed, grabbed his mug, ignored his cry of indignation, and tossed the rest of the drink back down her throat. She slammed that mug down on the table and said, "Can we track down the creep now?"

Josh stared at the mug, and then looked up at her. "But that was mine."

She scowled, and he couldn't tell if it was real or fake. "My offer of help ends in ten seconds."

He grabbed his coat and his bookbag and clamored to his feet. "Right! Offer accepted, tracking systems activated!"

She shook her head, sending her braids dancing again. "You loser," she said, before she grabbed his right wrist and pulled him out of the café.

When Josh knocked on Tori's door, her roommate opened it. Sadie huffed out a breath and said, "I don't even know why she bothers with you."

Josh said, "I like that shirt. Lana Del Rey is, like, a goddess, right?"

Sadie rolled her eyes in a very dramatic fashion and

said, "You wouldn't know a goddess if she tied you to a bed and-"

"Sadie Moore, don't you finish that thought!" Tori shouted from inside. Josh smiled at Sadie, closed-lipped and head slightly tilted. She narrowed her eyes at him, dark brown and deadly, and then whipped her head around, black hair coming at his face. He closed his eyes against the attack, felt her hair slap him across the face, and he winced, opening his eyes again.

Tori appeared in the doorway, bookbag slung over a shoulder and a red hat covering her head, hiding her hair from his sight. He blinked at her and where all the hair that had been a few days ago no longer was and said, "Did you cut your hair?"

"Pixie cuts are the way of the future," she said shortly. She looked over her shoulder and called, "Don't wait up, Sade!" before closing the door behind her. She turned to him and asked, "You ready? I've got the outline for the exam and all my notes on our novels."

"You are awesome," he said, grinning at her. As he turned to go back down the hall, he looked over at her and said, "Can you do me a teeny-tiny favor though?"

She sighed but kept pace with him. "Another one? Helping you study isn't enough?"

"I'll have you know that helping me study is helping you study," he countered, placing one hand on the stairwell as they stepped down to the main level. "But all that aside, it really is a super teeny-tiny favor. Like, miniscule."

She rolled her eyes, but pushed the door open, holding it for him. "Alright, let's hear it."

"If you see a kinda creepy guy who looks like he might've been in a cemetery at eight o'clock at night, let me know?"

She stopped in place, something he only realized happened when he glanced over and noticed she wasn't on his right. He stopped and turned around, looking at her looking at him. "What?"

She raised her eyebrows and said, "Do you even hear yourself? What kind of a description is that?"

"It was enough for Alden."

Tori relaxed, huffing out a breath. "Alden Gwinn is almost as much of a freak as you, Josh, of course it was enough for her."

"Don't call my friends freaks," he said simply. "I don't call your friends psychos."

"That's because Sadie would kick your ass if you did," she said with an eye roll.

"Whatever." Josh shrugged. It wasn't worth the fight, especially since she was right. Sadie Moore was an Amazon warrior. "We gonna study or what?"

"Yeah, okay," Tori said, beginning to walk again. When she reached his side, he started heading for the library again. They walked together for a few minutes, not saying anything. Josh had "Hey Ho" by the Lumineers stuck in his head, and he was biting his lip hard to keep from singing, *I belong to you, you belong to me, you're my sweetheart*. Tori never liked his tendency to sing whatever song popped into his head. Especially love songs after she'd dumped his sorry ass.

"So... you met a guy in the cemetery?" Tori asked, still walking briskly.

Josh huffed a sigh. "Yes, you were right: Josh likes creepy things and cemeteries are kind of inspiring. Thank you very much for your wisdom; we are not worthy; all hail the mighty Queen Victoria Halliday."

She eyed him out of the corner of her eye and grinned. It made his stomach swoop a little; she'd always been pretty when she'd smiled. Honestly, the thing he felt the worst about their whole break-up was that he didn't get to see that very much anymore. "I will be a benevolent ruler," she said. "So you got your photos then?"

"Uh, not exactly," Josh admitted. "I kind of blinded him with my flashlight and then called him an old man, and then we had a debate about the philosophy behind desperation…"

Tori had stopped walking and was gaping at him. "How are you such a disaster?" If it had been Alden, she would have sounded impressed. Tori just sounded baffled.

Josh shrugged in the most eloquent manner he could think of: with a lot of waving arms and exaggerated frowns.

Tori dropped her face in her hands. "What did that cemetery guy look like?" she asked, her voice a little muffled.

"Uh, tall. Taller than me, anyways. Dark hair, kinda pale. Y'know, like a guy that lurks in cemeteries."

She sighed again. "Descriptive."

He waved his hands again. "I think he was a couple of years older than us; he looked really tired, but, like, clean? His hair was neat, his clothes were clean, and he looked lonely and had really strong opinions but didn't seem used to voicing them. How's that?"

Tori narrowed her eyes at him. "Okay.... This is going to sound really crazy, but he sounds like a guy in Sadie's class."

Since Sadie was in her third year, Josh's second-year heart jumped in his chest. "Oh?"

"Yeah. She's taking this Psych course and has mentioned this guy who usually sits in the row in front of her. She says he takes really detailed notes and pays attention in class, but doesn't say anything... Except every now and again, they'll mention something, usually about trauma... And he'll suddenly start talking really articulately, y'know? She likes him, says he says some cool stuff...

"Anyways, she pointed him out to me one time, and he is tall and pale and clean..." her voice trailed off. "I think he hangs out by Washington Park."

Since that was pretty close to the Printing and Photographic Services building, he thought that was kind of weird. "Are you sure?"

She shrugged. "Pretty sure. C'mon, we might as well check it out. It's a nice day for a walk, and I can quiz you while we go."

It was a nice day, and it was a nice walk. Tori for all her gruffness was a good tutor, and since finals were starting next week, this was really nice of her. The sun kept shining, they passed people, they bickered as Tori questioned what exactly went through his brain (Josh wished he knew), and then, eventually and yet suddenly, Tori said, "There! I think that's him."

Josh looked up and felt something in his chest brake hard – because that was totally the guy! He was walking across the lawn, head low and coat sweeping around his knees. In the daylight, he looked less like a vampire-wannabe, and more like a super-stressed, slightly hipster student.

"Oh my- Dude!" Josh hollered, already striding towards the man, grabbing at his bookbag with one hand to keep it from falling off his shoulder. He walked faster, ignoring Tori's shout of, "Josh, you moron!" and called, "Irene's husband, stop right there!"

And, miraculously, the man did. He stopped, halting suddenly, body swaying with the motion, and his head snapping around like an animal's. He frowned, deep and angry, and snapped, "Seriously? That's what you're calling me?"

Josh jogged over the last few feet until he stopped an arm's reach away. He laid one hand on his chest and slumped over slightly. "Well, huff, I don't, huff, know your actual, uhhh, name," he panted.

The man stood straight and just looked down at Josh. "And there's a reason for that," he said, voice icy.

Josh peered up at him, and slowly straightened, chest still heaving slightly. "C'mon, man. Creeps of a feather should flock together."

The man raised his eyebrows, high arching things. "Excuse me?" he snapped.

Josh rolled his eyes. "Uh, we both like chilling out in cemeteries at night. Practically the definition of creep, y'know?"

"Not in my dictionary," the man retorted.

Josh grinned and pointed at him. "Ha! Funny." He dropped his hand back to his side. "Anyways, look, I need to ask you a favor."

The man pulled his head back, like a surprised snake, and frowned. "Do you even hear yourself? A favor?"

Maybe the man was friends with Tori. Hell, maybe they were twins. Whatever, not the point; the point was: "I need to take a few pictures of you. Please," he added, because he wasn't a total asshole.

The man stared at him for a long time – like, almost ten seconds. Then: "I don't understand." His frown was confused instead of angry, and he looked wary.

Josh huffed out a breath. "I've got this photography project due in five days, and everything looks stupid and awful, and you're the only interesting thing I've seen all month – and I'm totally not hitting on you, because let's face it, that would be totally creepy – and I can't fail this or my life will actually be over." He paused, took a breath, then added, "Literally."

The man's shoulders were loose now, and he had his hands in his coat pockets. "I think your definition of death and mine are, once again, very different."

Josh looked him straight in the eye and said, "My dad'll make me be an accountant if I don't pass."

The man's eyebrows shot up again, and then he ran his eyes up and down Josh's body, like he was looking at him for the first time. Then he said, "I'm trying to imagine that, but it's just not working."

Josh spread his hands wide. "RIGHT??"

The man huffed out a breath, but his lips were quirked up and he dropped his head, shaking it at the ground. He asked it, "What kind of pictures?"

Josh stopped, and then thought for a long moment.

He remembered the way the man had looked, one hand reaching for the tombstone, and he thought about the way his shadow had stretched out long and lonely before him as he walked away. He thought of the way his heart had jerked towards it, like the scene was pulling his heart on a leash. He said, "Maybe in the cemetery. Like, tomorrow afternoon, evening-ish?"

The man raised his head, and Josh saw his eyes were gray like smoke. He said, "Outside? So, no special clothes or anything?"

Josh laughed a bit at the very idea. "Like I've got a budget for costumes. Nah, dude, just like last week."

The man looked away for a second, eyes out of focus, and then he looked back. "4:30?"

Josh grinned, huge and happy and with his heart lifting high into the sky. "Yes! Yes, that'd be-- dude, you are a lifesaver; I owe you my first-born child. Or coffee. Or both."

"No one wants your kid, Josh," Tori said, punching him in his shoulder blade. He gasped in pain, bending over slightly, and she stepped around him. She offered the man an uncomfortable smile. "Sorry, I didn't know he was going to attack you like that."

The man shrugged, the motion loose and graceful. "Apology accepted; I should have built up a better defense." When Josh looked up, he saw Tori frowning at the man, eyebrows scrunched together. The man locked eyes with Josh and gave him a slight nod. "Until tomorrow, creep." Then he turned neatly on his heel and continued away, slipping past trees.

Josh straightened as Tori crossed her arms over her

chest. "He makes it sound like you're a weapon of war," she grumbled. "When you're actually just a mess."

Josh snorted and waved a hand in farewell, even though the man wasn't looking at them. "See ya' tomorrow, Mr. Burne!" he called.

The man turned his head just enough to send Josh a snarl, and Josh grinned at him, bright and happy and hopeful. He elbowed Tori gently in the side and stage-whispered, "I owe you big time, Queen Victoria."

She elbowed him back, vicious and sharp. "Damn right you do."

Chapter Three: Cemeteries, Chemistry, and Creepy Girls

When Josh wandered into Mount Hope the next day, he had his camera slung over his shoulder, and a bounce in his step. The gate creaked just as much at 4:28 as it had at 8pm, and he took some twisted sense of delight in pushing it open and closed.

Cree, crue; cree, crue; cree, crue; cree, crue; cree-

"Are you always this obnoxious?"

Josh jumped, catching himself on the gate, and stumbled slightly. He looked over his shoulder in a rather clumsy motion and blinked at the man standing behind him. The guy was frowning – already Josh could tell that was a typical expression for him – and his hands were shoved deep in his coat pockets. There was a slight gray tint to his skin though, and Josh squinted at him as soon as he saw it.

"Dude, you look awful. You okay?" He hitched the camera strap up further on his shoulder and watched as the young man's shoulders twitched.

"Fine." His eyes darted away from Josh and looked into the cemetery, his gaze going far away. "Did you have a specific area in mind?"

Josh blinked, leaned back – the man kinda screamed

Personal space, yo! – and said, "Uh, yeah. I actually wanted to take a photo of you by Irene."

His eyes slid over towards Josh's face, and his lips twitched down. "What is it with your fascination with that woman?" he snapped but started moving forward anyways.

Josh let him walk past, watched the way he hunched his shoulders and kept his head low and the slightly off-balanced way he moved. He glanced at the ground, saw the shadows long and skinny from the sun setting behind them, and grabbed his camera. He walked slowly behind the young man as he screwed off the lid over the lens and settled it in his hands. "I dunno," he said, raising the camera up to his eyes and coming to a halt. He made sure the flash wasn't on, only the automatic, and played with the focus. "I thought you were the one with the fascination; touching it and all."

The man stopped, body swaying forward slightly, and then turned to look over his shoulder. His eyes were gray in his gray skin, his collar was high and black, and there was a defensive curl of his lip and nostrils. "Now y-"

And Josh snapped the moment: the orange-red of dusk and potential and the brewing frustration of man. He lowered the camera and looked into the screen.

"-the hell?" the man snapped, and his boots were loud against the rotting leaves and concrete.

In the photo, the man looked like a hunted creature, with his shoulders hunched around his ears and his pupils reflecting the light from the lights beginning to turn on as the sun set just slightly. His expression was angry and wary – for all that he looked huge, as the close-up shot made him look broad shouldered where he wasn't, he also looked trapped.

"Daaamn," Josh drawled, flicking the shutter closed. He looked up and grinned at the man. "You and me got chemistry, baby."

The guy's fists were clenched, and his eyes were bright and narrowed. "What the hell was that?"

Josh turned the camera around and brought the screen up to the man's face. "See? That's a potential A right there!"

The man glared for a moment, and then he seemed to hold his breath as he studied the screen. Then, slowly, he deflated like a balloon. He licked his lips slightly, and said quietly, "Is that what I look like?"

Josh shrugged a shoulder. "Eh, not really. I mean, I kinda poked a sleeping bear, so of course you're gonna come across more bear-like than normal..." He brought his camera back as he spoke and slung it back over his shoulder, tucking it into his side. "Unless you mean the gray skin, in which case: yeah, dude. You look messed. Up."

The man eyes darted between Josh's camera and his face, still looking limp. He inhaled, and with it, he straightened his shoulders and stood tall again. "I didn't know about the, uh... skin thing." He paused, eyes glinting in the light and then: "Sorry."

"You getting enough sleep at night, man?" Josh asked, daring to take a step towards him. "'Cause, like, I can make this as fast as possible if ya' need to."

The man shifted his feet and said, "Yeah. That'd be good."

They stood there for another few seconds before Josh kind of rocked back and forth and said, "Soooo... We gonna go or what?"

The man shook himself like a dog. "Right."

They started walking.

Josh, never one to choose silence over a good old-fashioned conversation, said, "So, like, I realize that you totally don't know who I am besides that creepy camera guy from the cemetery. So, uh... I'm Josh. Josh Deering."

From the corner of his eye, he watched as the man nodded and said, "Adrian Cross."

Josh grinned and said, "Ooohhh. Fancy!" The man – Adrian – began to tense, and Josh scrambled to add, "No, man, it's totally cool! I mean, like, Joshua Deering is totally lame. Very, y'know. Blah. Not at all artist-material; way more... I dunno..."

"Accountant-style," Adrian filled in, raising an eyebrow and glancing over.

Josh flinched and ducked his head. He watched his sneakers stomp over leaves and followed without looking when Adrian turned to the left. He said, "Yeah. It really is."

"Thing about names though," Adrian said, sliding forward to walk in front of Josh, "is that they're chosen for you. They're really just someone else's expectations for you; you actually get to decide whether or not you care for it."

Josh stopped and stared at him. Something in his chest felt warm, like the first time his little sister said his name. He said, "Dude. You just said something nice."

Adrian stopped too, a few feet away. His face was

blank, perhaps even a little annoyed. "Don't get used to it," he said shortly, before he dropped to a squat. "Did you want me to do anything else here?"

Josh started; he hadn't realized they were back at the grave yet. "Uh, yeah! Mind reaching out towards it like you were last night?" He reached for his camera and pulled it around, taking a couple steps back and bending his knees slightly.

Adrian glanced over, and he was smirking slightly. "Made me look longing, huh?" But he obediently schooled his face and reached out to brush his fingers along the edge of the grave.

"Sorta," Josh admitted, bringing his camera up to his eye. He tried to find the focus and couldn't seem to figure out what had been so intimate about the scene the other night, intimate enough that he had felt awkward by stumbling upon it. "What were you thinking about the other night anyways?"

Adrian hummed softly. "Oh. I was just wondering why she was here. There's no one else in this area with her last name… Wondered where she came from, where her family was…" And his face seemed to soften, and his eyes unfocused, and he looked less like a wolf and more like a child. Josh remembered again that the man was likely only a little older than him; he seemed so mature in comparison to Josh's constant floundering.

"Guess I was wondering where I was going to be buried," Adrian whispered; and Josh snapped a couple photos. "If I was ever gonna get home again."

"Where is home?"

He traced his fingers over the grave; Josh shifted over

slightly so he could catch the way they brushed the dove's wing. "Flint. Michigan. You know, where they're having that water problem? But I haven't been there for… five years, I guess." A shadow seemed to pass over his face, and Josh made sure to capture it on film. Seriously, this guy attracted shadows like Hollywood attracted stars. "Don't know if I'll ever get back."

"I'm from Rockford, Illinois," Josh said, pulling out into a long shot, focusing on the shadows spreading around Adrian and Irene's grave for a few clicks. "Y'know, in case you cared."

"Home is home," Adrian said with a twist of his lips. "Everyone should care about it."

Josh lowered his camera and stared at him for a full five seconds. "Wow. You're totally, pathetically poetic, aren't you?"

Adrian turned his head, and the tips of his ears were red. "Asshole," he snapped weakly, putting his hands on his knees and pushing himself up. "That's it. I'm finished."

Josh pouted. "Aw, but we were totally bonding! Shared names, hometowns…" He examined the pictures he'd gotten; some of them were good – a couple would be really good with minor edits. "Dammit, dude. You should totally pose for me some other time."

There was silence for another moment, and then: "Are you hitting on me?"

Josh looked up, and Adrian looked totally bewildered and a little afraid. Josh, in a move that gave him the nickname "The Flash" (not really; but he'd always wanted someone to call him that, and maybe if he kept at it, someone would finally start using it), brought his camera up and took a shot of that expression. He lowered his camera, held a very solemn expression, and said, "Hey. I was being serious. You are very dramatic, and the camera loves you. This isn't about sexiness; mostly because, let's face it, you're kinda sickly looking and you totally need, like, a week's worth of sleep. And I'm not gay, but if I was, I'm not into skinny chicks, let alone dicks."

They both stared at each other for a long minute. The cars zoomed past in the distance, the wind made the branches click together, and somewhere a crow cawed.

Josh had to admit it was all very dramatic.

Finally, Adrian exhaled and said, "Thank… you?"

Josh said, "Yeah, that was pretty weird; sorry, man."

Adrian rolled his head back, stared at the sky, and quietly began to chuckle. His shoulders shook, and his lips curled a little; the sun dipped into the horizon, turning the sky a dark red, and Josh snapped another picture.

"And I thought I was crazy," Adrian said, shaking his head before he let it fall forward again. "Believe it or not, that wasn't even the weirdest thing that's happened to me this year."

Josh frowned at him and pulled his camera back to his chest. He said, very seriously because this was a serious matter, "Dude. I am so sorry. Your life must be hella freaky."

Adrian laughed again. It was a soft, quietly hopeless thing. Josh knew laughs: they usually made him want to laugh too. They were silver sparkly things, or brass rounded real things. Adrian's laugh was a whispering wind that made something inside Josh's chest ache, like when you watched some stranger get their heart broken, or when you walked away from a puppy sitting in a pet store.

"It's life, I guess. Can't change it too much." He rolled his shoulders and said, "I feel like we did this whole thing really fast."

Josh shrugged. "Photography shoots actually don't take too long. It's all the preparation beforehand that's lengthy. Pictures are speedy." And he thought, but didn't say, And I don't want to take up any more of your time. You look like you're gonna fall over. He turned on his heel and gestured down the path. "Shall we?"

Adrian rolled his eyes. "Right; now you're chivalrous." But he stepped forward, heading down the path. Josh walked at his side. "So, that wasn't too bad," he said, voice sounding weird.

Josh turned his head. "Are you feeling awkward? There's no need for awkwardness!" He slung his left arm over Adrian's shoulders. "We have bonded! You, my creepy friend, are my A-plus muse!"

"I take it back," Adrian said, shoulders hunching up to his ears. "This is bad. Very bad."

Josh laughed his loud, brass, booming laugh that exploded out of sheer happiness. And he would have kept laughing if Adrian hadn't stopped abruptly. As it was, Josh almost tripped over his feet.

"Dude, what the…?" but he trailed off as he straightened up and saw what was standing at the crossroads.

It was a very tall, skinny young woman; she had long, white hair that was blowing about in the wind, and a huge pendant that glinted in the streetlights nearby. As a complete juxtaposition (yeah, Josh was totally going to ace his English exam), she wore a light green hoodie, and skinny jeans.

Nevertheless: "As a Photography Major, I recognize that this is super symbolic and dramatic, and I don't like it." But he sure did feel the urge to photograph it.

"Josh, shut up," Adrian hissed.

She bobbed her head, hands tucked neatly into her hoodie's pouch. "Cross," she said; her voice carried well.

"Blanche," Adrian said, voice dull.

Josh straightened up, and his head swung from one creepy figure to the other. "Wait; your name is Blanche? Isn't that French for white?"

Her eyes glanced in his direction. "Yes. To both."

"Seriously, just stop talking-"

"What is that, a stage name or something?" Josh said, taking a couple of steps backwards, closer to Adrian. It was weird, because for all first impressions, Adrian was the creepier one; but they had bonded. They had shared names and hometowns, and this girl was using a stage name.

"Or something," she said easily. "You catch on fast."

Josh's shoulder brushed against Adrian's, and when Adrian bumped it back, Josh let it stay. "I'm actually a bit of a dumbass. Actually."

Her lips curled up and something inside Josh screamed, *She is so scary and kinda hot; we are so screwed!* Her eyes narrowed with her smile, and she said, "That's fairly obvious."

Something dug into Josh's left side at that moment, and Adrian hissed, "Shut. Up."

And, because Josh was a dumbass, he said, "'Kay."

And winced when Adrian pinched him again.

"What do you want, Blanche?" Adrian said, his voice a little tense, but altogether rather strong. Josh approved.

She tilted her head down and said, "You left and didn't say goodbye..."

Her lower lip jutted out in a pout, and Josh thought, This all seems like a very obvious ploy.

Adrian scoffed. "Right. We shared fencing class, not vows. Try again."

Josh turned his head towards Adrian and said, "Fencing class? You had a fenc- Ow!"

"Oh, do stop pinching him," Blanche said, pulling her hands out of her pouch and crossing them over her small chest. "I'm not actually going to hurt him."

Josh mouthed, Actually? even while Adrian said: "Then get to the point. Some of us have studying to do."

"Like me!" Josh chirped, stepping a little behind Adrian so he couldn't pinch him again. He got a very sour look sent his way over Adrian's shoulder.

"Alright, Cross," Blanche said. "I just thought you'd like a little mystery." Her lips twisted down as she added, "You sure kept to yourself in school."

"He still does," Josh assured her from behind Adrian's shoulder. Although he really could only assume this was the case, but judging by Adrian's overall everything, it was probably true. And it must have been, because this time he got a swift, bony elbow to the gut, causing him to exhale everything in his lungs all at once.

She stuck her hands back in her jacket pouch. "I wanted to know if you wanted to come with me."

"I wasn't aware you were going anywhere," Adrian

responded, shoving his hands back in his pockets.

Josh watched very carefully, still trying to catch his breath. There was obviously an ulterior message happening with their hands. Otherwise, they were just super awkward people, which would be super disappointing.

She shrugged, causing her hair to ripple like a waterfall. "Me and a few kids have decided to try our luck living on our own. I mean, they had to be preparing us for something, right? So… we decided to see for ourselves."

Adrian's shoulders went back; they almost hit Josh he was staying so close. "And what does that have to do with me? I left almost a year ago."

"We know," she said, her voice very Do I look like I'm an idiot? (she didn't; not to Josh's eyes, anyways.) "You didn't even say goodbye. We were really upset."

Adrian scoffed. "Right. I'm sure the school had an assembly and everything. Look, Blanche, we weren't friends then and we aren't friends now. What is this all about?"

She looked away, rolled her shoulders, and then looked back. She met Adrian's eyes evenly as she said, "I want you to come with us. It's not safe for us alone."

"It's not safe for anyone," Adrian retorted. "Are you seeing the state of our planet right now?"

"Are you listening to me right now?" she demanded, face twisting as she mimicked him. "I mean us. People like you and me. We need to stay together."

"Cut the mystery bullshit and say what you mean," he snapped.

"Someone is hunting us," she said flatly.

The wind whistled between them as silence fell; her hair flew like a cape, Adrian's long coat whipped at his legs, and Josh felt very awkward and confused.

"Thank you for your concern," Adrian said finally. He took a step back, and Josh had to hurriedly move backwards so he didn't get his toes squished. "But I think I'm going to take my chances. I… I'm finally finding a place here."

Josh squinted at Adrian just as Blanche's eyes darted between the two of them.

She swallowed, raised her chin, and then shrugged loosely. "Whatever," she said, tossing her head. "Thought I should offer anyways. Here." And she stepped forward, one hand slipping out of her hoodie pouch, with something inside and held out to them. "In case you change your mind."

Adrian glanced between the paper she held between her fingers and her face. He inhaled before he stepped forward enough to reach out and take the paper. He stepped back, leaving about a foot between him and Josh. "Thanks," he said quietly.

"You're welcome," she said simply. She tilted her body to the side and sent Josh a coltish smile. "Bye, Josh. Nice meeting you."

He grinned, knowing it was a little bit wobbly. "You too, Whitey."

She smiled back, let it fade when she nodded at Adrian, and then she turned to her left and walked back towards the main gate. The boys watched her go, staying very quiet.

"That was totally scary in a kind of hot way," Josh said finally.

"Sure, if you say so," Adrian bit out, turning to follow

her back down the path.

"Wait, where are you going?" Josh said, jogging to catch up.

Adrian looked over his shoulder and sent him a confused look. "Home? Unless you need more pictures?"

And even though Josh had only just met this guy, he felt a wave of relief at knowing that he wasn't going to follow after the strange girl. Instead, he grinned and said, "Well, we could always have dinner. My treat?"

Adrian looked at him evenly for a long minute before he rolled his eyes. "It's gonna be something awful like burgers, isn't it?"

But he did agree to the free supper.

Chapter Four:
Stallone, Stalking, and Strippers

"So, wait," Alden said, holding up a hand. "Her name was Blanche?"

Josh nodded, a crazy grin on his face. He knew she'd get it! "Right? I think it might be her stripper name; do you think she's a stripper?"

Alden made a face at him from over the top of her can. "Just because you want every girl to be a stripper, doesn't mean that every girl is a stripper." She took a long, loud slurp from her Mountain Dew (not Diet because she wasn't a fan). Earlier this semester, Josh had taken a few shots of her drinking because she made the *craziest* faces. Every now and again he got the itch to take more, but he already had the Mountain Dew photo.... And they were in the middle of a serious conversation.

Josh rolled his eyes. "I don't want every girl to be a stripper. I'm not a pig. I'm just saying that she said it was 'something like' a stage name." He raised a hand. "If someone sounds like a stripper and looks like a stripper, I'm gonna call them a stripper."

She huffed out a breath before taking another swallow of her drink. "Whatever, Josh. I think there's a bigger picture here than whether or not the girl was a stripper."

He turned his head and squinted at her. "Liiiiike…?"

She turned her head to face him, and a couple of her braids hit his cheek. It was cool, he was a man, he could take it. "Like, how did she know he was there? How did she find this Adrian guy at Mount Hope?"

He blinked, turned forward again, watched a man walk his dog across the road opposite them, and said, "Huh."

She nodded, lifting her can up in the air like a victory cup. "Yeah. Exactly." She drank again, and then said, "Now that is creepy."

"The whole thing was weird," Josh admitted, fingers twisting a straw wrapper into a small, white ball. "I mean, Adrian gives off these major no-touchy vibes. Like, I was pretty sure that he would have ripped my arm off if we hadn't totally bonded-"

"Uh huh," she said, nodding like this was totally normal (to be fair, Alden and Josh were made of a very similar, oddly coloured cloth).

"-but when this Blanche girl showed up, he went cold. Like, total ice," Josh finished. He squinted down at his little wrapper ball and said quietly, "And he was pretty distracted throughout all of dinner."

She huffed out a breath, puffing her cheeks out and all. "See, the problem there is that we don't know enough about this guy to know whether that was weird or normal. Maybe he's always distracted at meals."

He nodded, curling the ball into the palm of his hand before making a fist. "You're right. Some people are really weird about eating."

"Like, my mom? She always holds a napkin in one

hand, and the whole time she's chewing, she has it held up to her face."

Josh turned his head, raising his eyebrows. "But... wouldn't that just draw more attention?"

Alden shrugged before chugging the last of her Mountain Dew. "Mom's just a weird bug," she said once she was finished.

He nodded, staring ahead again. They both sat on the bench for another minute, watching a couple students go by and a wind blow a couple pieces of garbage across the lawn. Finally he said, "Think those photos are developed yet?"

"Might as well check it out," she agreed, pushing herself up on her feet.

Sometimes, Josh honestly believed in fate. Like, how could it be possible for Adrian to be sitting with his head in a book on a bench halfway between Josh's dorm room and his English class?

Fate, man. It must have been fate, because otherwise Josh was just incredibly lucky, and his life up to this point had proven how untrue that was.

"Aiiidriaaaaaaan!" he called, drawing on his inner Sylvester Stallone.

The man in question flinched in one complete movement, and then raised his head, eyes wide. For a moment, Josh wondered if his massive grin and raised arm would scare Adrian off, and judging by Adrian's posture, he wasn't entirely sure himself. But then Adrian released a breath, relaxed back into the bench, and called out, "Are you referencing something?"

Josh huffed out a laugh and jogged over, feeling his bookbag gently and repeatedly thud against his spine. He came to a stop a few inches away from Adrian and said, "You've seriously never seen Rocky?"

Adrian blinked. "It's on the To-Watch list," he admitted, lips quirking slightly. "Haven't had a lot of time recently."

Josh glanced down and reared his head back at the massive size of the textbook Adrian was reading. "Dude! What the hell?"

Adrian glanced down and drummed his fingers lightly against the pages. "Finals next week," he said, as if Josh didn't have a calendar comprised of red X's counting down the days. "Gotta keep the GPA up."

Josh nodded, pulling the strap of his bookbag up higher on his shoulder. "Parents?" He knew all about parental expectations. Seemed some days all he was doing was consistently not meeting them.

Adrian's fingers paused on the page, and then moved to close the book. He made a slight face before saying, "Scholarship, actually."

Josh inhaled sharply. "Shit, dude. That might actually be worse." When Adrian cracked a smile and huffed a small laugh, Josh grinned before nodding at the bench. "Mind if I sit?"

Adrian blinked again, and then shrugged. "Free country."

Good an answer as any. Josh set himself down next to Adrian, sliding his bookbag off his shoulder to sit at his feet. "So. Got those photos developed."

Adrian raised his eyebrows. "And?"

Josh tapped his foot against his bookbag, mulled over the best way to answer him, and then finally decided to go with brutal honesty. Mostly because, why the hell not? "You look super creepy and shadowy, and pretty damn awesome." He raised his head and grinned at Adrian.

"Just what every guy wants to hear," Adrian deadpanned. But when Josh squinted slightly at him, he saw the corners of Adrian's eyes were creased, like a hidden smile. It would have been a nice picture... But Josh figured he'd gotten all the photos he was going to get from Adrian for quite a while.

So, Josh just shrugged again and said, "Eh, it should be worth a good mark. I just gotta finish the final product for Wednesday and we should be good." He leaned over slightly, not enough to touch the man, but enough to make the next sentence matter. "Thanks, man. I appreciate it."

Adrian scoffed slightly, but his fingers tapped on his textbook cover. "Well, you don't exactly look dangerous. Just insane."

"Not like that Blanche girl, huh?"

Even though they weren't touching, they were close enough that Josh felt it when Adrian stiffened. Glancing down, he saw Adrian's hand was flat against the book cover, and the knuckles of his other hand were white. Josh pursed his lips, dug his heel into the dirt at their feet, and said, "Probably should have played that a little bit better."

"Yeah." And Adrian's voice sounded slightly strangled. "Just a bit."

Josh rolled his shoulders, leaned back into the bench,

and stared at his bookbag. "Look, man," he said after a minute. "I know it's none of my business-"

"Exactly."

"-but I can't help but be slightly concerned," he continued, ignoring Adrian's snapped response. "I mean, you are my super creepy, life-saving muse. And, like, if someone's, y'know, hunting you-"

"You don't have any idea what you're talking about," he snapped again.

"You're right," Josh agreed, nodding to himself. "I don't have a clue. I mean, how is someone hunted? Like, is the IRS after you? A girl you brutally dumped? Or is it something serious, like the FBI?"

"Josh," Adrian said, quietly. "You really should drop this."

"But, see. I can't." Josh turned his head and waited until Adrian glanced over at him too. "Because I was there when she said it, and I watched the way you reacted, and you acted like it was a serious thing. Like, you don't think she was joking. You think someone's hunting you."

Adrian looked away, down at his book, and then sighed softly. He said, "I don't know what to think. Blanche wasn't... We weren't friends. I don't know why she would search me out."

Josh crossed his arms over his chest. "So, it was a deliberate meeting."

Adrian's head turned towards him and shot him a long, dry look.

Josh shrugged back, eyes and action wide. "What? It might've been a chance meeting!"

"In a graveyard?" Adrian said, voice as dry as his

look.

Josh opened his mouth, held it for a moment, and then slumped over in defeat. "Yeah, that's what Alden said too."

Adrian's eyes narrowed. "Alden?"

"My friend. She's a Music Major. She's pretty cool, plays the fiddle." Josh glanced over at Adrian and said, "Not the girl from the other day, that's Tori."

Adrian's eyes stayed narrowed; if anything, he looked tense again. "You have a lot of friends?"

Josh shrugged. "Nah. Only a couple. Alden, and Tori, and Dylan, my roommate." He looked up at Adrian and grinned. "And now you."

There were a few seconds where Josh watched Adrian process that. The way he took that information, let it settle around his shoulders and into his eyes, and slowly relaxed – as if he wasn't entirely certain it was safe to do so. "We're friends?"

Josh rolled his eyes. "Dude, we exchanged hometowns and went through a super dramatic, creepy, and apparently deliberate incident. And I took pictures of you." He levelled a look at him. "We're bonded for life."

The wrinkles around Adrian's eyes creased slightly, and he looked away. "Right. Friends." He was silent for so long that Josh was about to lean over and ask if Adrian even wanted to be friends – it wasn't good to force friendship on a person (no meant no!) – but finally he said, "She was there for a reason."

Josh blinked a couple times, and then sat up straight when he finally understood. "That Blanche girl?"

Adrian smiled slightly. "Yeah. Her. She doesn't just

stumble upon people. She finds them."

"Dude, that sounds super ominous. Are we sure she's not a hunter?"

Adrian shook his head, and his dark hair fluttered around his face like feathers. "She's got no stomach for violence. I'm not worried about that."

Josh sat for a moment, staring at him. When Adrian didn't add anything, he said, "Alright. Then what are you worried about?"

Adrian inhaled long and slow, then he exhaled it the same way. "Why was she looking for me? What do they want with me?"

Josh squinted at him. "Um. She was trying to warn you about this hunter dude?"

Adrian shook his head again, harder this time. "No. There're lots of other people she could have warned, people she actually liked. Why me?"

Josh raised his eyebrows. "Uh, because you guys shared a fencing class?" Admittedly that was a good question, but how the hell was he supposed to know what she wanted?

There was another batch of silence; Josh was beginning to figure out that that was just going to be part of being Adrian's friend (and yes. Another friend to add onto the list!).

"There's always something to watch out for," Adrian said quietly. "No point in focusing on a rumour."

Josh frowned but decided not to say anything. There was something about the way Adrian was looking away that made him think that maybe-

"Now, if I had more information," Adrian continued (Called it, Josh thought triumphantly; I am good), "like a name, or witness, then I'd start getting worried. But an unknown possibility?" He shook his head a third time. "Not worth it." He blinked once, and then huffed out a laugh. "Not with finals around the corner, anyways."

Josh nodded, deciding that it was better to be supportive than sane in this case. It wasn't like he was a prime candidate for sanity anyways. "Right. Gotta keep your priorities in check."

Adrian turned his head and grinned a small smile. "Exactly."

Josh sighed slightly, then bumped Adrian's shoulder with his own. "So, uh. If something changes, you'll let me know, right?"

Adrian's smile flickered off. "I don't think that's a good idea," he said.

"Too bad!" Josh sang with a shrug, pushing himself up onto his feet. "I demand to stay in the know." He grabbed his bookbag and slung it over his shoulder before pointing at Adrian. "That's what friends do."

"Right," Adrian said. "And I'm sure you're an expert on friendship."

Josh paused, looked up to the sky, and frowned up at it. "I'm pretty sure I'm a shitty friend, actually. I kinda do my own thing and don't care too much if people get it. But… Lost people need other lost people, so. You're stuck with me. Dude." He cocked his head to the side and grinned.

"I'm already sick of that word, Deering," Adrian called as Josh walked away.

Josh didn't bother looking back, just sent him the middle finger.

Chapter Five: Strangers, Studying, and Shadows

Almost fifteen months ago, Josh had walked into his assigned dorm room at Lundgren Hall and introduced himself to the guy the university had decided would be his new friend. He knew that it didn't always work that way. Sometimes roommates hated each other; that's why they had forms for new room assignments. But surprisingly, Dylan Bohyer-Hart was a cool dude and they got along really well.

...Okay, so Dylan wasn't really cool. He had dirty blond hair that he didn't wash enough, average height and weight, a gruff voice, a strong defence, and a lot of pride. But he also had pretty good taste in video games, and mostly refrained from rolling his eyes at Josh's totally justified panic attacks, and had even brought Josh food that one time he'd gotten the worst flu ever, oh my God last winter. He was more into sports than Josh was (by which Josh meant that Dylan actually had favourite teams and watched games, and used to coach pee-wee soccer in his hometown (both Josh and Alden thought this was adorable)), but didn't seem to care that Josh couldn't tell if the Lakers were a hockey or football team.

Essentially, he was the closest thing to a brother Josh

had ever had, and he probably owed him his life.

"I need a beer," Dylan grunted as he entered the room.

Josh lowered his notebook onto his chest and turned his head to watch Dylan kick off his shoes. "You do? But we're not legal?"

Dylan stopped and sent him a sharp look over his shoulder. "Isn't that why man created fake IDs?"

Josh blinked at him. "I feel like fake IDs were invented for far more nefarious purposes," he mused. "Like spy stuff; James Bond, y'know? Or, like, Mission Impossible? Is Simon Pegg in one of those, or--"

"No," Dylan grunted. "I'm not getting into this with you right now."

"Fine," he answered before turning his head back so he stared at the ceiling again. He raised his book into the air and said, "I'm studying anyways. Kindly take your negative energy elsewhere."

"Loser," Dylan barked back. Josh heard him thump down onto the other bed, and the shifting of cloth. "At least that exam's done," he said after a moment.

"Day One will officially be over innnn… how many hours?"

"Five and a half."

"Damn," Josh said, squinting at his notes. "That's less time than I thought."

"Is that Math still?"

"English now." Josh closed his eyes. "I couldn't stand looking at numbers anymore."

"When's the exam?"

"Nine."

"Damn," Dylan echoed.

"Yep." Josh opened his eyes again and lowered the notebook so he could read it better.

There was silence for another few minutes while Josh struggled to read his English notes and Dylan kindly kept his big mouth shut. Then Josh closed his eyes again, let out a huge groan, and dropped his notebook. It hurt when it landed on his chest, but not as much as his brain currently did. He rubbed his hands over his eyes and said, "I cannot study anymore."

"I like that. 'Cannot'. Very English," Dylan commented. "You might just pass it."

"Yaaay," Josh droned, lying still. "That still doesn't help me with Math though."

"Yeah, you're screwed for that."

Josh huffed out a breath. "Thanks, man. Super supportive." He opened his eyes and stared at the ceiling.

"Dude, go for a walk."

Josh turned his head to look at Dylan, who was sitting on his bed, passing a tennis-sized stress ball between his hands. "Huh?"

Dylan glanced up from his hands. "Go for a walk. Clear your head. Come back and study 'til midnight, and then sleep." He looked back at his hands and tossed the ball again. "Better that than killing yourself."

"Dude, that might've been the nicest thing you've ever said to me," Josh said, actually feeling touched.

"Asshole," Dylan snapped, eyes flicking up. "I'm the best damn friend you've ever had. Now, get outta here," and he tossed his head in the direction of the door.

"The sad thing is," Josh said, forcing himself up into

a sitting position, "you're completely right." Once sitting, his eyes got blurry for a moment, and he closed them tightly. "Ugh, my eyes."

"Break time. C'mon, get your ass going. March."

"Yeah, yeah," Josh grumbled, blinking his eyes open. He twisted his body around and pushed himself up onto his feet. When the world didn't spin, he started walking, heading for the door. "Thanks."

"You're welcome."

He decided he'd just stroll around campus, maybe do the circuit. It would only take him about an hour, which would be long enough to clear his head, stretch his legs, grab something to eat, and then run back to his room and study until his brain seeped out through his ears. He wondered if such a thing was actually possible, and if so, what colour would it be? Would it be gray like brain matter and noodly, or red like blood and liquid? Or would it just run out of his nose like snot?

He shook his head at himself and tugged his hoodie closer to his neck. He really should've grabbed a jacket; that showed how brain-dead he actually was. And what a terrible person Dylan was; didn't he know that it was freezing out here?

Annnnnd… he'd left his phone in his room. Dammit, Josh. Just because you didn't know how to answer your sister's texts didn't mean that you could hide the phone underneath your pillow.

…And his camera. Hell, Josh, didn't you have any brain at all? Sure, the project might be submitted, but there would always be another one; and how was he supposed to get good enough to be a travel photographer like he wanted if he didn't practice; and how could he practice if he left his camera in his room…

He sighed as he walked, knowing that his thoughts were swirling down the toilet of mental health and he should change the subject. But he was cold and tired and exhausted, and Lilly had asked about the holiday plans and what he wanted their stepmom to make for dinner when he came home.

Stupid. Everyone was stupid. Especially Josh, but that was normal now. He was stupid for being so upset over his dad marrying Jennifer, he was stupid for trying to date Tori in the first place, and stupid for being such a crap boyfriend that she dumped his sorry ass (in fact, he really wasn't sure why they were still friends. He suspected it had something to do with the fact that he tried to be super cool about the breakup, and then told her when that Li guy wanted to ask her out, and then told her where the free condoms could be found. But that was just a guess). He was also stupid for walking around Champaign, Illionois in early December without a coat.

Just. Brilliant.

He started walking towards Washington Park, and he glanced over at the bench he'd found Adrian sitting in last week. It was Monday now, seven whole days since their last conversation. He'd seen Adrian walking around since then – and it was weird, because he wondered if Adrian had always been walking the same paths as Josh had and he'd never even noticed, and how messed up was that? – but hadn't had the chance to go over and talk to him. The last week before finals was an anarchy of stress and study, and if the size of Adrian's textbook was anything to go by (and even in his own head, that kinda sounded like a euphemism, and wow, man, you are messed up), he had a lot of stuff to cram. Probably more than Josh did, and Josh was a bundle of nerves himself.

Still. It would've been nice to stop and chat for a minute. Check up on the man. The whole graveyard thing was super weird. But kind of cool, too. Like Alden had said the other day, maybe he wouldn't have been so focused on this Adrian guy if they'd had normal interactions.

Or maybe not. Josh liked people; he had always liked people. But he rarely clicked with people. So, when he found someone that didn't give him strained smiles or too many eyerolls, he tended to get attached. Like an abused puppy or something, maybe.

Damn that Psych course from his winter semester last year; it made him go all self-analytic or something…

The footsteps behind him were getting closer.

Josh had been hearing those footsteps for a while, and something inside him (gut instinct? Spidey senses?) had instantly gone on alert. Which was stupid; it was seven o'clock on a Monday night during finals week, which meant there were students milling around everywhere. But there was something about these footsteps. Maybe it was the distinct way they sounded, or the fact that they appeared right when he passed by Adrian's bench (wow, Josh, sentiment much?), or maybe that they had stayed right behind him.

He turned a corner, deciding against walking past the Sorority Building. Tori had considered joining last year, but hadn't for some reason she never shared with him… (There had been lots of things she hadn't shared with him, now that he thought about it.) The footsteps followed. He kept going down the street, the park on his left, and glanced over his shoulder to see a shadow following him. Something in his gut tightened, and he turned sharply to focus on the street in front of him.

He wasn't stupid (although he was usually foolish). He knew what happened in horror movies when someone was followed: they were picked off in abandoned, dark areas. Since he didn't want to be caught alone, he'd better make sure he was never alone.

He actually stopped walking at these thoughts. Like, seriously, man? A horror movie? It was seven o'clock; he was only a couple of blocks away from Student Housing. It was probably just some student going for some air, just like him.

But still… There was something in him that felt distinctly uncomfortable. Better to face the person, see their face for himself, and then he'd know. Yes. He'd do that. He swallowed, rolled his shoulders, and turned around.

She was small, probably only reaching as high as his shoulder (but he wasn't about to go over to check out his estimate). She had straight black hair, and a tight black jacket, and skinny black jeans, and she looked to be of Asian descent. Tori was always telling him he shouldn't say that, that he should ask about their country of origin, but for some reason he didn't really feel like getting to know this girl.

"Hey," he called.

She had stopped walking when he'd turned around. She was fifteen feet away with her hands in her jacket pockets. "Hey," she returned.

He waited for a second, wondering what was happening. Shouldn't she be continuing on her walk? "Can I, uh, help you with anything?"

She shook her head, her lips curling up slightly. "Not any more than you already are."

And that was... weird. That was just plain freaky even. "I... don't understand," he said. "I haven't done anything?"

She shrugged, a lovely fluid motion. He kind of wanted to take a picture of the way her hair rippled in the streetlight. "Honestly, I was just enjoying the walk. The calm before the storm or something."

The what? What calm? What storm? "...The storm that is finals week?" he guessed, somehow knowing even as he spoke that that was wrong.

She was still smiling. "Sure. Why not."

Okay. He was getting a really weird feeling about this whole thing. "Are you... lost or something?"

She took a step towards him. It was a loose step, open and graceful, like the first touch of a dance. "Not lost. Just haven't found what I'm looking for yet." She took another step towards him, and her smile was easier to see now. It was... not a friendly smile. It was smug, like she was enjoying a joke at his expense. "But I think it'll turn up any time now."

Okay, that was it. This was crazy. "Okay, I have literally no idea what you're talking about."

She looked at him for a long moment, seemingly weighing something in her mind. Then she shrugged easily. "I'm looking for your friend."

And suddenly Josh understood, like when Dylan tried

to tutor him in Math, and smacked him across the face with a pillow. This was about Adrian. This was about the hunter. That Blanche girl had been right; someone was hunting Adrian. And it looked like that someone was standing right in front of him.

Because if she had been friendly, she would have introduced herself, right? Instead of stalking him in the streets like a wanna-be supervillain.

"Oh crap," he whispered, having no idea what he should do. From the ten feet between them, he saw her lips open in a dreadfully victorious grin, and her face relax. He huffed out a breath and took a step backwards. If only he could keep his stupid mouth shut.

"Well, uh, actually, I have a lot of friends," he stammered, swallowing sharply. "I'm super popular."

She tilted her head, smiling at him. "Ah, of course. That's why you're walking alone at night."

Crap. "Well, y'know, sometimes you just need a break from your adoring public, right?" He took another step backwards. Did he lace up his shoes before he left his room earlier? He glanced down quickly; nope. They were hella loose. Shit.

"I wouldn't know. People don't tend to like me." She took a step forward, still acting totally at ease. "Don't know why…"

It sounded like a lie.

"Maybe if you didn't sneak up behind people at night?" Should he run? Dammit, he should have gone right at the Sorority instead of left, then he'd be near the Police Institute. There were only streets and the park in this direction. And, shit, he'd left his phone in the room.

"Maybe. But where would I get my entertainment then?" She frowned at him, but even that seemed amused. "You look like you're thinking about running away from me."

She was pretty astute. "Well, you're kind of creepy."

Her frown turned into a pleased smile.

"Annnnd I have exams to study for?" he tried. "So, like, I should really be getting home." He took another step backwards. "So, um. Good luck finding whoever you're looking for! I hope you find him."

Except not. Go to hell, you crazy woman.

She watched him for another few seconds. "Oh, I'm pretty sure I found him. Also." She shifted her weight in a way that Josh instinctively understood as an offensive position. "I'm not finished with you yet."

"Yeeeeaahhhhh, nope. Gonna nope right out of this one." And with that, he turned on his heel towards his left and bolted down the street, heading away from campus and towards the main streets of Champaign, Illinois.

It was too bad his shoes were so loosely tied; he might have gotten farther than forty feet if he'd been more prepared. Instead, something grabbed onto his shirt and yanked him backwards.

He yelped, and his feet slipped out from beneath him, and a hand grabbed his right arm, and suddenly something – some *things* – dug into the meat of his bicep, sharp and painful and present. He cried out as the hands on his bicep and shirt spun him around, his feet stumbling to catch up with his torso; and then there was a sharp knee jammed high and sudden into his gut.

He doubled over, gasping for breath. The hand on the

back of his shirt let go, only to grab at the fabric over his chest. The sharp things in his arm released, and another hand joined the first at his chest, and then a leg swept his feet out from under him and he fell sharply to his knees, even while his torso was forced upright. His knees hit the cement with a sharp crack of bone, and he gasped again from the pain of it, head reeling.

The woman looked down at him, and her face was disgusted. "Well, that was even easier than I imagined it to be."

"Yup," Josh gasped. "I suck."

She rolled her eyes. "Once upon a time, men used to be men;" and on this last word, sharp things pierced through his hoodie and shirt, and pricked the skin underneath. "Now, well. They're just boys."

"Sorry," he gasped again, closing his eyes against a wave of pain. And then the sharp things on his chest dug in slightly, causing his eyes to open wide again.

"That's it; eyes on me," the woman said. She frowned at him and said, "You don't have any idea what you're dealing with, do you?"

"Not a clue," he admitted with another gasp.

"What a waste," she said, as if she actually pitied him. Then she released him with one hand – and when she raised her hand, Josh saw that her nails were long, like three inches long, and that the edges were glinting red in the streetlights. Blood. It was her nails stabbing him. She then grabbed the back of his head with that hand, scraping her nails against his scalp – he felt the skin open beneath them – and yanked his head back. "I'll make this quick then," she said, voice brisk.

"Make… what… quick?" he gasped, eyes suddenly watering.

"This," she said with a smirk, and released his shirt and flexed her arm-

And then cried out, sharp and surprised as her head was yanked back as if by the hair. Her grip on Josh's hair released, and he fell forward, managing to catch himself on his hands, panting, still bent over. He heard another sharp cry, and then the scrape of shoes over cement, and he forced himself to raise his head and look. And the breath left his chest again.

Adrian was standing underneath a streetlight, long coat open and two arms in front of him. One arm seemed to be balancing him almost, while the other hand was clenched tight in a fist, holding nothing. His skin looked washed out – was that because of the streetlight? – and his shadow stretched long and thin over the pathway, all the way to the woman…

…who seemed to be fighting two black tentacles that grew out of the cement path. One tentacle had a grip on her hair, while the other was dodging her random kicks. As they moved, Adrian's fisted hand moved back and forth, almost as if he was controlling them.

Josh blinked, and with the air he'd managed to collect again, wheezed out, "-the hell?"

Adrian glanced up, eyes locking with his, but as he did so, the tentacle holding the woman's hair loosened, and she wrenched her head free with a snarl. She twisted, spinning on the ground, one hand swiping at the tentacle. Slashes of light appeared like cuts in a pair of jeans, and the tentacle collapsed on itself.

Adrian winced, then raised his other hand. The other tentacle lurched forward, headed for the woman's legs. But she was too fast, and she kicked out with a sharp heel, slashing it the same way she slashed the other one. It, too, collapsed.

Adrian seemed to swear and wilt slightly, shoulders hunching.

The woman climbed to her feet and faced Adrian, her back to Josh. "That's it?" she said, panting slightly. "That's all you've got?" She paused and rolled her shoulders. "This'll be even easier than I thought."

Adrian's eyes darted between the woman and Josh. He raised his eyebrows at Josh, before looking back at the woman. "Bite me," he said, his voice winded.

Josh huffed out a laugh and pushed himself up into an upright position. His vision went fuzzy, and the back of his head felt wet, and his knees and chest were throbbing, so he waited, swaying slightly on his knees.

"And no imagination," the woman continued, taking a step forward. Adrian looked back at Josh and widened his eyes. "I thought for sure I'd have to take the boy before you came to his rescue," the woman said, taking another step.

Josh drew in a hard breath and forced himself to stand up. For a second, his vision went white with pain and dizziness, and then just went fuzzy. He bent his head forward and stared at the cement path, waiting for the blurry red dots to sharpen. Huh. He was bleeding.

"Happened to pass by," Adrian said, and he cleared his throat. "Lucky for everybody, I guess."

"For me," she said. "Not you." Josh heard the click of

her heels, and slowly raised his head. Everything throbbed to the beat of his heart. "Now, are you going to run too?" she asked Adrian.

"Not really my style," Adrian said, rolling his shoulders. He shifted his feet, getting into a better position. "Rather go down fighting."

"Admirable," she said. Then, with no warning, she pushed off her heel and shot towards him, running at full speed.

Josh opened his mouth to shout something – maybe he could be a distraction! – but Adrian set his shoulders, flattened his hands, palms up, and pushed up, like he was pushing up the sky. And his shadow, spread wide around his feet, rose up like a gas; and Adrian clenched his hands and pushed out away from his body, and the shadow turned vertical and rose up as a shield between him and the woman, who twisted her body and slammed her shoulder into the shadow.

It stopped her, but Adrian winced as if he somehow felt some of it. He grimaced, and gritted out, "Back. Off." Then he spread out his fingers, and pushed back, sending the shadow backwards.

It covered her like a thick blanket, settling around her and wrapping her up like a cocoon. She grunted and wriggled; Adrian shot towards Josh, face set into a heavy frown.

"Move!" he barked, reaching for Josh. His hand curled around Josh's right bicep, and it was cold and clammy and right where she had pierced his skin, and Josh inhaled sharply.

"Dude, my-" he began.

"Move!" Adrian repeated, and he used his grip on Josh's arm to spin him around and force him to run down the path between the streetlights and the lawn. Josh stumbled – his head was throbbing, and his chest hurt with each breath, and his knees were screaming at him – but kept pace, mostly because Adrian was pulling him along. Behind them, he heard a ripping sound, and a victorious shout: "Ha!"

"Oh shit," he gasped, stumbling slightly.

"Shut. Up," Adrian said, between pants. "Run."

Behind them, he heard the repeated click of heels against the cement pathway.

Ahead of them was another crossroad – Josh was so tired of crossroads – and Adrian led them straight through it, heading off campus and towards the city streets. The sound of her steps was getting louder, and Josh's headache was getting worse. Adrian looked over their shoulders, swore softly, and pulled Josh along faster.

Now the pathway led towards an intersection, a busy one, and traffic was heavy. The light ahead of them was red, and cars zoomed past them, and shadows zipped along at their sides.

Adrian looked to their left, and then stopped, pulling Josh around behind him. As Josh stumbled, he saw Adrian's hand reach for the shadow of the streetlight beside them and conduct it – Josh didn't really know how else to explain it; Adrian never touched the shadow, just directed it with a full body motion – towards the running woman just a few meters behind them. The shadow leapt towards her, covering her in another black cocoon. She screeched and fell to the ground, hitting it with a chorus of muted cracks and thuds, as if the shadow had muffled the sound.

"C'mon," Adrian ordered, grabbing Josh's right wrist. He turned them back around – the traffic and walkway light were green now – and pulled them across the street. As soon as they hit the sidewalk, he turned to the right and led them to a small deli. "We should be able to hide there for a bit."

He pulled the door open, pushed Josh in, and then led him to the back of the store where the salads were stored. He pushed Josh into the wall, which he hit with a bodily thump and slid down slightly, his knees giving out on him. Josh rested his head against the wall and watched Adrian through half-narrowed eyes. Adrian was panting, and in the bright light of the deli, his skin was gray and damp with sweat.

Josh felt sweaty and bloody and scraped raw. He glanced over the counter and saw a guy about his age, staring at the two of them with wide eyes.

"Um," the guy said. Josh squinted at his nametag and read, 'Matt!'. "Um. Can I help you guys?"

Adrian turned around and swallowed, suddenly looking sick. "We, uh. We…"

"Dude, you got any bacon?" Josh asked, voice rather wobbly. Both Adrian and 'Matt!' turned to look at him, wearing the same disbelieving look.

"Uh. Yeah," 'Matt!' answered after a long moment. He wore braces. Josh sympathized; he'd worn braces for two years, too. Lilly probably would too. The poor Deering genes did not include perfect teeth. "How much did you want?"

"It's finals," Josh said. "Give us, like, five pounds."

"Josh," Adrian said, and his voice was tight. "I don't have any money."

"It's on me," Josh said, waving a hand. It fell limp against his jeans. 'Matt!' had stepped away and was busy getting the bacon ready or something. "Is she there?"

Adrian turned back, and his shoulders were low and his chest still heaving. He looked like he was about to faint. "She won't come back with witnesses around," he said, his voice a whisper.

"Thank God," Josh said, closing his eyes.

There was peace for a while. Quiet except for his breathing, Adrian's breathing, the hum of the overhead lights, and then the whirl of a cutting machine. Josh wondered what those things were called; he really should learn. Details like that impressed people.

"Uh, hey?" 'Matt!' called after a minute.

Josh blinked his eyes open and forced a smile. "Yeah, dude?"

'Matt!' looked at the wall behind Josh, and then back at him. "Did you know you're bleeding?"

Josh blinked at him, and then looked towards Adrian. He was slumped over the counter by the cash register, his elbows seemingly holding up his entire weight. Josh turned back to 'Matt!' and said, "A'yup. We were, uh, skateboarding. And I crashed. So, bacon!" He forced another grin and lifted his head off the wall. His scalp felt raw and damp.

'Matt!' looked between the two of them and the five pounds of bacon in his hands. "Uh... huh," he said. He obviously didn't believe them, but just as obviously didn't think it was worth arguing about. Skateboarding, Josh? It was December. Honestly, he was kind of disgusted with himself. 'Matt!' stepped over to the cash register and looked down at the top of Adrian's head. He looked back at Josh. "And him?"

"Studying crash," Josh said, nodding twice before his vision went blurry. He closed his eyes, waited for the sudden nausea and dizziness to pass. He slowly opened his eyes again and smiled weakly at 'Matt!'.

'Matt!' watched him for another moment before ringing in the bacon. "That's $12.89," he said, eyes still darting between the two of them.

Josh pushed himself off the wall and pulled out his wallet as he limped towards the counter. He opened up the wallet, pulled out his Visa, and waved it weakly in the air. "Visa, please." He stood by Adrian and gently bumped his hip with his.

Adrian groaned, and raised his head. He blinked unfocused eyes at Josh.

"Gotta pay," Josh said.

Adrian exhaled, nodded slowly, and then stood up. He swayed slightly, and then shifted over a few inches.

Josh grabbed his bicep, holding him up, and then paid for the bacon. He grabbed the bag, gave 'Matt!' a grin, and said, "Thanks." Then he turned to Adrian and said gently, "Dude, we gotta go."

Adrian nodded and they slowly limped out of the store.

They stood in the doorway; Josh looked down the street. "I can't see her," he said, squinting. If his hands hadn't been full of Adrian's bicep and the bag of bacon, he would've raised it to his forehead like in those old pictures of lookouts.

"She's around," Adrian said, and it sounded like a promise. "But she'll keep away until we're alone again."

Josh looked across at him. "So, what's the plan?"

Adrian rolled his shoulders and stood up straight. "Campus." His voice was weary. "We'll stick to the main roads and the most used paths. I'll walk you to your dorm, and then spend the night in the library."

Josh blinked at him. "Dude, that sounds awful." The library was not a good place for shuteye; he should know.

Adrian shrugged a shoulder. It was a sluggish movement. "Better that than getting caught by her."

Josh stared out into the street for a good few seconds and mulled that one over. "Point." He inhaled, and then exhaled. Everything still hurt, but at least he wasn't dizzy anymore. "Let's go."

Chapter Six:
Of First Aid, Fractions, and Friendship

When Josh opened the door, Dylan was sitting on his bed with his laptop on his lap. He squinted at the screen, glanced down at the book beside him, and said, "That wasn't an hour, dipshit."

Josh blinked into the room and felt Adrian's presence behind him, solid in a way Josh wasn't. He glanced at the clock on the wall, saw that it was only 7:05, and thought, My entire life changed in less than thirty-five minutes. Who'd have thought?

He cleared his throat and said, "Change of plans. Too cold outside."

Dylan slowly raised his head, and as he did so, said, "Then grab a jacket and get your ass- Shit, dude, what happened?"

Josh tried to smile for Dylan's wide, horrified eyes, but it felt as weak as his knees. "You wouldn't believe me if I told you." He looked over his shoulder at Adrian and peered at his ashen face. "Man, just come in for a few minutes," he said quietly. "You look like you're gonna pass out."

Adrian simply stood there for a couple of seconds, eyes scanning the room. Josh wondered vaguely what he thought of Dylan's soccer posters, Josh's calendar of exotic places, the half-full laundry basket, and the cluttered desk they shared. He exhaled slowly and said, "Okay. But. Just for a bit."

Dylan said, "What the hell, man? What's going on?"

Josh tugged Adrian into the room. He pointed at his bed which, because they had a corner room, was tucked into the corner, on a longitude as opposed to a lateral. "Just… sit over there, okay?"

Again, Dylan was saying, "Josh, what on earth is happening? Who the hell is this guy?"

Josh glanced weakly over at Dylan and gave Adrian a gentle push towards the bed. "Dylan, Adrian. Adrian, Dylan. Best bud meet creeper friend."

"Hey," Adrian wheezed, stepping over and then collapsing on Josh's bed, a limp body in a pile of dark, sweat-soaked clothes. Josh was glad he was in the habit of making his bed.

Dylan's head whipped back and forth between the two of them before his eyes settled on Josh. "Shit, dude, you're bleeding!"

"Yeah," Josh said, slumping into their desk chair. "Yeah, I think I need, like, the first aid kit."

"Infections," Adrian mumbled, his voice mostly muffled.

"Yeah," Josh said, spinning the chair enough so the back was settled against the wall. He rested his head against the wall and closed his eyes. "Don't want infections."

There was silence for a long few moments, where Josh just tried to find the energy to move. Then: "Okay. I'll grab the first aid kit; but then you're gonna explain things – got it, Josh?"

"Dill?" Josh said, his voice surprisingly steady. "I honestly don't have an explanation to give."

Another pause and then: "Adrian, was it?"

"I don't know much either," answered Adrian's muffled voice. "Honestly."

Dylan snapped out another curse and then there were footsteps, the creak of the door, and the slam afterward.

Josh opened his eyes a crack to make sure Dylan had actually left, and then closed them again when he saw they were alone. "Do you mean you don't know much about that crazy chick, or about your shadow thing?"

There was silence for a while; Josh listened to the clock tick away the seconds. "The woman," Adrian finally answered. "I've never seen her before. And… well. The shadow thing is… Just. Part of me, I guess."

Josh exhaled and willed everything to just stop hurting for ten seconds. "Are you like a science project or something?"

"…Something like that. I guess."

"Is that why she was after you? Because you're something like a science project?"

"…Probably."

That was when the door opened again, and Josh opened his eyes. Dylan came over and placed the first aid kit on the desk next to Josh and his spinney chair. He opened it, staring into the contents, and said without looking at Josh, "Alright. Where to?"

Josh blinked and said, "You mean, where to first?"

Dylan's head snapped around and he frowned.

"There's more than one?"

Josh pushed himself into a straight-sitting position, and slowly pointed at his head. He grimaced as he did so and looked down at the red circular stain on his T-shirt, right over the centre of his chest, then glanced over to see the skinny rivers of red running down his right arm. He gathered his strength and his breath and reached behind his head to pull his shirt off. He leaned back in the chair, dropped the shirt onto the floor, and said, "Yep. Think so."

Dylan stood there for a long moment, staring at Josh's chest with wide eyes. Josh let him look until he got uncomfortable. "Dude, I kinda feel like a girl now. Please stop."

Dylan shook himself, looked away, and pulled stuff out from the first aid kit. He said, "You might want to close your eyes."

As Josh did so, he heard Adrian call out, "You're gonna have to clean it first."

Dylan snapped, "Do I look like an idiot?"

And Josh said, "Ladies, please, stop fighting over me." It was weary and weak, which was rather fitting because so was he.

There was a wet cloth touching his skin then, and he gasped because it was cold and unexpected. Dylan swore again, and said, "Sorry." But he kept at it, and then moved to Josh's arm. Then he said, "Lean forward, man. Let me look at your head."

Josh did, leaning forward until he hit Dylan's shoulder. The cloth started dabbing at the back of his head, and he whined when it hit a sensitive part. Dylan paused and said, "Just a bit more, okay?"

Josh said, "Do you think her nails were poisoned?"

Dylan froze again, cloth pressing against the back of Josh's head. He said, "These are from nails?" even while Adrian answered sleepily, "I have no idea… Hope not..."

Josh nodded into Dylan's shoulder. "Great. Guess we'll just have to wait and see."

"Guys, this is seriously freaking me out," Dylan said, and his voice was shaking a little.

"Just pour rubbing alcohol on everything," Adrian said, his voice still lazy. "I can't imagine she'd stab you so much if she was poisonous."

Josh blinked his eyes open and stared at the light pink of Dylan's shirt. It used to be white before Dylan had thrown it in a load with his red boxers. "True," he agreed. "Just soak me, man."

"Aw, hell," Dylan said, but he did shift away, thoroughly wet a cloth with rubbing alcohol, and start dabbing at Josh's head.

It hurt. Like, a whole lot. Josh might have cried a little, and whimpered too, but Dylan didn't say anything except, "Well, nothing's foaming. I don't think. Should we shave your head?"

"Not my haaaair," Josh moaned, squeezing his eyes shut.

"Should be fine," Adrian said, and his voice was clearer now. "Just make sure to get the others clean."

"If you're so smart, why don't you do this?" Dylan snapped. His voice was hard, but his hands were gentle as they pushed Josh back into the chair and started dabbing his bicep.

Josh turned his head to see that Adrian was rolled up on his side, watching the cleaning process with half-lidded eyes. He was still very gray, and he looked like he might vomit any minute. "Because I don't think I can stand up," he said, and Josh watched his hands tremble before he managed to curl them into fists.

"Aid saved me, Dill," he said quietly, wincing at the alcohol stinging his skin. "Don't be mad."

Dylan just looked at him, and then started dabbing his chest.

Adrian said, "What did you call me?" His voice sounded confused and he frowned like a small child.

Josh said, "Aid. It's a nickname. We've gone through a life-changing event, man; that means nicknames."

Adrian frowned deeper and said, "I should have left you alone."

Dylan stopped touching Josh's chest and stepped away, back to the first aid kit. Josh's chest was suddenly very cold from the water and alcohol drying on his skin, and he shivered, goose fleshing appearing on his arms. Dylan turned back with bandages and said, "Lean forward again."

Josh did so, and said, "I went after you, asshole. It's my own fault."

Adrian shook his head, still pressed into the mattress. "Blanche warned me. And I knew something like this was possible. I should have avoided you-"

"Look, dude," Dylan said, wrapping a bandage around Josh's chest. "I don't have a clue who you are, or what you're talking about, but if Deering here wants to be your friend, there's really no way to stop him." He tugged on the bandages, and Josh gasped in pain. Dylan waited a second, and then tugged again before clipping it together. "So, whatever happened, Josh isn't gonna care because he figures friends aren't friends until they go through some serious shit together."

Josh rolled his head back and said through the fog of weariness, "He's right. We're bonded for life, dude."

There was silence for a long while as Dylan wrapped Josh's bicep in another bandage. Finally, Adrian said, "I think crazy hunters go beyond the usual level of serious shit."

He wasn't wrong, but still… Josh closed his eyes. "The worse it is, the better the friend."

Adrian was waiting for him outside his math exam.

Josh faltered and then decided to just stop walking, because there was no one coming behind him. He just stood there for a moment, thinking about how it was 11:50am, and just four hours ago he'd woken up and stared at this guy sleeping on his floor. His scalp was itchy and achy, and it still hurt to breathe, and it had been a very painful math exam -- not only because he sucked at math but also because he was pretty sure his dominant arm was bleeding again.

He exhaled, inhaled, and then said, "Hey. What'cha doing here?"

Adrian shrugged from where he was leaning against the opposite wall and said, "Waiting for you. Do you have someone who can stay with you?"

Josh blinked in confusion, and scratched his left arm

(that, at least, was pain free). "Uh. Not really. Dill's got a study group, and I'm sure the girls are busy too-"

"You should invite one of them over to study," Adrian said, face intent.

Josh frowned and took a step forward. Adrian's skin was still slightly gray, and – Josh took a couple more steps toward him – his eyes were bloodshot. "Uh, you really think that's necessary?"

Adrian's lips thinned. "She won't attack you if there're witnesses."

Josh huffed out a breath. He was getting really tired of this repetition. "Alright, fine. That helps me. But what about you?"

Adrian raised his chin. "I can handle myself."

Josh rolled his eyes and turned around so he could lean on the wall beside Adrian. "Right. 'Course you can. I mean, I thought I heard her call you pathetic, but..."

They were close enough that Josh could feel Adrian tense, and then a couple seconds later wilt again. "Look, this has nothing to do with you. You should just leave while you can. It's not that hard."

Josh thought about that for a minute and stared at his shoes. He kicked the air a couple of times, making sure to scuff his heel against the floor as he did, and said, "You're right. And, like, I know we barely know each other. Hell, I know I called us friends, but we really don't know anything about each other. But... She's gonna come after me, dude. She already did once, and you came running. So... why not try again, y'know?"

Adrian didn't say anything, and when Josh glanced over, he was glaring at the ceiling.

Josh quirked a small grin and leaned over to bump his shoulder against Adrian's. "Hey. I was planning on being your friend anyways, right? So what if things got way more serious than we were expecting? It just means that we're gonna be awesome once we get through it!" He grinned at Adrian's upturned face, waited for a reaction, and then sighed when Adrian didn't change expression. "Aw, c'mon. If I wanna help you, that's my choice."

"You're just a kid," Adrian muttered, closing his eyes. "What do you know?"

Josh scowled and kicked at Adrian's calf. "I'm nineteen."

"That's a kid."

"It's old enough to vote!"

Adrian winced but didn't react otherwise. "Yeah, well, I'm twenty-three, and I say you're a kid."

"Screw you," Josh snapped, stepping away from the wall so he could fully glare at him. "I'm a target no matter what happens; there's no point in cutting me out now."

Adrian lowered his chin and opened his eyes. He looked so much older than twenty-three at that moment, all wispy dark hair, gray skin, and bloodshot gray eyes. He was too thin Josh thought suddenly, noticing the sharpness of his cheekbones, chin, and nose.

"And you think being my friend is going to make up for the rest of it?" he asked, his voice a monotone.

"I damn well hope so," Josh said, scowling at him. "Because if not, my life is even crappier than I thought it was."

Adrian huffed a small laugh, looking away. "Yeah, that would suck, huh."

Josh straightened and rubbed at his injured bicep. "Didn't even ask me how my exam went; some friend you are," he grumbled.

Adrian's eyes flashed back to his, and he said, "Dylan said that you weren't very good at math, so I didn't think I'd bother asking."

Wow. That was rude. "Dude, you can't say stuff like that! Now you've jinxed me!"

Adrian rolled his eyes and pushed himself off the wall. "You already wrote it, moron. Can't jinx what's already done. Now, c'mon; I've got an exam at one, and you've got a friend to call."

Adrian ended up dropping him off at Alden's dorm in Barton Hall, like some kind of 19th Century chaperone. He slinked off around the corner before Alden could open the door, which meant that Josh had to deal with a crazed Medusa all by himself. She grabbed him by the shirt, causing a lot of pain that he tried to deal with like a man (Okay, so he yelped, but apparently that was common enough that she wasn't startled? Rude.) shoved a pair of noise-cancelling headphones at him, and then pushed him down onto her bed before she started waltzing around the room playing her violin. It was a common enough sight that the lingering stress of the exam and Adrian's insane intensity started to slide off Josh's shoulders and he felt he could devote some time to studying.

Alden had a single room which was a necessity as a Music major, or so she claimed. Since they'd become friends, they tended to flip-flop fairly equally between hanging out at her dorm or his and Dylan's back in Barton's twin, Lundgren Hall. At least, they would until Dylan showed up, because sometimes Dylan was… weird around Alden.

Seriously, it was like he'd never been around a pretty cute girl before. (Not that Josh exactly had swarms either, but you know what he meant.)

Which was why, a couple of hours after Adrian had dropped Josh off, he was surprised by a hand roughly yanking the headphones off his head. Josh yelped (again, sue him) and raised his head to squawk at Alden and instead came face to face with Dylan.

"You know where Alden lives?" he blurted instead.

Dylan sighed a heavy thing right in Josh's face, and about five feet behind where he was kneeling, Alden made a face at Josh. "We are friends, Joshua," she informed him.

Josh looked back at Dylan. 'Since when?' he mouthed.

Dylan sent him a glare that almost (almost) distracted Josh from the tips of his ears going red, and snapped, "How's the bleeding today?"

"Bleeding?" Alden echoed, her entire body going slack with surprise.

Josh scowled at Dylan. "I don't want her involved," he whispered.

Dylan blinked an unimpressed look at him. "Since when?" he said in a normal voice. "Alden, any chance you can pass me my bookbag?"

"Sure." She grabbed it from the floor and stepped over to hover over Dylan's shoulder. Josh noticed that her violin was resting on her desk. She glanced at Josh. "What does he mean by bleeding?"

Josh sent her a queasy smile. "Uh, you know. Artists bleeding for their, uh, work and, um. My final project?"

"The one you submitted a few days ago?" she countered, crossing her arms over her chest. She turned her head. "Dylan, why is Joshua bleeding?"

"Came home with it last night after going for a walk." By now, Dylan had his bag open and a fresh roll of bandages in his hands. "Come on, shirt off."

Josh leaned back, pressing his back against the wall. "This is a girls only dorm, dude."

Dylan shrugged. "Fine. Bleed to death for all I care." He turned, sliding off his knees and falling onto his butt. He looked up at Alden. "Apparently him and some guy named Adrian fell into trouble."

"Wait, the cemetery guy?" Alden shot Josh a hard look before looking back at Dylan. Slowly, she lowered herself to sit on the floor just a couple of feet away from him and leaned into his face. "Tell me everything."

It was a strange thing, to be so horrified by what was happening but also so crazy amused by Dylan's dawning realization of what he'd started. Normally Josh tried to help Dylan out with his ridiculous crush on Alden (ridiculous because his method of courtship was mostly snapping one-word answers and avoiding her eyes, not because Alden wasn't worth it. Alden was a queen) by keeping the conversation going, but he also really didn't want Alden involved.

Dylan sent Josh a very dirty look, swallowed hard against a rising blush, and then started talking. And he was actually honest, for all that he didn't know much. Josh listened for thirty seconds before he grabbed the headphones that Dylan had dropped on Alden's bed minutes earlier and shoved them back onto his head. Maybe he couldn't stop this, but he could ignore it. And ignorance was bliss, just like that song said.

He thought it was a song. It was a song, right?

Minutes later, someone tugged on his ankle. Josh looked up and saw Dylan scowling at him. Alden had gotten to her feet and was running one hand over her violin while the other was pressed against her face. Josh slid the headphones down to rest against his neck and said, "Dude, did you make her cry?"

"Shut up, Josh," Alden said in a thick voice.

"C'mon, man," Dylan said, his voice calm. "Shirt off. I wanna check those cuts. And then we can all just hang out until Adrian shows up, okay?"

"How do you know he's coming over?" Josh asked carefully.

"Because we exchanged numbers after you left for your exam. Now, c'mon. Off the bed; that'll look super bad if the RA comes by."

📷

When someone knocked on the door at 3:20, all three of their heads rose and stared at it. Josh glanced over at Alden, who looked back at Dylan. Dylan shot her a nod and got to his feet. Josh thought, Sheesh, when did I get a pair of guard dogs?

Dylan went to open the door.

He swung it wide, and Adrian flinched back on the

other side. Josh watched as Adrian's eyes flicked from Dylan to Josh where he had stayed on the floor. Josh gave him a grin and a wave with his left hand. "Hey! How'd the exam go?"

Adrian inhaled, and his whole body moved with it. It was kind of cool actually. "I survived, if that's what you mean." He looked back at Dylan and said, "Hello."

"Hey," Dylan said. He stepped aside. "We gotta talk."

Adrian's eyes went back to Josh, who shrugged, feeling guilt sink super heavy in his gut. "They saw the scratches. But I didn't say anything."

Adrian gave another full-body inhale and stepped inside. Dylan closed the door behind them and leaned against it, arms crossed over his chest. Adrian looked over towards Alden and said, "Hey."

"Hey," she said, and she closed her book and folded her hands on top of it. "Adrian, right?"

"Yes. Alden, right?"

"Mmhm," she hummed. "Adrian, why is my Joshua hurt?"

Adrian's eyes darted over to Josh, and his eyebrows rose high on his forehead. Josh shrugged and said, "I had no say in this sudden possessive streak, dude."

"He's my friend, and the only Josh in my life," Alden said. "That makes him my Joshua. Duh. Now, to return to my question."

Adrian looked back and forth between the two of them, and then slid his hands into his coat pockets. "He got hurt because of me."

"Thought you saved him," Dylan countered, pushing himself off the door and walking over to the bed Josh was leaning against. He slid onto the bed and leaned back against the wall, stretching his legs out so his feet were inches away from Josh's head.

Josh leaned over slightly, nose wrinkling. "Dude, ew, feet! But yes," he added, looking back at Alden. "He did save me."

Adrian rolled his shoulders and said, "Okay, yes. I saved you."

Josh grinned a small grin. "See? Hero."

Adrian scoffed and looked away.

"Okay. Fine," Alden sighed. "Adrian, are you in trouble?"

Adrian's head snapped back to her and he said "Huh?" with incredible intelligence.

Alden scowled – which was such a cute expression on her itty, bitty face. "Are. You. In. Trouble?"

Adrian continued to look blankly at her, so Josh considered the last week and answered for him: "Yeah. He's in a whack of trouble."

"Great. So much for an easy week," Dylan sighed.

Alden sighed and unfolded her hands, leaning back in her desk chair and propping her chin on one fist. "Alright, Adrian, I'm gonna tell you what I told Tori when we met her." She frowned and then said, "Actually, it's gonna be a bit different because, y'know, of the situation, but I think our stance is the same."

Dylan said behind Josh, "How'd I get roped into this?"

His feet wiggled by Josh's face and Josh whined, "Duuuude. Feeeeeeet."

"You see," Alden said, sitting back up straight in her chair, "Josh is our friend. And, well, people think I'm weird, so I don't have a lot of friends, and Dylan is a jerk, so he doesn't either—"

"Do too," Dylan snapped. "I hang out with loads of people!"

Alden rolled her eyes. "Dylan doesn't have a lot of real friends," she corrected. "Josh, on the other hand, only believes in real friends. He has some acquaintances—"

"I do?" Josh asked, deciding to put a hand on Dylan's feet to push them away from his face.

"-tends to cling. Like a loyal puppy," Alden finished, speaking over him.

"A dumb puppy," Dylan added, pulling one foot out of Josh's grasp so he could place the arch of his foot on the back of Josh's head. It was rather gentle though; unlike the shove he'd usually give him, which rather touched Josh because it was still super tender back there.

That didn't stop him from whining. "Gerroff me, asshole!"

"Which means that whoever Josh decides to befriend, we have to befriend," Alden was saying. Adrian was watching her with a slight frown on his face and a crease between his eyebrows. "So. Adrian. Dylan and I are willing to give you the benefit of the doubt unless you do something to hurt Josh. We are now friends on a trial basis." She suddenly grinned a quirky smile. "Kind of like a three-month probation at a new job."

Adrian stared at her for a long time, long enough that Josh actually turned around and punched Dylan in his lower leg so that he swore and kicked Josh's left shoulder, and Josh tried to grab Dylan's ankle again.

"Just like that?" Adrian said, his voice was completely bewildered.

"Yeah. Just like that," Alden said, voice calm.

"You forget, dude, I saw you last night," Dylan said, still trying to dodge Josh's grabby hands. "You looked just as bad as Josh did. Whatever happened, you were caught in the middle too."

"But you don't even know me!" Adrian said, his voice louder than Josh had ever heard him.

Josh paused, turned around, and said, "Yeah, so?"

Alden had a funny look on her face. "You tolerate Josh and let him take pictures of you. You're trying to keep him safe and you look fairly intelligent, if creepy." She rolled her eyes suddenly. "Plus, Josh was in that crazy sooky state for days, and the fact that you shook him out of it is enough by itself to give you a try."

"Yes," Dylan said, prodding Josh's shoulder again. "That."

Adrian still had that angrily confused look on his face, and he turned to look at Josh. "Are you listening to this?"

Josh grinned and reached out behind him on a whim; he caught Dylan's foot, and his grin grew when Dylan swore. "I pick good friends, don't I?"

Adrian's mouth was open just a little, and his skin was still rather gray, and his hands were trembling a little, and he looked really, well, conflicted. "I can't believe this," he said, finally closing his eyes.

"Believe it, man," Josh said, giving Dylan's foot a punch before he released it and pushed himself up onto his feet. He stepped over to Adrian and put a hand on his shoulder. "Mis amigos son tus amigos."

"That was crappy Spanish," Dylan said.

"No one asked you," Josh snapped back. "Now, I want some grub and answers. You down?"

Adrian frowned and said, "Now?" His voice was still strangled, like his confusion was blocking his ability to speak properly.

Josh shrugged. "Why not? I haven't eaten anything today and I'm starved." As if on cue, his stomach grumbled. He looked down at it with a fond smile and thought, What a good stomach.

Adrian closed his eyes and sighed. "Yeah. Sure. Pizza good?"

Josh grinned. "Pizza's great." He turned slightly to Alden and said, "You cool if we go?"

She picked a small ball of paper off her desk and flicked it at him. It bounced off his injured arm, and he watched it fall to the floor, feeling something like betrayal lick at his edges. "Yeah, moron. We're cool. Just..." and she frowned, glancing over at Dylan before looking back at Josh. "Just be careful, okay?"

Josh saluted, swore when his arm yelped in protest, and then grumbled, "Why'd it have to be my right arm?" He inhaled, drawing on his strength, and grinned at Adrian. "Food?"

"Okay," Adrian said, picking at a piece of pepperoni. "First things first: I'm not the only special person out there."

Josh swallowed his bite of pizza and said, "Is that what

we're going with? 'Special person'?" He used his left hand to make air quotes because his right hand was full of pizza and he wasn't joking about the starving thing.

Adrian merely looked at him. "You've got a better phrase in mind?"

Josh thought for a minute, shook his head and took another bite of pizza.

"Didn't think so," Adrian said, sighing a bit. "So. There's, um, actually a lot of us. Like, enough that there was a school."

"Dude," Josh said, mouth still full. "This is totally copyrighted—"

Adrian shook his head. "No, it... Port Haven didn't really teach us anything about our... abilities. It was just a place for us to stay safe. I mean, we did practice and explore our potentials, but... It wasn't a recruitment drive or anything."

Josh reached for his Orange Crush and took a loud slurp before nodding at Adrian to continue.

"Right," Adrian said, sighing again. "So. I went to Port Haven when I was eighteen. That's where I met Blanche."

"Whoa, wait," Josh said, lowering his pizza. "You mean Blanche is her real name?"

Adrian glared at him. "No. It's a nickname. Her last name is Blanchard, and she constantly dyes her hair-"

"You mean that's fake, too?"

"-kids called her Blanche. I don't know her real name."

Josh paused and looked down at his half-eaten pizza slice. "I almost feel sorry for her," he said, then he took another large bite.

Adrian rolled his eyes. "Anyways. Blanche liked it at Port Haven and she was still there when I left. That's why I was so surprised to see her last week; I thought she was still in California."

"Dude, you lived in California?" Josh said, after swallowing.

Adrian's lips thinned. "Yeah. Why?"

Josh waved a hand at all of Adrian's self, ignoring the twinge of pain from his arm. "Dude, you're so pale! Like, you're gray!"

Adrian looked down at his pizza and picked another pepperoni piece off. "Side-effect of the shadow thing," he said before popping it in his mouth.

"Oh." Josh finished off his slice of pizza, then grabbed another one. "Why are you telling me this?"

Adrian reached and played with the straw of his Pepsi. "She said someone was hunting us. Blanche was still at the school when I left. What if 'us' meant 'students?'"

Josh swallowed his latest bite. "You mean, there might be hunters going after Port Haven students?"

Adrian nodded with his eyes still focused on his straw. "Maybe. Yeah. Except, I can't figure out how they'd find us."

Josh blinked and said, "Is Port Haven a secret?"

"Yeah," Adrian said. "I mean, it's not a deadly secret, but it's not known either. Normal people don't go there." He paused. "At least... not a lot of them. There's enough. Just enough that you could trick yourself into thinking it was a normal school."

Josh rubbed beneath his nose. "This is getting weird."

"My entire life has been weird," Adrian admitted, pulling his glass over to him. "This is just violent."

Josh nodded slowly. "So. Um. Now what are we gonna do?"

Adrian frowned and took a sip. "We can't really do anything until we get rid of that Woman." (Josh kinda smiled a bit when he heard the capital letter of her title.) "And I want some answers."

"From Blanche?" Josh said, already knowing the answer.

Adrian glanced over at him. "From the Woman."

Josh frowned at him. "You totally don't seem like the kind of guy who'd be willing to walk into a trap."

Adrian shrugged. "We're already trapped, Deering. Now it's just a matter of fighting our way out."

Josh stared at him for a while, watched him pick at his pizza, and felt his body throb where the Woman had stabbed him. "I'm not a very good sidekick."

"I know," Adrian said softly. "And I'm a crappy hero." He grabbed his drink and took a long swallow from it, ignoring when the straw fell against his cheek. He lowered the glass. "But we're all we've got."

"We're gonna die," Josh said.

And Adrian said, "Maybe. But at least we won't have to write our exams then."

It was a bad joke; Josh shouldn't have laughed, he was nineteen and had years ahead of him, but-- "Well. At least you're thinking positively." He looked away, out of the window. The sun was almost finished setting, and the atmosphere was that perfect hush of almost-winter. "Mind if I take a few pictures then before I die?"

Adrian's lips curled slightly. "Yeah, that's fine. Just not of me."

Josh nodded. "Terms accepted."

Chapter Seven:
Of Blankets, Bookbags, and Bargains

"Wait, so you've got two exams today?"

Adrian closed his eyes. "Do you really have to repeat everything I say? Yes, I have two exams today."

Alden said, "That's almost as bad as having an exam on a Saturday." She paused, then added, "Like me."

"Poor baby," Dylan mocked, wincing a second after when Alden punched him in the shoulder. "Ow, woman!"

"Don't call me 'woman'!" she snapped.

"So, should I, like, just hide in my room all day?" Josh asked, picking out a chip. Mmm, BBQ.

Adrian opened his eyes to glare at him. "Well, that'd be the smart thing to do." His tone very clearly said exactly what Dylan quipped a second later: "But Josh isn't very smart."

Josh scowled at Dylan. "No one asked you, asshole," then he turned back to Adrian. "Should we meet up after your exams are done then, or something?"

Alden grabbed her own chip. Josh let her because he was pretty sure she didn't eat much during finals week. "You know, I'd still love to know what's going on."

"Ignorance is bliss," Adrian retorted, glancing at her.

(And ha! That's what Josh had said! He was totally smarter than they all gave him credit for.) "I really shouldn't even be talking to you."

"She can't exactly go after all of us," Josh said, popping a chip into his mouth. "I mean, the more people she goes after, the more attention she draws, right?"

When all three of them turned to look at him, disbelief written all over their faces, Josh said, "What?"

"That was… actually true," Adrian answered, frowning at him.

Josh glared back. Hey! He was smart! Maybe not book-smart, and maybe his social-skills were lacking because he lacked a brain-to-mouth filter, but he was observant! He had talent! He had skills! He had super crummy friends, apparently, but whatever, man. "You suck," he said, summing up all of his feelings.

Adrian frowned deeper, but his eyebrows creased the opposite way than his grumpy face, and Josh wondered if maybe that was the face Adrian made when he wanted to apologize. "I'll come by after my exam," he said.

"Or. I could meet you somewhere," Josh suggested, sending him a grin.

"I thought we just agreed you were gonna hide," Dylan said, reaching over to steal a chip.

"Hey! My chips!" Josh snapped, pulling away and pulling at his side. He winced at the sudden flare of pain and pressed a hand against his chest.

"Dumbass," Dylan sighed, knocking his foot against Josh's gently under the table in a wordless apology.

Josh sighed and offered him the bag. "You just had to ask," he grumbled.

Alden clapped her hands twice, her bracelet knocking against her other wrist. "Alright, boys, playtime's over. This is serious." She pointed at Adrian. "You pick him up after your exam and then you guys can do… whatever secret thing you're gonna do." She frowned. "If we don't hear from you by 8:30, we're gonna come after you. Got it?"

"Why do you keep saying 'we'?" Dylan asked, picking out a chip.

"Because I may have a five-pound purse, but you're the ex-soccer coach," Alden answered, glancing over at him. "And you know first aid."

Dylan frowned and cracked his chip in half.

Josh thought for a minute about questioning whether coaching pee-wee soccer during summer camps counted as being an 'ex-soccer coach,' but ultimately decided it wasn't worth the energy. Instead he looked over at Adrian. "Well. Okay. Uh… Good luck?"

Adrian actually cracked a smile. "It's Biology and Psych; should be a breeze."

Josh made a face; from the corner of his eye, he watched Alden make a very similar face. "Dude. That sounds awful."

Adrian shrugged. "I like it. It all makes sense to me." He pushed himself off from the table. "I should be around by seven, okay?"

Josh said, "Okay. Well, uh. See ya'."

Adrian gave him a small smile and a salute, before nodding at Alden and Dylan.

Josh watched him walk off and ignored the ache that was most of his body. "How's this trial friendship going?"

he asked without looking at his friends.

"I think I like him," Alden said. "He seems sensible. You need sensible."

"It'll be nice to hang out with someone that isn't a total hipster," Dylan added.

Josh turned his head and gaped at him. "I am not a hipster!"

Dylan looked pointedly at the camera that sat securely in its bag at Josh's hip.

Josh felt a wave of betrayal. He knew without knowing that his camera felt the same way, tarred with the same insulting brush. "I'm not a hipster," he grumbled. "I'm an artist."

"Okay, boomer," Dylan agreed.

"But will she actually come after us tonight?" Josh asked, keeping his voice low. They'd already been walking around for an hour, and nothing had happened. Josh didn't even have a chance to take pictures since Adrian had pointed out that hunting a violent person might lead to damages to expensive equipment, convincing him to leave the camera in his dorm room. Adrian's exams had gone well, Josh's day had been boring, enough that he'd told Adrian the stories of how he became friends with Alden and Dylan just to pass the time. Adrian had explained how he lived off campus in his own apartment and was majoring in Health Studies until he figured out what specialty he wanted.

Adrian shrugged his shoulders. "She's already failed once, and she didn't get a chance last night. I can't imagine her just sitting around waiting for us."

Josh nodded. "Yeah, she's not exactly subtle. What with the whole stalker thing."

"None of us were subtle," Adrian corrected. He nodded to the right, and they took that path. "It's amazing that no one else saw."

"Or," Josh said, raising his pointer finger – and ow, that hurt his arm – "maybe they saw and didn't care."

Adrian glanced at him, frowning again. "You mean, they were high," he guessed, his voice very dry.

"Or they thought they were hallucinating," Josh suggested. "It is Finals Week. Exhaustion will do things."

Adrian looked at him for a long moment, and Josh wondered what exactly he was thinking. Then he exhaled through his nose and said, "I doubt it, Deering. I really doubt it."

"Well, what else could it be?" Josh asked, waving his left hand – because it was safe to do so. "Drugs or stress, man. It's gotta be one or the other."

Adrian shook his head. "No, Deering. It doesn't. I just think no one noticed."

"Well, how'd you find me then?" Josh asked, bumping his left shoulder against Adrian's. "If it was such an unnoticeable thing?"

Adrian frowned, but it was a thoughtful thing and not angry. "I usually hang out in that area. And I guess I'm used to being on the watch for suspicious activity."

Josh blinked. "Wait. You thought me talking to a girl was suspicious?!"

Adrian's mouth quirked. "Sure, let's go with that."

"Are you saying I don't got game?"

Adrian turned just enough to raise an eyebrow at him. "Do you hear yourself? Anyone who says that definitely does not have game."

"Heeeey!" The word cracked in the middle, which probably didn't help Josh's case at all. "I'll have you know that I totally had a girlfriend."

"Congratulations." It was as dry as a bag of chips.

"Hey, man-" Josh began, but he was interrupted by a couple of very slow claps.

Josh stopped and stared at Adrian, who was equally frozen in place. Any actual anger he felt towards Adrian – and let's face it, it was more annoyance than anything, and probably stress talking (and maybe there was a part of him that was impressed with Adrian's trash talk) – suddenly turned cold with fear, and he took a very slow breath in. Keeping his eyes on Adrian, he thought, You still with me, bro? And Adrian nodded his head very slightly.

Josh exhaled. "Are you seriously slow clapping us? Because that's just rude."

"I had to get your attention somehow," the Woman said – and it was the Woman, he knew her voice; he wondered if he would always know her voice. "After all, that whole thing was rather pathetic."

Josh swallowed and turned to his left, facing the voice. "Well, like I told you earlier, I'm a super pathetic person."

The Woman slid her small (vicious, evil, sharp, and please God not poisonous) hands into her skinny jeans. She tilted her head to one side as she stood in the spotlight and smiled slightly. "I can't help but agree," she said – and it was her sugary sweet voice that offended Josh more than he might have otherwise been. Her dark eyes glanced off Josh, and her smile grew slightly. "Hello."

Josh felt Adrian shift beside him, shoulder brushing shoulder. "Hey," Adrian said, his voice low. "Don't suppose you know the answer?"

She blinked and straightened her posture. "Answer?" she echoed.

"How you've managed to trap us," Adrian said, pointedly looking around. Josh blinked and finally noticed that somehow they were behind the library – and Josh had never been here before of his own volition. "And kept everyone's eyes off of us."

The Woman's face cleared slightly, and her eyes widened. "Oh. That." She ducked her head slightly and grinned a small, feral grin. "How else am I supposed to hide the bodies?"

Josh frowned, suddenly terrified and confused and frozen in place. "Wait, is that why you're here? To kill us?"

She glanced over at him, head still ducked slightly. It made her look young and innocent and almost hot. Which was possibly scarier than her nails. "Oh no. Well actually, I don't have orders concerning you. Dead, alive, mutilated, scarred beyond belief… Whatever happens, happens. But him…" And she raised her head to look straight at Adrian, suddenly all playfulness falling off like a cheap cloak. "He's coming with me."

"Like hell," Adrian said immediately.

Josh couldn't find words as his brain was still stuck on whatever happens, happens. God, that was terrifying. Random violence was so much worse than purposeful violence. It wasn't personal, just uncontrolled chance and a desire to have a good time.

She smiled slightly. "That's what they all say." She rolled her shoulders and shifted her feet.

"All?" Adrian echoed.

Josh watched the Woman position herself, pushing off one heel. He grabbed Adrian's wrist and yanked him to the side, a sudden movement that meant her reach just missed. Their momentum made Adrian's bookbag fall off his shoulder and into the Woman's path.

Adrian inhaled sharply – Josh heard it – and then moved by pushing Josh into the streetlight the Woman had been in moments before. Josh stumbled over his feet, and reached back for Adrian: "Dude-"

Adrian reached out towards the ground, just as the Woman turned on her heel to face his back, and he pulled Josh's shadow out of the ground and twisted, throwing it on the Woman in another black blanket.

Josh blinked. "Oh. That's what you were doing."

Which was when the Woman growled and started slashing at the shadow; Josh gulped as little cuts of light began to appear in the blanket. Adrian's face was already set, and Josh saw that any lingering redness had been washed out. He glanced behind him, towards Josh, and then shifted a couple of steps into the streetlight. His own shadow appeared, and Adrian bit his lip, glancing between it and the viciously wriggling Woman.

"Her feet," Josh said, suddenly understanding Adrian's issue. "Grab her feet, keep her from moving."

Adrian exhaled a long breath, and pushed out with his hands, causing his shadow to slink across the ground and join with the shadow blanket. At that moment, the Woman managed to break her head free and she gasped for breath. Adrian flexed his hands, and suddenly the ragged leftovers of the shadow blanket slipped off the Woman and joined with the shadow on the ground. The joined shadow climbed up the Woman's legs to her knees. Adrian clenched his hands and dropped them a couple of inches, and the shadows seemed to solidify and merge with the ground.

The Woman teetered, suddenly immobile from the knees down. She looked down at the shadows and scowled. She raised her head and said, "This won't stop me for long, kid."

"Her hands," Josh said, slipping off his jacket and holding it away from his body. It cast another shadow, square and squat. "Can you stop her hands, Aid?"

Adrian glanced behind him, and when he did, Josh saw that there was sweat beading along his hairline. Adrian looked at the jacket's shadow, inhaled slowly, and then nodded as he released it. He moved one hand towards the shadow and pulled it out of the ground. It hovered for a moment, like a giant black softball.

Josh stepped forward, dropping the jacket, and touched Adrian's shoulder. "Bring her hands down, Aid," he said quietly, hoping she couldn't hear.

Adrian blinked and shook his head slightly, and Josh watched as a couple drops of sweat flew off his face. He threw that softball-shaped shadow softball at the Woman.

She stood her ground and slashed at the shadow, cutting it in half. With Adrian's hand leading it, the two ripped shadows circled back, one slapping her shoulder and the other reaching her wrist. They curled, the first slipping down her arm and the other spreading over her hand when she tried to use it to grab the first. When the first reached her other wrist, Adrian clenched that hand and brought it down to join his other, and the Woman with a sharp, startled yelp, fell forward. The wrist shadows joined the ground shadow and she was stuck with her hands and feet in the ground, bent completely over.

She pulled as much as she was able and started swearing in a language Josh didn't understand. Adrian said, "I can't hold her, Josh," and his voice was weak and strained.

Josh gulped again but dropped the jacket and stepped away from Adrian, inching his way around the straining woman, who was rocking her entire body back and forth. He leaned down and grabbed Adrian's bookbag then turned back, looking over at Adrian. Adrian looked like he was losing the fight – the shadows were beginning to loosen their hold on the ground – and he took a deep breath, then raised the bookbag high over his head, ignored the searing pain of his right arm, and slammed it down onto the Woman's back.

She gasped and her knees buckled. The shadows seemed to understand what Josh was doing because they slipped down to her ankles, letting the Woman fall to her knees. She turned her head and said, "Don't you dare-"

Josh raised the bookbag and hit her with it, making her face snap back the other way. Then again in the back of the head. And then a third time, same place, which was when she fell forward into the shadow.

He stopped, watching her body rise and fall with heavy breaths. When Josh saw her open her eyes, he said, "Oh my God, not again," and with a groan, he slammed the bookbag into her head again. Her head fell forward, and she gasped, "I'll kill-" before he hit her again. And again. And then once more before she fell limply onto the ground, and her entire body went slack.

Adrian exhaled loudly, fell to his knees, and the shadows dispersed, fading into the ground like mist. Josh stared at the Woman, waiting for her to move. He couldn't quite breathe right, and the only thing he could think of was, I just knocked someone out with a bookbag. He felt the crazy urge to apologize to her limp body, even as he knew how stupid that was since she'd seemed totally cool with possibly killing him.

He raised his head and looked towards Adrian, who was on his hands and knees, head hung low and panting. "Dude, I think I got blood on your bookbag."

Adrian huffed out a weak laugh.

Which was about when Josh heard the footsteps. He stopped and looked around, feeling ridiculously like a gopher or guard dog.

"What is it?" Adrian asked weakly.

Josh would have raised a hand to quiet him, were his whole right arm not throbbing.

"Dude, someone's com-"

There was suddenly a man at the mouth of the path, the source of the footfalls. He was of average height and wore dress pants, a crisp white shirt, and a dark purple vest. His skin was the color of mocha, his hair black and cropped. There was a gun in his hand.

I should've seen that first, Josh thought. Why did I focus on the clothes?

"Well, this all went terribly," the man said, in some weird bastardization of a French accent. He cocked the gun.

Behind Josh, Adrian huffed out, "Shit," and suddenly Josh knew that there was nothing Adrian could do. He'd seen how awful Adrian looked, and how much effort it had taken for him to keep the Woman down. He didn't have the power to stop a gun.

Again, Josh didn't have any words to say. Instead he stared at the gun and swallowed. He looked up at the man and wondered if he was the kind of bad guy – because he had to be a bad guy; he came at them with a gun! – who liked to rant about their evil plans or the kind to shoot first and ask questions later.

The Man in the Vest, as if he had heard Josh's wonderings, raised the gun and aimed it at Josh. He said, "You're of no use to me."

And just when Josh thought he was going to die, he felt something grab him around the upper legs and pull him down with a yelp. He felt something whish above his head and then the ground meeting his back. His breath escaped him in a wild gasp of pain and his chest felt too tight. He had closed his eyes with the impact and heard the Man in the Vest above him: "Interesting;" and then Adrian: "Back off."

When Josh opened his eyes, he saw that there were shadows wrapped around his upper legs and lower torso. "Holy-" he gasped, because they felt cold, like a slightly damp blanket, and then he stopped talking because he was suddenly being dragged across the ground, all the way to Adrian's side.

Adrian was still on his knees, but at least he'd straightened up. His skin was super gray though, and Josh's stomach twisted at the sight.

"Dude-"

"Shut up," Adrian gasped.

The Man in the Vest frowned. He didn't say anything, raising the gun again and aiming it at them. Josh couldn't tell which one of them it was aimed at and didn't really care because he was dead if Adrian was knocked out. He grabbed Adrian's sleeve and said, "Aid-"

But he was interrupted again (and why was everyone so keen on keeping him quiet?) by his phone ringing. That super cool song from that awesome Spider-Man movie sang out between the three men, and all three of them paused.

Josh looked down at the jacket that he'd dropped minutes earlier and said, "Uh, sorry," before stretching his left arm along the ground to reach for the cell phone in the right pocket. He pulled it out and saw Alden flashing on the Caller ID. He thumbed the screen and said, "Hey, monster."

He could almost feel the looks the other two were sending each other. But letting a phone keep ringing was just rude and would have probably ruined whatever aesthetic these hunters were going for, right? So what else was he supposed to do?

"Are you guys okay?" Alden said without an actual greeting. It would have been rude except…

Josh looked up into the gun still aimed at them, glanced

down at the body of the unconscious Woman, and then back up into the Man in the Vest's incredulous frown. He said, "We are in deep shit, Alden."

The Man in the Vest swore, then clicked the gun again. "Enough."

"You should call the police," Josh said, staring at the man, watching as a trembling shadow shield situated itself between him and the gun. "We're behind the library; there's a man with a gun-"

"I said that's enough," the Man in the Vest repeated. "Give me the woman and I'll let you go."

"Like hell," Adrian gasped. He sounded like he was fighting for each breath he got.

"Deal," Josh said. He heard Alden's cry of alarm, and Dylan in the distance asking what was going on--

The Man in the Vest nodded once, lowered the gun to face the ground, then lowered himself to one knee. Behind him, Adrian swore and started arguing with a weak voice, but the Man in the Vest simply grabbed the Woman around the waist, threw her over his shoulder with a pained huff of breath, then stood up. He swayed a moment, and Josh thought, He's not that tough, actually; and then the Man in the Vest walked away backwards, watching them the whole time.

On the phone, Alden was still panicking. "Okay, Dylan is gonna call the police, you just stay there and-"

"It's okay," Josh said, as he grabbed his jacket with his other hand. "You saved us. We're okay."

Chapter Eight:
Of Packing, Phone Calls, and Port Haven

The first thing Josh did once he finished his final exam was flop onto his bed face first because he wanted to suffocate himself. Dylan was out studying – unlucky goon had one last exam tomorrow – Alden was packing for home, Tori had already left for home, and Adrian was – well. Josh actually hadn't seen him since he'd managed to half-drag-half-carry him back to Josh's dorm room four days ago. Adrian had been gone when Josh had woken up in the morning, and it turned out that if he didn't want to be found, he couldn't be found.

Josh rolled over onto his back and stared at the ceiling for a long moment, breathing in the air of relative freedom. He hoped Adrian was okay. He was so gray and weak after the fight with that Woman, and so silent after Josh had let them go. But what the hell was Josh supposed to do? He couldn't fight a gun. And what were they gonna do with that Woman anyways?

He sighed and drummed his fingers on his chest for a bit. It was still tender from the scratches that had scabbed over a couple of days ago and was now super itchy. It was the same with his right arm and the back of his head; and Dylan had commented on how his back looked like he had a serious case of carpet burn. He thought about scratching, then reached over for his phone and swiped the screen for his contacts. He took his time, making note of how few people he actually had on his phone, people he could actually count on anyways, and stopped at Lilly of the Lake. He tapped her name and texted his sister, Freedom is mine.

Sometimes he wondered about the world they lived in. He wasn't allowed to have a cell phone until he was fifteen – his first day of high school. His sister had gotten one for her twelfth birthday. Double standard, for sure. But useful, especially when she was the only family member he wanted to talk to.

His phone buzzed on his stomach and he picked it up to see: omg! U coming home now?

He groaned and dropped his head back into his pillow, letting the phone drop onto the bed. Home. Home where he and his dad would tiptoe around each other as he waited for his marks to come out. If they were good, his dad would be reluctantly approving, and spend the rest of the visit reminding Josh of all the things he could get with a Business degree. If they weren't, Josh would feel sick while his dad would strut around the house full of pride because he had won. Jennifer would try to play mediator between the two of them, and maybe it would work if Josh respected her as a mother figure at all. But he didn't; he liked her fine as long as she remembered that she wasn't his mom and she was never gonna be.

And Lilly, well. Lilly would be on Josh's side no matter what, he knew that. But a twelve-year-old girl was only so powerful against a fifty-year-old man and his forty-four-year-old wife.

Someone knocked on his door.

He blinked at the ceiling and said loudly, "You're either Adrian or Alden. Which is weird because I think both of them are pretty pissed at me."

There was silence for a moment before: "I'm not pissed, Deering."

Josh exhaled all of his breath in a heavy puff before he forced himself to get off the bed. He walked over and opened the door slightly, peering around it. "You sure you're not pissed?"

Adrian closed his eyes and sighed. "I promise I'm not pissed. I'm tired and worn out and slightly paranoid, but not pissed." He opened his eyes, and Josh was relieved to see they looked relatively normal. "Can I come in?"

Josh opened the door further and grinned at Adrian, gesturing him in. "Sure, man. You look almost normal."

Adrian stepped in but paused long enough to shoot a dirty look over his shoulder. "Thanks," he said. He took another couple of steps inside, and then stopped. "Uh. Should I…?"

Josh closed the door behind them and said, "Ah, take my bed. I'll take the chair."

Adrian glanced at him again, and then walked over to the desk chair and settled himself in with a frown in Josh's direction. Josh rolled his eyes – touchy dude – and dropped back down into his bed. He stretched out, humming happily.

His phone buzzed again, and he glanced at it to see, Soon? R u coming soon?

He made a face at it, then turned to Adrian. "What do

you tell a hopeful sister?"

"Depends on what they're hopeful for. And how old they are."

"Me coming home and twelve," Josh said, spinning his phone around with a single finger.

"Oh," Adrian said, and Josh glanced up to see him leaning back in the chair and wincing. "Yeah, my sister is still waiting for me to come home."

Josh propped himself up on an elbow. "When's the last time you were home?"

Adrian blinked his eyes open lazily and looked away at a corner. "Five years ago."

Josh's eyes widened, and he gaped at Adrian. "Duuuude. That's crazy."

He shrugged, and spun slowly back to face Josh. "It was necessary. I was at Port Haven for almost four years, and since then I've mostly been hiding-"

"Hiding from what?" Josh interrupted, squinting at him.

Adrian glanced over at him, scratched at his elbow, and then sighed heavily. "It's a super long story."

Josh stayed where he was, blinking as obnoxiously as possible at him. Honestly, did it look like he had anything better to do?

Adrian huffed again. "Okay. So, uh, around two years ago, a teacher at Port Haven was killed-"

"Whoa whoa whoa," Josh said, sitting up completely. "Like, murdered?"

Adrian closed his eyes, sighed, and then reopened them. "Yes. Murdered. Killed means murdered. Can I tell my story now or what?"

Josh pressed his lips together, dragged a finger over them, then tossed an invisible key over his shoulder.

Adrian looked at him for another long moment before his shoulders relaxed again. "So, a teacher was murdered, and no one could tell us why or who or, well, anything really. And right afterwards, two students left the school without really telling anyone, one right after the other, and…" He stopped and frowned into the distance. "It was just… weird, you know? Something was happening, something was changing out there in the world, and it had something to do with our school.

"I didn't feel safe there anymore. Most kids didn't. This kind of thing happens at public schools, but Port Haven was supposed to be better. It was the sort of place where if your parents had to ask how much enrolment was, they couldn't afford it. You know?"

Josh nodded.

"And over the next few months, we started getting more and more students, and the teachers were having more and more meetings… Some of us had connections to the outside world, and they told us that… special people were beginning to draw attention. There were rumours from the East Coast, a girl bursting into flame, and a murder house run by some kind of fanatic… Even though there was nothing special about it, there wasn't anything normal about it either, and…"

Adrian's face made about eight different expressions in about five seconds, and then he settled on a slight frown with a shrug. "So, I left. Wasn't like I was learning a lot there anyways. Started wandering the country – like I'd always wanted to – and finally stopped here. Close enough to home that I can go back if I need to, but far enough away that I wouldn't put them in danger."

Josh drummed his fingers on his leg. He thought about it all: the murder, the special people, and Adrian's road trip. He said, "So, you're not an orphan?"

Adrian looked back at him and smiled a small smile. "I've got a big sister and three older brothers. Mom and Dad are still going strong... I've even got a few nieces and nephews wandering around the East Coast."

Josh blinked, and then grinned at him. "Dude! That's awesome. All I've got is my dad, stepmom, and Lilly. And, well, a couple of grandparents, I guess..." he added with a frown. He hadn't spoken to his maternal grandparents for months... He should probably give them a call. "They want me to go home now that exams are over. Which was the plan, but..."

"But?" Adrian said, crossing his arms and frowning at Josh.

Josh opened his arms, as if to encompass the space around them. "Uh? You're being hunted? You need a friend? I've got a couple of people willing to kill me?" He dropped his arms. "I just... Don't know how I'm supposed to go home now, y'know?"

While he spoke, Adrian's shoulders hitched higher and higher, and his arms tightened around his chest. By the time Josh stopped talking, Adrian looked like a tense little tin man full of awkward guilt.

Josh made a face and slumped his shoulders. "Dude, I didn't mean that this was your fault.."

Adrian looked up at him. "Except for how it is," he said shortly.

Josh sighed and rolled his eyes as dramatically as he could because Adrian was a little drama queen too. "Okay, fine. It's all your fault. Since we can't do anything about it, let's move on, 'kay?"

The corners of Adrian's mouth twitched slightly. "Getting tired of hashing out the same argument?"

"Waste of energy I could spend eating," Josh agreed with a nod. When Adrian barked out a sudden burst of laughter, Josh felt something warm settle in his chest. "So. Now that we've got that out of the way, what do you think we should do?"

Adrian relaxed. "I honestly don't know. All I've got is a lot of questions. Like, what do they want with me? And what did she mean by 'all'? And who is that guy, and what's his power? Who's giving her orders? When are they gonna try again?" He looked up at Josh. "See what I mean?"

As Adrian spoke, Josh felt something heavy settle in his gut, something like guilt. He had let the Woman go, even knowing that Adrian had questions for her. He said quietly, "Sorry for letting her go..."

Adrian huffed a bit and rolled his eyes. "Well, what were we gonna do with her? I could barely walk, and you-"

"Suck," Josh supplied with a knowing nod.

Adrian scowled at him. "I was going to say, 'Couldn't carry both of us,' actually. Josh, you did great. You beaned a sadistic crazy woman with a bookbag."

"That was really only effective because you had a crazy heavy bag," Josh admitted, smiling a little anyways. Maybe he really wasn't that useless. Maybe he wasn't that crummy a friend! "Like, dude, you should be ripped carrying that thing."

"Instead I've got bad posture and potential back problems," Adrian countered. He grew a slightly crooked grin.

In the unexpectedness of that snark, Josh let out a short burst of laughter.

Adrian grinned at him for a moment, then settled back into a more serious expression. "Honestly, though, I don't have a clue. There's not much point in running since we don't know what we're running from, and we know that we're no good against both of them…"

"What about that Blanche girl?"

Adrian paused, halfway through a spin of his chair. "Blanche?" he echoed.

"Yeah! She's the one who warned us about this whole hunting thing! And she gave you contact information, right?" Josh felt a wave of relief and rightness about the whole thing. "Maybe she has some information! And, hey, if she's 'special,' then maybe she can help fight those guys!"

Adrian sent him a very dry look. "Blanche's specialty is finding things," he said slowly.

Josh paused and said, "Wait, so she can hunt people?" Because that was kinda super freaky… but also useful. But also… how did they know she wasn't hunting them? Would hunters hunt other hunters? Man, this was confusing.

Adrian shrugged a shoulder. "Sort of? If she needs to find something, or someone, she can. That's how she found me at Mount Hope."

"Dude." Josh whistled low – or at least, he tried to. He'd never quite managed to learn how to whistle. Instead it was just a low, long exhale. "That's so cool."

Adrian shrugged again with an odd smile on his face, but he pulled his wallet out of his jeans' pocket, opened it, and took out a slip of paper. He frowned at it. "I really didn't want to do this, but... She did say there were others..."

Josh grinned and pulled his legs up onto the bed so they were folded under him. He curled his hands into fists and gently banged them on his legs in time with his chant of: "Call her, call her, call her, call-"

Adrian scowled as he started punching in numbers on his phone. "Shut up, Deering; I'm on the phone."

"Yessss!" Josh breathed as he punched the air with both hands and fell back onto his bed. Which was when he glanced down at his own phone and saw that Alden had texted him: Call me asap.

Josh frowned in confusion but picked up his phone to dial Alden's number. On the chair, he could hear Adrian saying, "Uh, hi, Blanche? This is Adrian, Adrian Cross?"

Alden picked up almost right away: "I think I'm being followed."

"Shit," Josh said, very clearly and concisely.

"Yeah," Alden answered, and her voice sounded taut like a too-tightly strung fiddle string. "I don't know how I know, but there's this... woman practically everywhere I go the last couple of days."

"Asian?" Josh said, sitting up. "Long, black hair?"

"Yes," she whispered.

"Shit," Josh said. And then he chanted that word over

and over again, looking over at Adrian. "Aid?"

"...ck man with a gun," Adrian was saying into his phone. "They said they wanted me alive." He paused, and glanced over at Josh and mouthed, What?

"The Woman's following Alden," Josh said, ignoring Alden's very soft Crap, crap, crap, I was right, in his ear.

Adrian froze. "Blanche? The situation just got worse. Can I call you back in a couple of minutes?" He paused again, then blinked once, face clearing. "Oh, yeah. That works too." He pulled the phone away from his ear and pressed the screen. "She's on speaker; put Alden on too."

"Wow that's smart," Josh said. "Hold on, Alden, we're putting you on speaker."

After a little bit of manoeuvring, Josh and Adrian both sat on his bed and the two phones lay between them.

Adrian sighed a soft. "Alden, meet Blanche. She's a... friend from my last school."

Josh knew he wasn't the only person to hear that pause before the word "friend." Either Adrian was still super awkward about the idea of friendship or he wasn't completely sold on Blanche.

"Hey," Blanche said from Adrian's phone. "I hear you're being followed?"

"Yeah," Alden said from Josh's phone. "I noticed her last night, and nearly all day today."

"But how do they know about you?" Josh asked. "I mean, you and Adrian have only hung out once publicly, and only with me..."

Adrian frowned for a long time before he raised his head. When he spoke, his voice was a soft thing in the back of his throat. "You said her name that night. On the phone."

Josh froze, thought about everything that had happened – it was a strange mix of blur before the fight and after it, and total clarity during the fight – and said: "Oh, shit."

"Alden's not that common a name," Adrian said, sitting up. "Wouldn't be hard to track her down."

"Craaaap," Alden moaned. "Now what's gonna happen?"

"You've got to get her out of there," Blanche said. "Where are you now, Alden?"

"In my room," she said quietly. "I live in a dorm."

"Good. Stay there until Cross can get you. Cross, you have to come here. All of you need to come here; you're useless by yourself."

"I've done pretty well so far," Adrian snapped back, shuffling his shoulders.

"Hey, man, you're doing awesome," Josh said. Because he really was.

"Yes, of taking care of yourself," Blanche countered. "But now there's normal people involved. You can't protect all three of you."

And Adrian looked up at Josh, and Josh knew from the look on his face that Blanche was right. He remembered how pale Adrian had looked after the two different interactions, and how tired he still looked four days later. "They'll just follow us," Adrian said softly. "I'll be leading them straight to you."

"We've already got someone around, Cross. And I'd rather have you here helping us than them catching you."

"Can someone please tell me what's going on?" Alden said. "I feel totally out of the loop."

"There are people hunting Adrian, Alden," Josh said quickly. "And they don't mind hurting us in order to catch him."

"Oh," she said in a soft voice.

Adrian shook his head. "I should have left-"

"Hey!" Josh said, pointing at him. "What did I say about this argument?"

Adrian glared at him. "That was before Alden was involved," he countered, his voice low and tense.

"Hey," came Alden's voice. "Are these hunters the authorities? Are they the police or something?"

Adrian blinked at the phone, even as Josh grinned at it. "Nope!" Josh answered, possibly a tad too cheerfully.

"Then shut up," Alden said. "No one should fight bad guys alone. Especially not someone who saved my best friend. Should I call Dylan? Will they be after him too?"

"Oh hell," Adrian said, dropping his face in his hands.

"Wow, Cross," Blanche said, voice wry. "You've sure been busy making friends, huh?"

"Shut up, Blanche," he muttered from behind his hands.

Josh chewed his bottom lip and said, "What if Adrian got Alden and I grabbed Dylan? We can all call home and say we decided to go camping at some ski lodge for break instead-"

"They'll be so pissed," Alden said.

"Better pissed than dead," Blanche said.

Silence fell over them all as they realized what exactly

they were talking about: people who were willing to kill them. Josh rubbed at where the Woman had stabbed his chest, and when he looked up at Adrian, saw that he was watching the movement with a deep frown.

"I'll give Cross instructions on how to get here," Blanche said, breaking the silence. "I'll expect you here on Tuesday. Good luck." And then she hung up with a click.

Adrian sighed. "I'm so sorry, guys."

Josh punched him lightly in the shoulder. "Yeah, we know." He turned back to the phone. "Adrian's on his way right now, okay?"

"Okay," she said, her voice wavering slightly. "I guess it's good I'm practically packed, huh?"

Adrian was staring at his phone and he said, voice frustrated, "Anyone know where we can get a car?"

Josh blinked, even as he heard Alden's watery laugh from over the phone. "Oh, crap," he said.

"Cory to the rescue!" Alden said, before she hung up with a click of her own.

Adrian raised an eyebrow at Josh, who grabbed his phone and frowned at it. "I hate that car," he grumbled. He did. It was awful. One day, he was going to set fire to it.

"Better that than nothing," Adrian said with a small smile.

They both walked over to the door, with Josh reaching for the doorknob. "So, we'll meet back here with Alden and Dylan?" Josh said, checking with Adrian.

"Right," he said with a nod, just as the door opened.

Josh swore: "Dude!

Dylan squinted at them from across the doorway.

"Why are we meeting Dylan?"

A transcript of the phone conversation that occurred approximately an hour later (Josh wasn't really keeping track of the time, especially with Dylan swearing and shouting at him for a good period of time):

Alexander Deering (aka Dear Old Daddy-O): Hello?

Josh: Hey, Dad.

Dad: Josh! Good to hear from you. How are you doing?

Josh: Oh… You know… Still breathing, ha ha… (Hissed: Shut up, Dill!)

Dad: Josh? Is everything okay?

Josh: Oh, yeah! Totally cool. Exams just finished, so-

Dad: Right, Lilly was saying! I guess you'll be catching the bus back right? Should we expect you tomorrow or Tuesday?

Josh: Uh, actually, Dad, that's the thing… I'm, uh. Not coming home.

Dad: …Excuse me?

Josh: Yeah, see, I met this guy the other week and-

Dad: You met a guy?

Josh: Yeah, he helped me out with my final photography project. Met him in a graveyard. It was pretty cool, actually. Cinematic, y'know?

Dad: Right. Sorry. So, what does this guy have to do with anything?

Josh: Well, um. You see… He needs help.

Dad: …Help?

Josh: Yeah. Help. And… I'm gonna help him. We're

gonna help him.

Dad: 'We'?

Josh: Yeah, Dylan, Alden, and me.

(Shouted from distance, Dylan: Yeah, and Alden's car!)

Dad: Help him with what, Josh?

Josh: Nothing illegal! Just, uh. Some, uh. Personal… stuff…

Dad: …That doesn't exactly fill me with confidence, Joshua.

Josh: Dad, look, he doesn't have a lot of friends. And we're gonna be fine. Really! It'll be great experience for when I'm a travel photographer!

Dad: …Josh, I think you should come home.

Josh: Yeah, well… I don't. And I'm not.

Dad: Josh, this isn't up for debate-

Josh: Mom would want me to help him, Dad. So, I'm gonna help him.

Dad: (sigh) You can't use that every single time you want to do something-

Josh: I can if it's true! (pause) Mom knew me, and I knew Mom, and I'm gonna help Adrian. Tell Lilly I love her; I'll call if I'm not gonna make it home for Christmas.

Dad: Josh-

Josh: Bye, Dad.

-click -

"This is bullshit," Dylan said, folding another shirt.

Alden rolled her eyes and crossed her arms. "Just shut up, Dylan."

"It is!" Dylan cried, straightening. "I should be studying for my exam tomorrow, not packing up all my worldly goods!"

Josh tossed his small stress ball at the ceiling and then caught it again. "Dude, I told you I'd pack for you. There are solutions."

"Shut up, Deering," Dylan snapped. "This wouldn't be a problem if you didn't have such a man crush on that creep."

Josh turned his head and glared at Dylan while still lying on his bed. "I tried to keep you guys out of this. You're the ones who had to butt in."

Dylan held Josh's glare for a few seconds before he deflated, falling back to sit on his bed. "I just don't know how all this happened. Last week, my biggest problem was listening to you whine about your math exam."

Alden sighed from where she sat on the desk chair. "Look, Dylan, just think of it this way: Adrian would be going through this whether we were friends with him or not. At least this way he's not alone."

Dylan ran a hand through his hair. "I barely even know the guy," he muttered.

"He's good," Josh said firmly, still watching his friend.

"He's lonely," Alden continued, nodding once. "And he feels awful about the whole thing. The least you could do is be quiet."

Dylan stared at his hands and Josh watched, holding the stress ball in both hands. It was too bad Dylan was so against having his picture taken; the conflict on his face was brilliant. He could understand where Dylan was coming from; he'd probably do the same thing if the situations were reversed. Dylan could at least pretend to be excited about an adventure, though.

Dylan sighed and said, "I guess I had to pack anyways. And it's not like I want to see Grandma forget my name again."

Josh huffed out a small breath and said, "Thanks, dude." He turned back to face the ceiling, tossed the ball again and said, "How you holding up, monster?"

"Oh, fine," she said. "I mean it sucks that I can't go home, but I figure I'll just consider this part of my karma collection. If I do this awesome thing, I'll get something fantastic later in life, right?"

Josh smiled at the ceiling, tossed the ball and said, "Exactly! Fantastic things for all of us!"

"Whoopie," Dylan muttered out of sight.

Josh dropped the ball back onto the bed and picked up his phone. He found Adrian's number that he'd gotten earlier and texted, U coming back soon?

He held the phone and said, "Dill?"

A pause and then: "Yeah?"

"I'm sorry for getting you caught up in this," Josh said, still staring at his phone.

Another pause, a long sigh, and then: "What's that thing you say? About real friends going through shit? I guess we're just proving that right."

Josh smiled slightly as Alden said, "Aw, that was sweet!"

A new text message popped up just as Dylan said, "Knock it off, Alden." Josh read, 1 minute.

He dropped the phone back onto the bed, grabbed the

stress ball, and began playing catch with himself again. He listened to Dylan and Alden's bickering; thought fondly to himself, Sheesh, guys, get a room; and waited quietly until he heard a knock at the door.

He turned his head, watched Dylan stop packing, and Alden chirp, "I'll get it!" before hopping out of her chair and trotting over to the door. Dylan said, "Be careful, Alden," right before she opened it. She paused, hand on the doorknob, then said, "Who is it?"

"It's Adrian," came the answer.

She opened the door carefully, and Adrian slipped inside, pushing the door shut behind him. He looked around the room, frowning at Dylan, and raising his eyebrows at Josh.

Josh shot him a wave. "Hey, man."

Adrian's lips quirked up slightly and he gave a quick nod. "Hey," he said quietly.

"Welcome to our lovely abode," Alden said with a grand wave of her hand.

Dylan looked up and said, "It's not your abode; butt out."

Alden frowned, fists on hips and cheeks puffed out. She said, "It's the thought that counts, jerk face."

Dylan made a face at her and went back to packing, this time his jeans.

Josh stared at Adrian and said, "So. When we heading out, buddy?"

Adrian frowned and turned his cellphone over in his hand. He said, "It's a thirteen-hour drive, so Tuesday morning at the latest, I guess."

Alden gasped behind them, hands falling off her hips.

"Thirteen hours? How far away is this place?"

"Rapid City," Adrian said, looking at her over his shoulder. "South Dakota."

"Seriously?" Dylan snapped. Josh narrowed his eyes at him – dude, don't be a jackass – and Dylan scowled and focused on his suitcase again. "What a racket," he grumbled.

At Dylan's comment, Adrian's shoulders hunched high, and he glanced down at his feet. Josh felt a wave of hot protectiveness flare up like a wave, and he said, "Cool! I've always wanted to leave the state!" And then grinned at Adrian with all of his might.

Adrian glanced up, smiled slightly, straightened, and then rolled his eyes. He said, "South Dakota's not that exciting, Deering. It's just a place."

"Not like your Port Haven, huh?" Josh asked.

Adrian huffed and said, "There's no place like California."

Dylan's head shot up and he said, "You're from California?"

Adrian turned to face him, and his posture seemed wary to Josh. "Lived there for the last few years. Why?"

Dylan looked Adrian up and down before saying, "You're as pale as a ghost, man! Didn't you leave your house?"

Alden snorted from where she had returned to the desk chair. "Ha!"

Adrian turned back to Josh and raised an eyebrow. "Guess you haven't told them, huh?" His voice was rather downcast, and he was still super tense.

Josh shrugged. "Your life, your story. I'm just the guy

who's a small part of it."

"Whatever it is, Adrian," Alden said from her seat, "we're still gonna help you." And then she smiled at the back of Adrian's head.

Adrian locked eyes with Josh, who sent him a thumbs-up. "Dude, whatever you want, I'm behind you."

Adrian sighed a very long sigh.

Chapter Nine:
Of Chips, Cory, and Crushes

Alden took the first shift because Cory was her car, and she had decided. They left at seven in the morning (Josh was still yawning), and the trunk was full of three suitcases, a duffel bag, and a knapsack. Dylan had called shotgun and Adrian was frowning at his phone, trying to figure out Google Maps. Josh leaned against the window, yawned again, and closed his eyes.

Alden and Dylan weren't really speaking. They hadn't said much at all since Adrian had given them a shortened version of what was happening-

("Okay, so, there are these people with special powers. Like in the comics, except real. And there are these other people that are hunting them. I have special powers, and a couple of people are hunting me. The house we're going to has other special people there, and they're going to help us deal with the hunters."

Josh thought that was an A+ summary and had applauded him. Alden and Dylan had demanded some confirmation and proof before they thought they could believe him. Since Adrian wasn't too fussy on passing out before a thirteen-hour drive, he had said that had to wait. Dylan and Alden had looked sceptical. Adrian had looked at Josh like, They still don't believe me; Josh had shrugged. Whatever. It was the truth, and their unbelief wasn't gonna change that.)

-and their silence was really unnerving, actually. Not that Josh was gonna tell them that; that would be a jerk move. But every time he looked over at Adrian, he looked incredibly uncomfortable, and Dylan kept twitching randomly, and the next time Alden caught Josh's eye in the rear-view mirror, he was going to stick his tongue out at her.

"I think hour-and-a-half-long shifts would work," Adrian said suddenly, still looking at his map. "That would be two shifts each, plus one extra hour."

"I vote Josh does the extra shift," Dylan said, his voice a surprise after all the silence.

Alden said, "Excuse you? This is my car; I'll do the extra shift."

Adrian said, "This whole thing is my fault; I'd really prefer if I did the shift-"

Dylan said, "Yeah, but Josh is the idiot who got involved; he should do the shi-"

"Oh, don't be a jerk!" Alden snapped, slapping his arm.

Josh yawned again and said, "Y'know, if everyone does an hour and forty-five minutes for the last shift, then that covers the extra hour."

Silence reigned again, and Josh raised his head to see the three of them exchange looks. He frowned and said, "I'm not an idiot, y'know!"

Adrian reached out and patted his shoulder. "I know, Deering." His voice was almost condescending; and it must have been, because Alden snorted, and Dylan huffed out a laugh.

Josh slumped back against the window, frowning at the snow-covered ground past the highway. "Hate you all," he grumbled.

"Okay, but what if these 'hunters' are following us?" Dylan asked. His air-quotes were obvious in his voice, even if he was gripping the wheel too hard to do it physically.

Josh chomped on a chip, then offered the bag to Adrian. Adrian pulled out a single chip, frowned at it, then said, "There's no 'if' about it. They're following us." Then he ate the chip with a solid crunch.

From shotgun, Alden said, "But maybe we lost them when we left the school?" Her voice was hopeful, and Josh watched as she reached for the bottle of apple juice sitting between the seats.

Adrian said, "I went all across this country, and barely made contact with anyone. They found me; they'll find us." He reached for the bag of chips and took a handful.

Josh grinned at him. "They're good, aren't they?"

"Addictive," Adrian agreed with a full mouth.

Dylan rolled his shoulders. "So, aren't we leading them straight to these other 'special' people?"

"We went over this already. Safety in numbers and all that. Did you eat them all?" Josh asked, peering into the bag.

"Should get a bigger bag next time," Adrian said, looking out the window.

"Duuuude..." Josh mourned, shaking the bag.

Alden shook her head, and her hair beads clapped against the seat's headrest. "Boys," she said simply, before slurping down the juice.

"I can't believe this," Alden said, resting with her head on the steering wheel. It had been several hours and each of them had already done a shift. Josh leaned over between the front seats to see that her eyes were closed. "We just left that gas station."

"Yeah, well, I didn't have to go then," Dylan said, opening the car door, climbing out, and shutting it with a good thud.

Josh heard Adrian sigh, and when he looked over, he saw that Adrian had rested his head against the window. "We're losing time."

"Man, the dude's just gotta piss," Josh said. "It's not that big a deal." Also, the view was rather remarkable. The way the light slipped between the branches of the trees and skipped off the few mossy rocks at their base, contrasted with the gravel shoulder of the highway... Josh reached for his camera nestled safely in the middle seat.

"This is so, so gross," Alden muttered, forehead still pressed against the wheel. "Boys are so gross."

"I dunno. At least we have the option of doing it in the woods. You girls have to wait for a bathroom." Josh shrugged his shoulders. "It's kinda nice actually. Freeing, you know." He rolled down the window and lifted his camera to his eye, trying to frame the shot he wanted.

"Gross, gross, gross, gross, gross," she chanted.

Adrian said, "You get used to it. I had to do it all the time while I was traveling last year."

Click! Shot taken: nature and capitalism meeting in a mutually satisfied handshake.

Pleased with his photo, Josh turned to face him and grinned. "Yeah? Couldn't wait for a gas station?"

Adrian shrugged, glancing back. "Half the time I didn't even have a car. Hitchhiked and took buses. Walked sometimes."

Josh gaped, feeling like he'd managed to find a pot of gold. "Are you serious? Dude, why am I listening to them flirt when you could be telling me all about your Epic Quest?"

"We are not flirting!" Alden snapped.

Josh glanced over, noticed that she'd raised her head in order to glare at him, and shrugged his shoulders. "Uh, it sounds like flirting to me. You and Dill pretty much interact like me and Tori did." He paused for a moment. "Before we broke up, I mean."

Josh caught Adrian's nod out of the corner of his eye. "There is some serious tension in this vehicle," he agreed.

"Sexual tension," Josh added, leaning in and wagging his eyebrows.

Alden squawked and slapped his arm while Adrian said, "That was immature."

And while Josh said, "It was not!" Dylan opened up the car door, slid into his seat and sighed, "Ahh, that's better. Carry on!"

"I spy with my little eye-"

"Don't. Even. Start," Dylan snapped, voice lowered.

Josh made eye contact with him through the rear-view mirror and stuck his tongue out at him. "Fun sucker."

Alden made a soft sound in her sleep and shifted, head against the window. Josh watched as Dylan's head turned in her direction before he looked back at the road. Josh huffed a sigh, rolled his eyes, and slumped down in his seat, leaning against his window. Seriously, though: he was the one who introduced the two of them, and now they were gonna date and make him the third wheel. How was that fair? How was that right? Being the third wheel was the worst thing in the world, especially third wheel to your two best friends. It made it look like you couldn't make friends by yourself, that you craved company or something.

Adrian made a sound beside him, and Josh turned his head to squint at him. Adrian was frowning at his phone, and then texted something, thumbs flying across his screen. Josh thought for a second about kicking him, but that would require effort, so he just turned his head back to the window. Josh was really, really bored. They had been in this car for over ten hours. He needed a break. He needed to do something. He needed to scream.

He needed Dylan to stop staring at Alden like she was some sort of angel. Just because they were stuck in gridlock didn't mean it was okay for him to be out of focus.

Worst thing about gridlock: there was nothing pleasing to take pictures of.

Something poked him in the arm, and he glanced over to see Adrian's phone prodding him. He looked up and saw Adrian frowning at him. "Hey," Adrian whispered. "What's wrong?"

Josh blinked once, and then again. "I'm friggin' bored," he said.

"Shh!" Dylan hissed.

Josh rolled his eyes and slumped further down against the seat. "Well, I am," he grumbled, lowering his voice.

Adrian poked him in the arm again with his phone and said, "Then take a nap. You've got the next shift."

Josh glanced over at him. "Thought it was your turn." Not that he was upset. Just curious. Adrian seemed to take plans very seriously.

"You need to do something, and I gotta talk to Blanche for a bit. Do you mind?"

Josh shrugged, rested his cheek against the window and said, "Whatever, man. Whatever."

If they got married, did he get dibs on Best Man? And if so, would it be like that scene from When Harry Met Sally – "Thank God neither of us was attracted to Josh, or we'd never have gotten together."

Stupid friends. Just wait until it was his turn to make a speech.

"So, like, how many people live in this house?" Josh asked two hours later.

Adrian glanced over at him, and then Josh watched as Adrian checked the backseat. Josh looked through the rear-view mirror and saw Alden slumped up against her window, legs thrown over Dylan's lap (she was very groggy when they woke her up for a bathroom break and shift switch an hour ago; it was kinda cute actually). Dy-

Ian had managed to lean his seat back and was snoring softly away, one hand on Alden's leg.

It was cute. Too cute. Josh's stomach did this weird pinching thing, and he focused on the road again. It was dark out and the headlights of oncoming traffic were bothering him.

"Five, I think," Adrian answered, voice quiet. "When I spoke to Blanche, I could hear TJ in the distance-"

"His parents actually called him TJ?" Josh interrupted, feeling the first bits of giddiness he'd had in hours.

"Well. I mean. Those are his initials, so… I guess?"

Josh whistled – or tried to, and just managed to make a low, long exhale. One of these days, he was going to learn how to whistle – just watch him! "This is like a dream come true."

Adrian was quiet for a minute, and Josh glanced over to see him making a face. "Right. Well, if TJ's there, it's probably a safe bet that Marcus came as well – unless something happened in the last year and they're no longer friends…" He frowned out the main window. "Can't see that happening, though. They were pretty close."

"So, Blanche, TJ, and Marcus," Josh listed. "And the other two?"

"No idea. Blanche just mentioned that there were others." Adrian was quiet for another bit, and then said, "It wasn't like a high school, y'know, with cliques and stuff. Most people only had a couple of friends, or people they shared classes with."

"So, special people have trouble making friends, is that what you're telling me?" Josh said, grinning at nothing in particular.

Quiet again. Josh was getting used to Adrian's tendency to think before answering. It was a bit rough, waiting for it all, but he usually said things worth waiting for, so Josh would just have to exercise patience (his dad would be so proud).

"Well, for some of us, we've known we were different for years; some people have only figured it out recently. For the first group, you spend so much time knowing you're different that you forget how to be normal, and how to interact with normal people. You've been isolated for so long, usually by your own choice, it's hard to make connections. For the second group, they're so freaked out by what they are, that they're afraid to make connections. What if they reach out and accidentally hurt someone... y'know?"

Josh peered out of the corner of his eye and said, "Which group do you fall under?"

Adrian's mouth twitched. "The first one. Figured out I was different when I was… Six, or so."

Josh blinked out the window and thought of a baby Adrian pulling shadows off the ground and throwing them at people. He imagined a skinny, dark-haired child with a gap between his teeth and eyes filled with tears, and suddenly felt incredibly sad. So, so sad. "That's young."

"Some guy broke into our house and I found him," Adrian said, his voice very casual. "Freaked right out. Shadows everywhere. Think I almost suffocated him or something. Sophia had to stop me. She never told our parents."

Josh frowned. Although Adrian's voice was casual, his sentences were weird. Choppy. It didn't take a genius to figure out that he wasn't exactly cool with the whole situation. "Who's Sophia?" he asked instead.

"My sister. She's, uh, eight years older than me?" Adrian was quiet for another moment, and then, "Yeah, eight. She got married before I left for Port Haven; Patrick's his name. Has a little girl, Marta, and, uh, last I heard, she was pregnant, so…"

Josh made a face at the window. He thought- "Didn't you say you hadn't been home in five years?"

"I still call them. And email. It's not like I'm estranged, or anything. I just… Don't go back."

"Oh." Josh wondered how that must be, not seeing your family in forever. He couldn't imagine going five years without seeing Lilly. "What're your brothers' names?"

"Daniel – he's six years older than me – and Martin's a year younger than him. Paul's three years older than me, and he's almost finished medical school." There was a note of pride in his voice, and Josh realized that Adrian really, really loved his family. "Dan's got a kid – name's Alex – and Martin just got engaged. I haven't met her yet, but Sophia says she's funny, so I guess she's good enough for him."

Josh blinked into the distance and said, "And… you're the only, uh, special person?"

Adrian was quiet for a bit. "Yeah. I mean, Sophia knows that I'm, well, different. I don't know if she told any of the others. But she would've told me if someone else was. She was always big on making sure I knew I wasn't alone."

Josh grinned at the window. "She sounds pretty awesome."

"She is." There was quiet for a bit, and then: "You said you had a sister?"

"Oh! Yeah, Lilly. She's twelve. She's cool, y'know? She does dance – tap mostly because she doesn't like the ballet outfits, crazy kid – and she's super good at math, and she used to play the piano, but decided that she didn't like it – can't really blame her, I can't play either – and… yeah." Josh chuckled a bit, thinking about that wildfire sister of his. "She's kind of a brat, but… I love her."

"I hear little sisters are like that," Adrian said, voice low. "And… you said stepmom… your parents are divorced?"

And something inside Josh froze a little, cracked slightly like when you stepped on too-thin ice. "No. Mom died about ten years ago."

"Oh." There was quiet, and then. "Oh shit. I didn't—damn."

"Yeah." Josh drummed his fingers on the steering wheel, forced himself to breathe through his frozen lungs – they felt heavy and thick, like they were coated in too much syrup or left out in the rain overnight. "It was, uh, cancer. Took her about a year to die."

"Oh. Man. Josh. I'm so sor-"

"It's cool," Josh said, cutting him off. Because if he had to hear anything about how sorry anybody was, he was going to have to pull over, and he still had a long way to go. "It was a while ago, and Jennifer's pretty cool. For a stepmom, I mean. So… Yeah. Just. Yeah."

There was quiet in the car as Josh struggled to not think of his mom, who used to play outside with him, and taught him how to sing, and used to make cookies with marshmallows because Josh liked them that way, or how she used to wear scarves over her head for the last few months, and how sad Josh was when he realized he was the only blond left in the family. It was a stupid thing to be sad about, but there it was.

He didn't think about the last couple of days spent in the hospital at all. Or how much he wished for someone to swoop in and save him and his family. Or how no one came. And how difficult it was to make friends after that, because everyone knew he was the kid who lost his mom to cancer and no one knew what to say to him.

Junior high had been awful, hormones plus mourning plus total isolation and a baby sister and grieving father. High school had been better, but then Jennifer had shown up, and suddenly Dad was happy again and Lilly had someone else to make cookies for her, and…

When Jennifer and Dad had married two years ago, Josh had sat next to his best friend at the time and said, "Nah, man, she's cool. I like her, really."

And he did. But he didn't love her. And the whole house was just… different.

Dylan snorted suddenly in his sleep, and Alden yawned a long, loud thing. And Adrian sighed slowly, and Josh said loudly, "Oh thank God you're awake; can I turn on the radio again? I'm dying."

📷

Josh peered at Adrian's phone and said, "Dude, you've gotta turn soon, you've gotta-"

"The phone will tell us when, Deering, just calm

down-" Adrian said, his voice annoyingly chill.

"How can you even see anything?" Alden asked, her voice very close to Josh's ear. She must have been leaning in again. "It's so dark."

"Maybe that's his superpower," Dylan said from the backseat. "Night vision."

"Ha ha," Adrian said as Josh snapped, "That's not funny, dude;" and the phone said calmly, "Turn left in 750 feet."

"Oh man," Josh said, staring down at the phone. "That's soon."

"There," Adrian said calmly as Alden slapped Josh's headrest and called out: "There!"

"Ow," Josh said, his ear ringing.

Adrian flicked on his blinker, slowed down, and turned into the street with calm. Everything Adrian did was calm. Except, when Josh looked over at his hands on the steering wheel, his knuckles were pale and tense where they curled. Alden was bouncing on the backseat, and Dylan snapped, "Would you stop that?"

"I can't help it; I'm excited!" she snapped back.

"It's number 145," Josh said, looking at the phone screen again. "That's on my side."

"We just passed 47," Alden informed them. Her hair whipped Josh in the face.

"Ow!" he said again.

"Just keep swimming, just keep swimming, just keep swimming, swimming, swimming," Alden sang, not even bothering to apologize; what a dumb friend.

"Sit down, Alden!" Dylan snapped. "You're blocking my view."

"It's just houses and yards," Adrian said simply.

And he was right. It was a very simple, sparsely developed area. Each house was different, and each house was large with a decently sized yard. They all had enough elbow room to spread out – in fact it looked kind of nice. Josh could totally imagine living here. He just couldn't at all imagine five Adrians living in a house on this street, or a couple of freaks like the Woman or the Man in the Vest crouching in the snow-covered bushes.

It was actually super pretty. Josh felt something in his chest lighten where he didn't know it was tight before.

"95," Alden chimed.

"Good job," Dylan said, voice very patronizing. "What a good girl."

"Oh, shut up!" she snapped.

Josh stared at the phone. It was saying that the house was 2500 feet away. He blinked at it, looked back up at the world outside and said, "You've got a bit to go yet."

"Thanks," Adrian said, and his voice was just a little bit tense, like an elastic band just starting to pull.

"-can all read the house numbers," Dylan was saying. "You don't have to read them out for us."

"I'm just trying to help."

"Alden's doing fine," Adrian said. "Can you two stop fighting?"

Josh looked down at the phone. 1500 feet. "Coming up."

"Calm down," Adrian said. "We're fine. They're friendly."

"It's because we're tired," Alden said. "We'd be totally chill if we all didn't feel like death."

Josh couldn't help but agree and judging by the snort that came from the backseat, Dylan felt the same.

House number 145 was large, like most of the others. It was also at the end of the street, on an L-corner, where the backyard and rightyard opened up into woodland. Snow covered everything, and there were two cars in the driveway – a blue Honda Civic, and a grey-green coloured Jeep. The driveway and walkway were clear, but the front porch still had snow on it, and there was even a swinging bench on it that had a good inch of snow settled into the cushions. Adrian pulled into the driveway next to the Civic, and Josh watched as the front light came on – motion sensor. The house itself was a light-brown colour, with dark brown trim and two large windows in the front with the curtains pulled right across. As Alden groaned out a stretch, and Adrian turned the ignition off, Josh watched as one curtain opened up a smidge, a head of light-coloured hair poked out, and then the curtain shut again.

"Well. They know we're here," he said.

"Should we get our bags now, or greet them first?" Dylan asked, clicking the seatbelt off.

"Might as well grab them now," Adrian answered, rolling his shoulders. "They know why we're here, and we don't have a lot."

Josh exhaled slowly, feeling his nerves wash up like a swarm of bees in his gut, spreading out down his arms and into his fingers and legs. He clicked his seatbelt off and opened the door, slowly pulling himself out of Cory. He stood there for a moment and stared up at the house, wondering what was going to happen next. Would this be where they all died?

A pair of arms curled around his right arm and Alden pulled herself into his side, resting her head on his shoulder. It hurt his still-aching arm a little, but the comfort was worth it. "Don't worry, Joshua," she said. "We're gonna be okay."

The bees settled down ever so slightly. Enough that Josh felt he could breathe again.

The slam of the trunk woke him up a little, and suddenly a bag bumped his other side. "Here," Adrian said, passing him one of the suitcases.

Josh took it, settled the handle in his grip, and said, "Thanks, man. I can take something else."

Adrian, who had one knapsack slung over a shoulder and a duffel bag in his other hand, shrugged. "I got it. Don't worry." His eyes met Josh's, and there was a glint in them and something about the set of his jaw that seemed to say, Yeah. I get it. This is scary; but don't worry. We got this.

Dylan passed them, breaking the moment and pulling the two suitcases behind him. "Well, c'mon, guys. It's cold out here."

For a moment, Josh was torn between being grateful to Dylan for being so normal and wanting to kick him for ruining the perfect shot: Friends Staring Out at the Future. Unintentionally-framed shots were the best shots because they were real and sincere.

Alden obviously felt the same because she glared at Dylan's back. "You jerk. We were having a moment!"

Adrian huffed out a breath and followed Dylan towards the steps. Josh kept his arm linked through Alden's and led her quietly behind the other two. "Yeah, well, this jerk wants to get things settled," Dylan called over his shoulder.

As soon as he hit the porch, and Josh and Alden reached the bottom of the steps, the front door swung open. Dylan swore, stopping in his tracks, and Blanche appeared in the doorway, a slight frown on her face. "It's late," she said.

"It's a thirteen-hour drive," Adrian retorted, seemingly unsurprised by Blanche's appearance as he stepped onto the porch. "And we had exams all week."

Blanche's eyebrows rose. "Exams?" she echoed even as she stepped aside to let them into the house.

Adrian slipped into the house without explaining; Dylan followed him with a muttered, "Thanks;" and Josh stopped at the door. "Hey, Whitey!" he chirped, ignoring Alden's sharp elbow snapping into his side.

Blanche smiled, a slightly cruel edge to the curve of her mouth. "Graveyard Boy."

Josh led Alden into the house, and she said, peering up at him, "I thought Adrian was the Graveyard Boy?"

"Creeps of a feather," Adrian called out from their left. Josh turned his head, stuck somewhere between surprise and pleasure. He remembered! He actually listened when Josh spoke!

The door closed behind them and Blanche said, "Living room." She slipped around them, and Alden slipped her arm out from his and followed her off to the left. Josh's side suddenly felt cold, even though Alden herself didn't generate much heat. It was more of a loneliness thing; with someone by his side, the world didn't seem nearly so frightening. He sighed, trying to dispel his sudden loneliness and fear, and followed the girls out of the hallway.

And then stopped in the open doorway between the hall and living room.

A demigod was sitting in an armchair.

"Oh my God, it's that guy from the Creed movies!" Josh gasped, almost dropping his suitcase.

The boxer grinned a big grin. "Well, that's hella flattering."

"You asshole, he's not actually him," Dylan snapped from where he had dropped onto the couch.

Alden glanced over at Adrian. "Do you know who they're talking about?"

Adrian shrugged, dropping his bags on the floor next to the couch. "I'm guessing some famous jacked black man. Probably sports related."

Josh gasped at him. "Dude! How do you not know the Creed movies? Don't you have Netflix?"

Adrian blinked at him slowly, like a cat. "I'm a poor Health Major student living alone in a cheap apartment," he said calmly. "What do you think?"

"Hey, Health Major! You planning on going into med school, Cross?" the demigod asked, nodding at Adrian.

Adrian glanced back, and his lips quirked slightly. "Not sure yet, Marcus. I've got a way to go, though. Port Haven set me back a couple of years."

"That's a matter of opinion," Blanche said, from the corner of the room. She looked up from her phone and eyed Adrian.

Adrian looked steadily back at her. "Guess it is," he said; and suddenly the tension in the room shot up about a thousand degrees.

"Whoa, Cross-man, chill!" said a new voice.

Josh started and looked around for the slightly accented voice, finally finding a man sitting at the top of the stairs that filled the room to the right of Josh and the doorway. The railings on top of the stairs were spaced well apart, enough that the man had both his legs between railings, with his arm looped loosely around the railing dividing his legs. He swung his feet back and forth. His socks had green stripes on them.

Josh instantly liked him.

"You know Blanche is fussy," the green sock man said, his face leaning against the railing. He was tanned and had a mess of short, dark hair. He grinned as he spoke. "No need to be uptight about it."

"Shut up, TJ," Blanche said, voice slightly hard. In the armchair, the supposed Marcus grunted and shook his head, leaning back in the chair.

TJ, the green sock man, rolled his eyes and leaned back, using his hold on the railing to keep from falling. "Can't do that, babe," he said. "This mouth can't be stopped."

"Wow," Alden said, perching on the arm of the couch furthest away from Dylan. "He's even worse than you, Dill."

Dylan raised his head to scowl at her.

From high up, TJ grinned again and said, "Ain't no one worse than me, stranger." He threw her a wink, and Josh felt a stab of amusement when Alden bristled.

Suddenly there was a sudden loud handclap, and everyone turned to look at Marcus, still sitting in the armchair like a king on his throne. "Alright, y'all," he said, voice carrying through the room. "Maybe we should get some introductions."

He threw a thumb towards the corner and said, "Blanche." He moved it to face towards the top of the stairs and said, "TJ." He pointed the thumb towards himself and said, "Marcus. Hannah's getting the rooms ready, and Erik won't be back until late."

Josh paused for a moment, then looked over at Adrian. He mouthed, Five.

Adrian rolled his eyes, mouth twitching at the corners. Then he gestured with his head towards Josh. "That's Josh. Dylan's on the couch, and Alden's the girl."

There was a pause before Alden spoke. "That's it? I'm the girl?"

Adrian looked over his shoulder at her. "Should I have said more?"

She frowned at him. "Where's the description? Am I the pretty girl? The annoying girl? The girl with the great fashion sense? What kind of girl?"

"The short girl," Josh supplied, grinning when she aimed her frown at him.

"Listen, you," she began.

"Okay, that's enough," Blanche interrupted, before they could continue.

Everyone turned to look at her and she pushed herself off the wall. "You guys have had a long day, and there's no point in discussing everything until we're all here. Here's the situation: We've got five bedrooms here. Marcus has volunteered to bunk with TJ-"

"You da bomb, Marcello!" TJ cut in from above.

Marcus very calmly sent him the finger. Josh mouthed,

Marcello? at Adrian, who shrugged his shoulders and mouthed back, Don't ask.

"...and Hannah's given up her room for Alden," Blanche finished, having actually stopped when TJ spoke. Josh didn't really know what to make of that; none of his friends stopped when someone interrupted them. "Which leaves the three of you boys to decide who wants the couch and who wants to share Marcus' bed."

Dylan said, from his seat on the couch, "Wait. This couch?" At Blanche's nod, he said, "Dude, I call dibs. This couch is gold."

Josh said, "Whoa, wait. You want to sleep on the couch?"

Dylan turned to Adrian and said, "He's all yours, man. When he starts talking in his sleep, I just throw something at him."

Adrian frowned, and Josh felt a wave of angry embarrassment wash through him. "Dude! I don't talk in my sleep!"

"Thanks for the pointer," Adrian said, obviously ignoring Josh. Which was totally rude. They were going to have words later.

"Well," Blanche said, looking up at TJ, "that was easier than I thought."

TJ kicked his feet, smooshing his face against the railing again. "The couch is pretty great though, babe."

Blanche rolled her eyes, then looked over at Alden. "C'mon," she said, stepping over. "I'll show you your room; it's upstairs. TJ, clear the way."

As Alden started and then grabbed her suitcase, TJ slid his legs out from between the railings and pulled himself up. It was only when he did so that Josh realized that TJ was a tall, skinny man, all bones and sharp angles. He said, "Yeah, yeah," and disappeared around the corner.

When Alden and Blanche headed for the stairs, Marcus groaned and pushed himself out of his chair. He said, "Guess I'll show you the room. It's this way." He walked towards the doorway, and Josh sidestepped out of the way, suddenly feeling tiny when Marcus stepped past him. Marcus stood at about the same height as Adrian, but he was easily almost twice as broad as either of them, with a thick neck and massive shoulders. When he walked past, Josh just gaped at him.

He heard a sigh behind him, and then a bag hitting him in the back of the knees. "Get walking, Deering," Adrian said behind him.

"He's so big," Josh whispered.

"That's what she said!" Dylan called from the couch. Apparently, Josh needed to work on his whispering skills.

Still, just because Josh sucked, that didn't mean Dylan had to be an asshole; so: "You know what-" Josh began, turning around.

"Not now," Adrian said, grabbing the sleeve of Josh's coat. "You can wrestle later."

"And that was kinky," Dylan called out.

"You shut your-" Josh tried again.

"Move, Deering," Adrian said again, pulling him along.

Marcus was leading them down the hall, away from the front door. He stopped at the corner and pointed down the new hallway. "Kitchen's on the left; bedroom's on the right. Bathroom's on the end."

Josh stopped between the two men and looked down the hall, seeing the open kitchen doorway just a couple feet away, the gray door with the frosted windows at the end of the hall, and the gray door on the right, almost six feet away. He realized that they were right next to the food. He looked over at Marcus. "You've got the best room in the house."

Marcus shrugged. "I think so. Girls might disagree."

"You are a good man," Josh said solemnly. Adrian scoffed.

Marcus huffed out a laugh. "You should check it out first, man. It ain't that nice of a room."

"It's next to the food, so it's beautiful," Josh said, walking down and opening the bedroom door.

It was a dark room: the blinds were shut, and the light was off. Someone stepped up behind him – Josh guessed Adrian – and reached out to flick on the lights.

Josh blinked into the illuminated room. "Thanks," he said.

"No problem," Adrian said.

There was one large window straight ahead – blinds closed – and a large dresser to the left of the door. There was a small TV on the floor next to it with a game console plugged in.

The double bed was tucked against the right wall.

Josh gasped and grabbed Adrian's sleeve. "It's a double!" he whispered.

"Ye-es?" Adrian agreed.

"I've only got a twin in mine," Josh explained, something giddy and bright bubbling in his chest. "And, like the song says, it's pretty depressing."

Another pause and then: "What song?" The question was hesitant, like Adrian wasn't sure he should ask it.

"You look so defeated lying there in your new twin sized bed," Josh sang, stepping into the room. "With your single pillow underneath your single head." He dropped his bag on the floor and turned to face Adrian. "Death Cab for Cutie? No?"

Adrian's frown deepened. "I've heard of them? I think?"

Josh nodded, undoing his coat and throwing it onto the bed. "You totally have. They've got some famous singles." He turned back to the window and said, "Those are super dark curtains."

"Those stay closed," Marcus said, voice booming from the doorway. "We don't want people looking in; especially on the ground floor."

And Josh's happiness began to deflate, the shadows of reality creeping back in. Right. They were in danger. They had to be careful.

Suddenly another coat landed on top of his, and he blinked up at Adrian's closeness. Adrian simply looked at him which, like before, was enough. They were in this together, and sometimes words weren't needed for that; sometimes a look was all you needed.

"I'll take the wall if you want," Adrian said quietly. "I don't move too much in my sleep."

Josh nodded. "Cool. Sounds fine." He twisted to look back at the doorway and said, "Thanks, Marcus."

Marcus nodded slowly. "It's the only bedroom on this floor," he said. "Everyone else's is upstairs." He shrugged a shoulder. "Just keep that in mind." Then he leaned away, disappearing from view. Footsteps sounded a moment later.

Josh looked back at the dark curtains, wondering what that was all about. With something bitter bubbling in his gut, he said, "They said they had people watching them, right?"

"Something like that," Adrian said quietly, sitting on the bed next to the coats. "They were pretty quiet about it, actually."

Josh glanced back at Adrian. "Suh-spish-ous," he sing-songed.

Adrian grimaced. "I know," he stressed in a low voice. "And if it wasn't for you, I wouldn't have come."

Josh eyed him carefully. "Me you or Dylan-and-Alden you?"

"Both you's," Adrian said, raising his eyes.

Josh waved a hand, turning back to the door. "Pssh; I can handle myself," he said, walking away. "I'm tough. Just give me a bookbag, and I'll knock that bitch-" and stopped.

Because there was an angel standing in front of him, a bemused expression on her face.

She had a round face, pale skin with flushed cheeks and a button nose. Her lips were pale pink and slightly shiny in the hall light, and her eyes were big and brown. She had freckles dotted along the bridge of her nose and sprinkled across her cheekbones. Josh wanted to plant a kiss on each one he could see.

The crown of her head was eyelevel to him; it was the most beautiful rich brown head of hair he'd ever seen. She had a side braid with a yellow elastic holding it together.

She said, "Gut evening."

He said, "Guh."

And then Adrian stepped up behind him and said, "Hello."

The angel turned her head slightly and smiled. It was like looking at a sunset over a lake – picturesque and breathtaking. Josh's chest actually hurt to look at her. "Hello!" she said. "You must be Adrian." And then she turned her head slightly and shone that sunset smile onto Josh and said, "And you are Josh."

Josh swallowed to wet his suddenly dry throat, and said, "Uh, yeah. Yeah, that's us. Josh and Adrian. Adrian and Josh. Yup."

He could feel Adrian's eyes burning the back of his neck. The angel before him changed her smile, made it slightly mischievous.

Suddenly, she was super hot. Like – WOW. Josh wished he could kick Adrian out of the room tonight. Not that, y'know, anything was going to happen because, hello, why would she ever want anything to do with him? But still. It would be nice to have the chance.

She merely looked at him, that same elfish look on her face. It made him nervous. Why was she staring at him? No one ever stared at him.

"Hi," he blurted.

She blinked and said, "Hello," her smile widening. "I see you have had a long day."

"Long week, actually," Adrian said, still hovering behind Josh like a shadow. "Final exams and such."

Her eyes brightened – he'd never seen such a lovely

pair of brown eyes. "Ah! I have always wanted to go to college. It must be a true experience."

"It has its pros and cons," Adrian said, voice rather neutral.

The awkward was strong in the air; Josh could practically smell it. And, feeling somewhat possessed by it, he blurted, "God, this is awkward."

Behind him, Adrian sighed. The angel glanced back towards Josh, eyes locking with his. "True," she agreed. "You boys have had a long day." She tilted her head slightly and added, "I have also failed to introduce myself." She offered a hand. "I am Hannah."

Josh stared at her hand. Shake it. He was supposed to shake it. His palms felt clammy. What if they started to sweat? He was starting to sweat. Why couldn't he move his arm? Crap. He had hesitated too long. Now everyone was staring at him. Crap. Crap, crap, cr-

Adrian punched him in the back. "Deering," he hissed.

Josh shot his hand out and took Hannah's – it was larger than he was expecting – and briskly shook it. Then he dropped the hand, spun on his heel, shouldered Adrian out of the way, and walked right back into the bedroom. He made for the bed but paused when he saw the coats covering it. Welp. There went his face-planting idea.

"He'll be better tomorrow," Adrian was saying to Hannah. "Between finals and the drive today and the whole, uh, powers thing… I think he's just… mentally wiped."

"Of course," Hannah said in her sunset voice. "It cannot be easy for them, after all… Poor things."

Great, Josh thought as he grabbed the coats. Pity. He

pushed them off the bed with a surprisingly satisfying slump. Just what he needed.

"He'll be better tomorrow," Adrian repeated. "I think we'll just crash for the night though."

"Of course," Hannah said. "I will see you in the morning then."

Josh crawled up on the bed-

"Yeah. It was good to meet you, Hannah."

-and face-planted into a pillow.

"You too, Adrian."

Josh listened to a grouping of footsteps and then the click of a door closing. "What the hell was that?"

Josh groaned into the pillow. "I derped."

"No duh. Are you always that dumb around girls?"

Josh groaned again, rolling onto his back. "She's sooooo prettyyyyyy," he whined.

There was silence for a minute while Josh stared at the ceiling and cursed himself. Finally, Adrian said, "You kept your shoes off the bed, right?"

Josh blinked, said, "Oops," and then kicked his shoes off. It took him a couple of tries.

"Don't worry, Deering," Adrian said, moving around the room. "I'm sure she'll figure out that you're not quite as moronic as you just sounded."

"I hate myself," Josh said simply.

"Join the club," Adrian retorted.

Chapter Ten:
Of Morning, Malls, and Mayhem

Josh woke up.

Thank God for that. It meant he was still alive.

Someone breathed behind him, deep and heavy. It took a few seconds for Josh to wake up enough to remember that Adrian was sleeping behind him, pressed against the wall. Josh blinked into the darkness, stared at the unfamiliar shapes of the items around the room, and knew that he wasn't going to be able to fall back asleep. Which was fair; after all, they'd been in bed before eleven o'clock last night and he didn't think he'd dreamt at all. His brain must have had a good rebooting or something.

He reached for his phone sitting on the nightstand. It blinked 6:23 back at him. He huffed and rolled onto his back in order to sit up, rubbing a hand over his face. He might as well get up. He already knew he wasn't going to fall back asleep. Maybe he could wander outside, take a couple of pictures of a South Dakota sunrise, or suburbia at its finest – bleakest? Which one would it be at 6:30 in the morning? Could it be both?

A quick glance over his shoulder let him see Adrian on his side, back pressed against the wall, and hands curled into loose fists on top of the comforter. Carefully, trying not to wake Adrian – it'd be nice to see a healthy colour in his face – Josh slipped out of bed, tugged his shirt down where it had hiked up in his sleep, and walked over to the dresser where he'd laid his camera down. He picked it up, cradled it to his chest, then stepped over to the door. He opened it as quietly as he could and shuffled out, closing the door behind him. He turned around and paused.

There was a light on in the kitchen. Intriguing. Wasn't today Wednesday? Did these guys have jobs? He had no idea; but normal people had jobs, didn't they?

Josh made a face at himself for that one. Oh yeah. There wasn't exactly an abundance of normal people in this house.

He stepped over across the hall and peered into the kitchen. Standing at the sink, filling up a kettle was a young man with a slight frown on his face. He was short and a little stocky and was wearing a vest and pressed pants.

Josh was suddenly overcome with the memory of the Man in the Vest, gun pointed at them and lips pressed into a thin line. He inhaled, long and slightly shaky, and forced the memory away with a slightly vicious shove.

The young man glanced over, although what caused him to do so Josh wasn't sure. He had a round face and glasses. "Oh. Hallo."

He had a slight accent, kind of like the male, groggier version of Hannah's.

"Uh, hey," Josh said. He pointed with his free hand at the kettle in the man's hands. "Coffee?"

The man looked back at the kettle and turned off the tap. "Not for me. For the others when they wake." He stepped over with a surprisingly light walk and set the kettle in its base. He flicked the switch to start it bubbling and then turned back to Josh. "You are Adrian?"

Josh blinked once. "Uh, no. I'm Josh." He threw a thumb over his shoulder and said, "Adrian's still sleeping."

The man nodded. "You normal?"

"Uh. Relatively speaking."

The man merely tilted his head to one side.

"I mean, I don't have the 'whooo powers' thing like you guys-" Josh expanded, and he wiggled one hand in a lame jazz hand in front of him because visuals helped, okay? – "but I don't think anyone would really consider me 'normal'." And he finger-quoted the last word because it was six in the morning and he wasn't really awake yet.

The man quirked a smile and something in his eyes softened. "'Whooo powers'," he repeated softly. "Gott, you sound like TJ." He reached up towards a cupboard. "Coffee or tea?"

"Uh, coffee. Please," Josh added, stepping into the kitchen. He watched as the man opened the cupboard and pulled out a light blue mug. There was a faded phrase stamped onto the side, and Josh wondered what it said. Maybe something cool like Aliens are here or terrifying like Believe in yourself and you too can be Hitler. "So... What's your name?" he said after a long pause.

The man pulled out a small bowl and glanced over. "Erik."

Josh heard the k on the end.

"I am Hannah's brother." The man raised the bowl. "Sugar?"

"Yes," Josh said with a firm nod. "All the sugar."

Erik rolled his eyes. "We have been speaking for two minutes and already I am not surprised." He set the bowl down next to the mug. "Milk and cream is in the fridge. Do not touch Blanche's almond milk; she will stab you."

Josh, who had started for the fridge, paused and looked back at Erik. "That… doesn't really surprise me." He set his camera on the counter beside the fridge, took the couple of steps to the fridge, opened its door, balked at the sheer amount of food – like woah man – and managed to spy a blue carton. He shifted enough things until he could pull out the milk. Walking back to the counter, he watched as Erik poured coffee grinds into the mug. "You always up this early, dude?"

Erik sighed. "I work overnights. It was fine before; the others had work, I slept, we spent the evenings together, and then I worked and they slept. But I do not like it now."

"Your routine's all wacky?" Josh guessed, leaning a hip against the counter next to the mug.

"My routine has always been 'wacky.' What I do not like is people following me and my friends."

Josh froze, suddenly wide awake without the coffee. "So… people really are following you."

Erik nodded. "At least two. A man and a woman. They have not tried anything yet, but Hannah says they are always nearby. They know our routines." He frowned at the kettle. "They are plotting."

The kettle clicked off then, and Erik sighed again, shoulders rising and falling with the motion. He picked up the kettle and turned, pouring the water into Josh's mug. He replaced the kettle all without looking at Josh.

Josh watched him for another minute. "You really don't like that we're here," he said quietly.

Erik huffed, growing tense. "The people watching us, they were waiting for something. Backup maybe. A bigger catch." He turned around and lifted his chin to stare right at Josh. His brown eyes were hard and his face set. He was older than Josh; and Josh could see it now. Older than Adrian even. "Now you are here, with people following you. They will have both: the backup and the catch. As you Americans say, 'The shit will hit the fan'." He scowled, a rather sharp expression on a face that looked rather passive. "We have enough shit already. We do not need more."

Josh swallowed and looked down at the mug. The faded words were Welcome to Disney World! He curled a finger around the handle of the mug and spun it around slowly to see the other side. A bleached Pluto grinned at him with tongue lolling out of his mouth. "Maybe we can help."

"Perhaps," Erik agreed, voice harsh. "Or perhaps we will all be dead before the weekend. Gott only knows."

"I don't think they want to kill you. I think they want to capture you."

There was a long pause, one of those where you know the other person is listening very hard and thinking even harder. Josh heard the sound of a drawer opening, and when he looked up, Erik was offering him a spoon. "Here."

Josh took it with a nod and got a spoonful of sugar. He dumped it into his mug as Erik said, "How do you know this?"

Josh got another spoonful of sugar. "The Woman told us. Said she was supposed to take Adrian with her." He gave a shrug as he stirred the sugar in. "I'm guessing she's got the same orders for you guys."

There was silence again, that same thought-heavy silence. Josh poured a splash of milk into his mug and stirred it around again. He raised his head, milk carton in hand, and froze at the scowl and glare on Erik's face.

"We are waking them up now," he said.

There went the photoshoot.

Alden yawned a deep yawn and snuggled deeper into Josh's shoulder. His shoulder and arm were still sore, but, like last night, the affection was worth the slight pain. Josh glanced over at Dylan who was sitting on Alden's other side and was very obviously not watching her. Adrian yawned from his place on the floor next to Josh's left knee and rubbed a hand into his eye. It was like watching a small child.

Erik and Blanche were standing, whispering to each other with set faces. TJ sat on the arm of Marcus' chair, blinking down at his phone, and Hannah was curled up in the corner of the couch, feet barely brushing Josh's leg. Barely, but still touching because Josh was super aware of every time she moved a little bit. She had a mug of tea in her curled hands, and every now and again she raised it to her lips and took a small sip. She noticed Josh watching her and sent him a small smile over the lip of her mug.

He turned his head away very quickly, well aware of

the hot blush he was now sporting. How was she so pretty? How did one ask to take a picture of someone without coming across as a creep?

"Coffee..." Alden moaned, hand weakly slapping his thigh.

Josh rolled his eyes and passed over his mostly empty mug of coffee.

Alden sat up slowly and took it from him, gulping it down quickly. She made a face. "Oh man. That was gross."

"Josh sucks at stirring," Dylan said, slumped down with his eyes closed.

Josh frowned at them. "Get your own coffee then."

"Alright!" Blanche announced, voice clear. "I think it's time we get everything figured out."

Beside him Alden froze, her small body suddenly going still. On his other side, Hannah shifted her feet, toes almost slipping under his left thigh.

"Sounds good to me," Adrian said.

Josh raised a hand. "Should we have a whiteboard? I feel like we should have a whiteboard." This was feeling very much like high school: half asleep with no worries about grades, your friends surrounding you, and a grumpy woman standing at the front of the room.

TJ raised his head. "Hey, yeah! A whiteboard; that'd be kick-ass!"

Marcus took a long swallow from his coffee. "We ain't getting a whiteboard, Romero," he said, voice low, groggy, and resigned. He looked like he hadn't slept very well. Josh spared a moment to feel kinda guilty about that. "Your girlfriend's groceries cost too much."

Blanche's eyes narrowed. "Organic food is something that benefits us all."

Josh was still frowning over the thought of Blanche and TJ dating. Like, he could see it. Maybe. But then why was Marcus rooming with TJ instead of Blanche rooming with TJ? Was it new? Was it a celibacy thing? Josh's curiosity was going wild.

Maybe he had put too much sugar in his coffee…

"Enough," Erik snapped, and his voice was hard like a branch whipping against the window in a windstorm. "This is serious. Bickering can wait until after we all survive." He straightened up and tugged his vest down.

Beside him, Josh heard a soft, slightly harsh phrase, and he turned his head to see Hannah frowning at Erik, forehead furrowed. He turned back to see Erik scowl and respond in that same language, voice deep and angry.

What language was that?

"Erik's right," Blanche said, rearing up like a snake. "We need to be serious now. Apparently, Josh and Adrian have news."

Josh blinked – news? – and looked down at Adrian.

Adrian craned his neck back to look back at him.

"We do?" Josh asked.

"Apparently," Adrian said, his voice dry as dust. He looked forward again. "Uh, so. We've got two people following us."

Erik nodded, sharp, brisk motions. Josh was completely bewildered by how someone stocky and square could come across so sharp… Kind of like a brick, now that he thought about it. "And we have at least two people watching us."

"That brings it up to four," Marcus said, voice booming and eyes glancing between Blanche and Erik.

"Oh good, we can math," Dylan grumbled, face mostly hidden in his hands. He looked like he hadn't slept at all.

"Josh, you said you had made contact with these people?" Erik asked, shooting a dirty look towards Dylan.

Josh rubbed a hand over his chest, feeling the soreness that still lingered there, like a bruise he might never shake. "Contact, yeah. You can say that."

Blanche arched a really nice eyebrow – like, had she actually bothered to do her makeup at seven in the morning? "How about you explain what exactly you mean by that?"

Adrian shifted, shoulder pressing into Josh's leg. "We've seen the Woman twice; she attacked Josh in an attempt to pull me out of hiding the first time, and the second time she attacked both of us."

"You do not seem to be too hurt by this," Hannah remarked, her voice soft.

"She hurt Josh pretty bad the first time, but we were ready for her the second time," Adrian said, tensing.

"Well, ready for her, yeah," Josh said, feeling a need to clarify. "That Man in the Vest, though; he totally caught us off guard."

"You saw both of them?" Erik said, voice sharp again.

"We managed to knock the Woman out," Adrian explained; and if Josh felt a thrill of pride at "we", then that was his secret. "Which is when this man came out and aimed a gun at us."

There was a strange silence at that one, as if no one really knew what to say to that. Adrian was still tense, so Josh said, "And then the Woman started stalking Alden, so we booted it over here."

"They got powers?" TJ said. He turned his phone over and over in his hands.

"The Woman's got long nails," Adrian said. "Very sharp; she uses them like knives. And the Man… If he does, it's nothing I understand."

"I believe the people watching us have physical powers," Hannah said, looking down at her mug. "One smells… burnt, like a storm of some kind. The other is very physical, very… present." She glanced down, swirling her tea slightly.

Alden shifted, pressing into Josh. "Wait, so you can, like, sense powers?"

"I sense danger," Hannah said, fingers tensing on her mug, and then relaxing like she had to think about it. "If I focus, I can… determine the measure of danger. It is… difficult to explain."

"It sounds vague, but it's been our saving grace," Blanche said, drawing their attention again. "When they start planning, the danger grows, and she senses it. This is our third house this year because we knew when to move."

"So, she senses danger and you find a safe place," Adrian said, watching Blanche. "And the guys stick around in case you don't get out fast enough."

"Haven't had to do much damage yet," Marcus said. "Except for the gas station."

"Oh my God," Blanche said, dropping her head into

her hand. "It is too early to talk about the gas station."

"Eh, Marcellus; don't bring up bad memories," TJ said, nudging Marcus with a bony elbow. "I flew thirty feet that day."

"It wasn't that much," Marcus denied.

"Sure felt like it," TJ argued, prodding him again.

"Back on topic," Erik snapped, voice like a whip. Everyone turned to face him. "It would seem we have four people after us, and at least three with powers. Josh and Adrian seem to believe they wish to capture us, not kill."

When everyone turned to look their way, Josh shrugged. "That's what the Woman said, anyways. If they're working together, it would make sense that they'd have the same orders."

He watched as Blanche, Erik, Marcus, TJ, and Hannah all seemed to have some kind of silent conversation. It was super hard to follow, especially when TJ started using hand gestures (Marcus slapped his hands away from his face), and Erik and Hannah started talking in that unknown language again.

Alden leaned into his side. He pushed back silently.

There was more silent and not-so-silent conversation, but either way, Josh was completely lost. He looked down at Adrian. "Maybe we should learn Spanish."

"I feel like Mandarin would be more beneficial," Adrian replied, as if he knew exactly what Josh meant. "There's a lot more people who speak that than Spanish."

"Well, yeah, but what about the Latino population?" Josh countered. "They all speak Spanish."

Adrian craned his neck around to stare up at Josh. "Wow, that was just a little bit racist."

"Yeah, dude," Alden said, jabbing him in the gut with a sharp elbow. "Don't be a moron."

Josh hissed in a breath but didn't argue. He should have known; Tori had been telling him for months to smarten up and fly right. He just didn't like to listen.

And then, the room fell silent, and something prodded his left leg. Josh looked over that way to see Hannah smiling at him – it was like a spotlight had fallen on them or something. Any second now, she was going to tell him that she'd been waiting for someone like him, and that they should go on a date, or maybe she'd just lean in to kiss him, or-

"We're going shopping," she said, eyes sparkling.

Three hours later, Hannah and Erik bundled the four of them all into the Jeep and took them to Rushmore Mall.

"Please, Gott, no," Erik groaned when he saw the parking lot.

"Hush," his sister said, swatting him on the thigh. "I still have shopping to do."

Half on Josh's lap, Alden clapped her hands together. "Alright! Maybe I can bribe my family into forgiving me. Bath and Body Works, anyone?"

Hannah's eyes glinted in the rear-view mirror. "Ja, that can be our first stop."

Adrian, his entire left side squashed up against Josh's right, was staring out the window. "I don't think there's anywhere to park."

"Welcome to Christmas," Dylan muttered, two fingers looped into the back of Alden's belt loops to anchor her

in place. Josh was watching those fingers very carefully -- it was very much a boyfriend move. Had something happened between these two after Josh had gone to bed? If so, when? And why? Weren't they going to ask for his blessing? "The most wonderful time of the year," Dylan finished, bitterly.

"You Americans, so commercial," Erik commented, his voice aloof. "In Deutschland, things are better. More wholesome."

Hannah shot him a very dry look right before she turned into a parking space that seemed to magically appear for her. "Ja, das Christkind is far more wholesome, as are our drinks." She set the Jeep into park and sent another look Erik's way.

He shrugged a shoulder as he undid his seatbelt. "Feuerzangenbowle is much better. I miss it terribly."

"Fur...whasit-bow-wow?" Josh repeated, staring at the two in the front seats.

Hannah twisted in her seat to look back at them. "Feuerzangenbowle. It is a traditional Christmas drink. Now come, we shop." And with that, the two pushed open their doors and climbed out of the Jeep.

Dylan grumbled as he undid his seatbelt. "First, we run for our lives, then we end up Christmas shopping. What a great break."

Alden bounced on their laps, and then slid off towards Dylan's door as he popped it open. "Oh, shut up, you Grinch," she snapped. "Or I won't get you anything."

Josh sighed as blood returned to his left leg. "Oh, thank God, she was heavy," he whispered, running a hand over his thigh.

He got a sharp elbow in his right side from Adrian and then, "C'mon, Deering, let's get a move on."

The shopping mall was, as could be expected, just as busy inside as it was in the parking lot. It took Josh a couple of minutes before he became comfortable with the crowd -- there was quite a difference between a crowded campus of students and a blocked mall of stressed-out Christmas shoppers. He kept close to Adrian, shoulders occasionally knocking into each other, and kept glancing at his face, trying to determine whether Adrian was uncomfortable. But besides the almost-ever-present frown between his eyebrows, Adrian seemed to take the crowd in stride, eyes darting around and lips slightly pursed in concentration. Dylan stayed slightly ahead of them, trailing the girls who were chatting with growing smiles and Erik whose shoulders seemed tense and prepared.

Prepared for what? An attack? Were they really going to get attacked in the middle of a crowded mall? What were they actually doing here -- were the others preparing the house for a siege or something? "I am so confused," Josh admitted, staring at a Dakota's Best store.

"You're not the only one. I didn't know tourism was so big in Rapid City." Adrian also seemed to be staring at the Dakota's Best store.

They continued down the long, straight corridor with storefronts on either side until it opened up into an intersection of sorts. Josh glanced to his right and saw more stores; to his left seemed to lead to a food court.

His stomach gurgled helpfully.

"Ooh! Who wants food?" he asked, pitching his voice so the others could hear him.

The other four paused and turned around, various degrees of interest in their faces. The girls exchanged a look and then Alden shook her head. "No can do, dude. We're on a mission."

Dylan looked hopeful. And hungry. "Please save me," he said bluntly.

Behind him, Alden rolled her eyes.

Hannah smiled and exchanged a look with her brother. "Perhaps we three can continue to Bath and Body Works and meet you for food after?" she suggested. "The others should have more information by then, ja?" she asked her brother in a lower voice.

He shrugged broad shoulders. "Maybe. Gott only knows what the three stooges will do." He narrowed his eyes behind his glasses. "Stay sharp. Do not go alone anywhere."

Josh sent him an admittedly sloppy salute. "Aye aye, captain!"

Erik rolled his eyes, took his sister's elbow, and then started to lead her further down the corridor -- a straight line from where they had come from. Alden sent them a smile, and hooked her arm into Hannah's free arm, and the three set off.

Dylan watched them go, and then said, "I'm thinking burgers."

"Yum," Josh announced before turning to the left and leading them that way.

"Coffee," Adrian stated. "Lots and lots of coffee."

"Amen, brother," Josh agreed, nodding. "Cup number three for me, please." Suddenly Dylan grabbed his sleeve, tugging him to a halt. If Josh overdramatically corrected himself, leaning back and moaning, "Whooooa there," then that was his business.

Dylan was pointing at a GameStop store with his other hand. "They have that Under… Over… Underswatch?" he said, eyes fixed on a sign in the display window. "Kyle's been talking about that game for months." Then, without another word, he released Josh's shirt and started for the store.

"Kyle?"

"His brother," Josh said, sighing as he realized he was going to have to wait another while for food. He followed Dylan into the store anyways.

"Guess the Grinch does Christmas shop," Adrian joked, frowning at the walls of games.

"Eighty dollars?" Dylan squawked, holding the game case in his hands. "Kyle didn't say it was expensive!"

"Yeah, siblings tend to ignore the fine print," Josh said, looking around at the games. Maybe if he got Lilly a game, she wouldn't hate him too much. His dad had said something about her really enjoying the Lego games...

"Maybe you two could split it?" Adrian was suggesting, walking towards Dylan. "Make it a joint present? I think that game's multiplayer anyways…"

Josh frowned slightly. Of course, he wasn't sure what games Lilly did and did not have, or even which ones she'd like. It was one of the major disadvantages of being away from home, and something that pricked at him in small ways. He used to know everything Lilly owned and everything that was happening in her life. Now he just got snippets of phone calls and SnapChats. It wasn't the same.

He turned around, looking at the mall spread out beyond the store's glass doors. Malls were great places for candid photos, and he wished Erik hadn't talked him out of bringing his camera. People walked in both directions: couples and friends, parents and children. Most were chatting amongst themselves with their hands waving and faces alight. A few groups were quiet; a couple of individuals were by themselves, heads ducked into their phones. One lady in a green dress was sitting on a bench and staring into GameStop.

Her dirty blonde hair was pulled back in a loose-looking braid with a thin green headband holding it away from her face. It was a fairly average looking face -- a small nose, pink mouth, light eyes and the kind of complexion that looked like it was usually tanned but now had winter's pale touch. Everything about her was rather fuzzy around the edges: her hair was a bit frizzy, her dress had frayed edges, and her brown boots were ragged around the heels and toes. Her fingers were curled under her cheek, and her head was tilted slightly as she looked through the glass doors and windows. It was almost like she was looking at… him.

He squinted at her, wondering if he was being paranoid. Her lips quirked upwards.

Josh knew he wasn't ugly. But he also wasn't attractive, or at least not attractive enough to get a lot of looks. So this woman, who looked at least five years older than him which meant she was probably a decade older, seemingly checking him out was just… odd. Very, very odd.

He swallowed and turned back to see Adrian pointing at another game and suggesting that a $35 game might be just as good as the other, and Dylan scowling at the one in his hand and then back at the one Adrian was pointing at.

Josh sunk his hands into his jeans pockets and curled his fingers around his phone. He let the familiar weight of it ground him and watched his friends talk and interact just a few feet away from him. He wasn't alone. He was safe. Everything was going to be okay.

The lights in the store flickered.

The three of them stopped and glanced up at the ceiling and the fluorescent lights. They buzzed just loud enough to hear it and shone a little too bright for comfort. Josh looked back at Adrian and Dylan and asked, "You saw that too, right?"

"Yes," Adrian said, voice taut. He glanced over at Dylan. "You should probably decide quickly."

The phone in Josh's hand began to buzz, vibrating in his pocket. Josh pulled it out and glanced at the Caller ID.

"Hey, Alden," he greeted as he answered.

"Josh, I don't know what you guys are doing, but you've got to stop," she said, voice hard in a way that meant she was worried. "Hannah is sensing danger."

"Uh, where you are or where we are?" he asked, turning around to face the front of the store again.

The lady in the green dress was gone. A cold shiver went down his spine.

"You," she snapped. "Hannah's sensing danger around you guys, that's why I'm calling you."

"Dylan's just gonna be another minute," he said, frowning at the bench that was strangely unoccupied.

"Should we meet somewhere or…?"

All the lights in the store went out. Just sudden silence in the store; he hadn't been aware of how much noise the lights, the fans, or the computers behind the counter made. Josh's fingers tightened around his phone, looked out at the bright mall just beyond the store's glass display windows, and said, "Shit."

"Josh? Josh, we're gonna meet you by the car, okay?" Alden was saying, her voice getting higher in pitch. "Just head towards the parking lot-"

"I'll come back for the game later," Dylan said, appearing at Josh's shoulder. "They just lost all the power in the store."

"But not in the mall." Josh inhaled, then exhaled. "Got it, Alden. We'll head there right now."

"Head where?"

Josh ignored Dylan as he hung up his phone and shoved it deep in his pocket. "Where's Adrian; we gotta go."

"He just got a phone call too," Dylan answered, pointing behind them to Adrian who was standing by the cash register and counter.

"Aid," Josh called. "We gotta go."

Adrian glanced up, phone pressed to his ear, and nodded at them. He started towards them, moving slower than Josh would have liked, but eh. He'd take what he could get.

He grabbed Dylan's sleeve and said, "C'mon," and led him towards the mall.

The second he and Dylan stepped over the threshold, the sliding doors slammed shut behind them, catching

Dylan's coat in the process.

"Shit!" he yelped, falling back against the glass doors. Josh spun on his heel and grabbed Dylan by the arm, pulling him forward, even as he stared inside GameStop. Adrian stared back at him with the glass separating them for a long moment. Shaking out of it, Adrian banged a fist against the glass, making a hollow sound, even as Dylan squawked, "Leggo, leggo of me, Josh. Just let me-" and he pushed Josh far enough away that he could get his hands between them and unzipped his coat, shrugging out of it. He stepped away from the door, and the coat fell limp against the glass.

Josh blinked at the coat. "Hell, that was smart. Where'd you learn that trick?"

"Movies," Dylan said, rubbing a hand over his opposite shoulder. "Ugh, that hurt," he grunted.

Adrian slammed another fist against the glass and demanded in a loud voice, "What the hell is going on?" At least, Josh assumed it was a loud voice -- it was muffled through the inches of solid glass.

Josh gestured wildly. "You think I know anything?"

Adrian started making a face at him, but then stopped, expression frozen in place. He turned his head slowly to the side and peered into the dark store behind him. He inched closer to the doors as he turned around.

Josh scowled and banged his fists against the glass. "Aid!" he shouted. "What's happening?"

Adrian made a gesture with his hand: a half-assed cutting motion that said, Shut up, Deering. And then, suddenly, his head snapped back, and he fell back against the door, the back of his skull cracking against the glass before he slumped onto the floor. Even as Josh shouted, "Aid-!" Adrian slid across the floor and deeper into the shadows of the store.

"What the hell was that?" Dylan shouted next to him.

"I don't know; why does everyone keep asking me things?" Josh babbled, turning his head to glare at Dylan.

"Josh!"

The two of them turned around to see Alden, Hannah, and Erik standing ten feet behind them. Josh's shoulders slumped in relief at seeing reinforcements. "Oh, thank God. The doors are locked, and Adrian is trapped inside-"

"Move," Erik grunted. His coat was buttoned up with four crisp black buttons, and he undid one quickly, shoved a hand inside, and pulled out a small handgun.

"Holy shit!" Josh yelped, gripping Dylan by the sleeve.

"What the fuck, man?" Dylan snapped, clutching at Josh's hands, scrabbling for grip.

"Move!" Erik barked, his voice sharp.

Dylan shoved Josh sideways, away from the door, still snapping at Erik. Josh, almost losing his footing, watched as Erik raised the gun to chest level, squinted slightly, and then shot off two bullets.

Bang! Bang!

Suddenly there were shrieks and screams all around them; Josh watched as a group of teenage girls dropped to the ground with their hands covering their ears, as two young men flinched back into a wall, and as a mother picked up her little girl and ran away. As if the gunshots created some kind of sound barrier between the five of them and the rest of the world, Josh viewed everyone's reactions to the gunshots with a distanced eye, oddly intrigued and confused by their actions. Why would she run in that direction? Why cover their ears and not their entire heads?

Why did Erik make him leave his camera at home? These were amazing shots!

Dylan was still shouting at Erik -- curse words and deities and Erik's ascendency -- and Hannah was holding a suddenly shrieking Alden with a surprisingly tight grip. Erik stayed straight faced as he lowered his arm and started to stalk towards the door with the hole in the glass.

Josh glanced over towards the doors, his grip loosening on Dylan's hands, and saw the small hole with the spiderweb pattern spreading across the glass. He gently pushed Dylan's hands away, still feeling somewhat separated from the rest of the party, and walked towards the door. He opened his mouth and croaked, "Aid?" He swallowed at his weak voice and tried again: "Adrian?"

He flinched violently back a step as Adrian was suddenly thrown into the glass door, just a few inches away from the bullet hole. Erik spat out, "Fick!" and stepped back as Adrian slumped down to the floor. The glass where his shoulders had hit cracked further as small pieces fell to the floor around Adrian's body.

"Holy-" Dylan was yelping again. Another couple of screams split the air behind them and Josh stumbled towards Adrian's body. He reached the glass and thought, If I punch it, I'll get cut, but I can't kick that high!

At his feet, another few shards of glass fell in soft, tinkling sounds, and on the other side of the mostly stable glass Adrian let out a low groan. He dropped his head against the glass, sending another couple of pieces falling around him and into his hair, and then peeled his eyes open. He blinked dazed gray eyes at Josh and croaked, "He still there?"

"Who? Who's still-"

There was a roar from inside GameStop, and Josh's head snapped up to see a very angry man stumble out from the dark, yanking at shadows around his chest and legs. The man growled a very loud sound, and in a couple of false starts, began storming towards Adrian, his steps measured. Adrian groaned lowly, then raised his fists; the recently ripped-off shadows began swirling around the Angry Dude's feet.

"Move, Josh!" Erik's voice snapped out again, and Josh flinched around, spinning out of the way just as another bang shot out and a bullet whistled into the glass between him and Adrian. It shattered just as the Angry Dude reached Adrian, grabbed him by the shirt, and then slammed his head into the back of the glass.

It was a cacophony: the shrieking of girls behind Josh (one sounded kinda like Alden); the low, hollow echo that came after a bullet shot; and the almost slow-motion shattering of glass surrounding them. Between the three bullets and Adrian's twice-slammed body, the door finally gave way, and Josh felt small pricks cover his back and right arm.

"Josh!" Alden shouted -- a sound full of fear and panic that was almost overshadowed by Adrian's loud gasp of pain.

Josh gasped himself, mostly out of fear -- because

what the hell was going on? -- and turned back just in time to see the Angry Dude in full view. It was a couple of seconds, but enough for Josh to see that the Angry Dude was tall -- like 6'4 easy -- and broad with that buzzed-cut nondescript brown-blond hair and a decent beard on his face. As Josh gaped at this beast of a man -- like, seriously, he should have auditioned for the live-action reboot of that Disney movie -- the dude raised Adrian's body, which didn't put up as much of a struggle as it should have, high over their heads. Adrian groaned again, a low, pained sound.

"Oy! Arschloch!" Erik shouted behind them.

The Angry Dude's eyes cut over to look past Josh's shoulder, and suddenly all the lights in the area -- including GameStop -- turned on with a bright, blinding white light. It was bright enough that Josh winced and cringed away from it, turning his head into his shoulder.

And then, suddenly, there was a choking sound, and Josh turned his head back to see the shadows from earlier -- stronger now, as if they had just been waiting for some light to give them shape -- circle Angry Dude's throat and tighten. Josh looked up to see Adrian sweating and panting but looking angry and determined with steely eyes.

"Josh, I swear to Gott," he heard behind him, and as if that was the trigger Josh didn't know he needed, he took in a deep breath, let it out, and then barrelled forward, through the barely holding glass, and drove his shoulder into the Angry Dude as hard as he possibly could.

Even if Josh wasn't very strong, the surprise seemed to be enough for the Angry Dude to stumble back a few steps -- which was good, because Josh wasn't very good at sudden stops, and he too moved forward a few feet -- and dropped Adrian into a pile at Josh's feet.

"You idiot!" Dylan shouted behind him, just as the Angry Dude raised his hands to his throat and started yanking at the shadows. They came off like wet paper, breaking beneath his grip.

"Oh, shit," Josh gasped, just as all the lights in the store went out again.

The sudden change -- dark to bright to dark -- made Josh's vision go fuzzy, and in those few moments when he couldn't focus, something long and strong wrapped itself around his right leg. For a split second, he thought it was a tentacle, and then maybe one of Adrian's shadows, and then it yanked him right off his feet. He fell backwards, the back of his skull and most of his torso slamming into the ground, and as he gasped from the combination of sudden sharp pain and the sudden loss of breath, he was pulled across the floor. He reached out, trying to stop, felt the brush of fabric against his fingers -- Adrian? -- and then was thrown leg-first. He slid against the floor, his head muggy and eyes burning, and then felt another sudden sharp pain, and then—

Nothing.

"-sh! Josh!"

Pain. Low, throbbing, aching pain. Josh groaned at it, felt the sea of darkness ebb away the same way you gently peel off a Band-Aid and forced his eyes open. The world around him was dark too, but not as dark as what had been behind his eyelids. There were shadows, and figures, and then, suddenly, sparks of light -- flashes of fire and danger.

Josh forced himself awake, focusing like he did when he was about to take a picture. Above him were screens: TVs and tablets and open laptops, and all of them were flickering on and off in rapid succession. There were sparks flying off several wires that were dangling dangerously close to his head, and one was swaying like a hypnotist's pendulum.

The pain thrummed low in his head, and he closed his eyes against it. Maybe this was all just a bad dream, and when he actually woke up-

Thud!

A very girly, loud shriek.

Josh opened his eyes and turned his head -- something crunched under his scalp -- and gazed through the dark room -- which didn't look that dark really -- and saw a large mass against what looked like a large glass window. On the other side of the window was a brightly lit open area and a girl with her hands pressed to her face.

Alden.

Rushmore Mall.

GameStop.

Adrian.

There was a deep, dark chuckle echoing around the room, and Josh's eyes focused on a large figure stomping over to the pile by the glass doors. The Angry Dude. He loomed over the pile and then with a loud grunt, reached down and pulled up two arms out of the pile. Attached to the arms were two bodies: Dylan and Erik. They didn't look quite conscious.

Josh exhaled slowly and turned his head to face the

ceiling and that slowly swaying sparking wire. He closed his eyes and bent his knees and pushed himself across the floor until his legs were straight. The sparking sounded louder. He could see the change of light through his eyelids as the screens flickered on and off. He bent his knees again, then straightened them again. Schoom; he slid himself a few inches. Schoom. A dual sound of thuds from across the room. Schoom. Schoom. Schoom. He opened his eyes again and found himself blinking at a row of headphones.

Cool.

He rolled himself onto his stomach, and then pushed himself up on his elbows. He commando crawled farther down the aisle, moving so very slowly because every jolt made his head spasm, and then peered around a shelf. He froze up, breath catching in his chest.

The Angry Dude held a weakly struggling Adrian off the ground, his feet dangling a couple of inches off the floor. His huge hands were curled around Adrian's throat, and he had his back to Josh… which meant that Adrian was facing Josh.

Josh couldn't tell the colour of Adrian's face from here, especially not with the darkness and blinding pain of his head. But he saw the moment Adrian noticed him, saw the hope that filled his expression, and saw the way he gasped when the Angry Dude tightened his grip.

What could he do? What could he — Adrian was going to die, and Dylan and Erik were probably unconscious, and Alden wasn't prepared for this, and why would she be? Josh wasn't ready for this, and he was the one who had dragged them all into this. And Hannah could only sense danger; she couldn't fight it! And all Josh had was a crazy headache and a wall of headphones—

He craned his neck around and blinked up at the wall of headphones. He blinked again, forcing the pain away. Then he pushed himself up on his knees and reached up with both arms and yanked off as many headphones as he could. Then, turning back to the Angry Dude's back, he pulled back his arm as far as he could, and chucked a headphone at the hulking man.

It hit him somewhere in his lower back, and the man flinched at it. Adrian gasped for breath.

Josh drew in another breath, pushed past a sudden wave of nausea -- oh, God, don't get sick now -- and threw another headphone. And then a third, and then a fourth, aiming at the Angry Dude's head.

He hit the right shoulder, the back of the neck, and then, as the Angry Dude turned his face to look at where the attacks were coming from, his cheek. The fifth throw hit him smack in the face, causing him to grunt and drop Adrian, who, again, fell like a sack of bricks.

Josh flinched back, trying to hide back in the aisle, just as the Angry Dude shouted a loud cry. Suddenly, all the lights in the store came buzzing on, bright and blinding, and Josh cried out as his head swarmed with sharp pain, and his stomach rolled with bile. He covered his head with his arms just as he heard another shout -- different from the Angry Dude's -- a sudden gunshot, and then, after a brief pause, an alarm ringing through the store, which went right through Josh in a shrieking banshee sort of way.

A fire alarm. Someone had set off a fire alarm.

"Dammit," he heard a low voice grunt, and Josh curled his arms tighter around his head. "Now what am I gonna— Ah." Josh felt a wave of fear shudder through him at the satisfaction in that voice. "That'll work."

Josh waited for something to happen, but all he could hear was the shrill ringing of the alarm. Carefully, he pulled his head out from under his arms and raised it. There was no one around. Exhaling a slow, quiet sound, he pulled all of his courage together to sit in his chest, and then peered around the corner of the aisle again.

The Angry Dude was nowhere to be seen, but Adrian was sprawled out on the floor, one arm outstretched towards the back of the store. From this distance, Josh couldn't tell if he was even alive.

A loud grunt broke through the wailing of the alarm, and Josh craned his neck around to see the Angry Dude walking back towards Adrian with a large TV cradled in his arms. The closer he walked, the higher he raised the TV.

"No," Josh breathed. His chest felt like someone had dropped a slab of concrete onto it, but still he tried to yell: "Aid. Adrian. Adrian!"

The Angry Dude loomed over Adrian, the TV raised high over his head. Josh struggled to get up onto his knees—

And then Adrian's eyes snapped open, a female shout sounded from the back of the store, and a gunshot cracked through the alarm. The TV screen shattered, and the Angry Dude let out a cry just as Adrian was suddenly pulled backwards towards the main door by a shadow Josh hadn't seen, and another body covered in green fabric was pulled towards the Angry Dude. The body hit the Angry Dude's feet, and between that and the very unbalanced TV, the Angry Dude teetered and tottered, and then fell in a pile of limbs. The TV landed half on them, half on the floor in a jarring crash!

Something touched Josh's arm, and he yelped, flinching backwards into the headphone wall.

Hannah flinched back as well, her hand pulled up to her chest. "Sorry," she gasped. "I am sorry. But we must go. Now."

Josh blinked at her and croaked, "Adrian."

She nodded. "Erik has him. And I have you. Now come." She curled her hand around his arm and gently tugged him towards her. He followed her on his knees and hands, head swimming and ears half-deaf.

She led him out of the store, past the dangling wires, past the pile of groaning limbs and shattered TV, and carefully through the glass shard surrounded doors. On the other side of the store were the others, with Alden crying as she spoke on the phone, and Adrian mostly collapsed between Erik and Dylan who were supporting him to the best of their ability.

Erik's eyes darted over to Josh and Hannah, who had one arm slung around his waist. "We must go. Now."

Josh swayed a little. "I think I'm gonna be sick," he groaned as his stomach heaved again.

"Concussion," Hannah said, voice as curt as her brother's. "There was blood on the shelf."

"Oh my God," Alden whined, before she focused back onto her phone conversation. "No. Yes, we're coming. We're coming right now."

"Where's the police?" Josh slurred, as his feet tried to follow Hannah's guidance. She led him to the side of the other three, and when Josh glanced over, he saw Adrian's eyelids were half-lidded.

"We do not know. And we do not wish to meet with them. Come, Josh."

Dylan bumped his shoulder against Josh's. "You okay, man?" he asked, voice low and concerned.

"Didn't get your game," Josh said, tripping slightly.

"Whatever, man," Dylan replied. "I'll get him a gift card."

And the chuckles that escaped his chest hurt like hell, but it was better than not having them at all.

Chapter Eleven:
Of Weapons, Waking, and Wrecking

An hour later, head still throbbing, Josh stared at Blanche's outstretched hand. "Dude, that doesn't look like Advil to me."

She sighed a long sigh through her nose. Josh tried to stifle a grin; Tori used to make that sound all the time. It was the sigh of Why do I put up with this? "You might have a concussion, Creepula; Advil aren't gonna help that much."

"But, see, I think they're gonna help and if I believe in something hard enough, my brain might trick my body into making it so." Josh looked up into her face and grinned his most obnoxious grin. "It's, like, a thing."

She narrowed her eyes at him. From the large armchair behind them, Marcus huffed a sigh. "I'll go get him some."

Which is about when Dylan stepped into the room. "Nope! No Advil. No painkillers, no nothing."

Josh pouted. "No nothing?" he repeated.

Dylan waved his phone around. "Google says that painkillers might increase bleeding in the brain. Has anyone taken a look at his pupils lately?"

Blanche rolled her eyes. "Guys, I had a purpose

here-"

There was a weight dropping onto the couch beside him. A hand grabbed his chin and he was forced to look into Alden's eyes. They were big and hazel and very concerned.

"I am looking at his pupils," she narrated. "What am I looking for?"

"Enlarged or two different sizes," Dylan's voice said.

Josh looked back at Alden, then at her hair. It was quite nice today, which was rather incredible considering the morning they'd had. "I like your hair," he said.

"His pupils are wacked," Alden announced. "And so is his brain."

"I'm calling it." Dylan's voice was decisive. "Concussion."

Blanche sighed that long sigh through her nose again. "I told you that."

"No, you said he may have a concussion—" Alden started.

"Oh my God," Blanche cut in. She thrust her hand and the strange object she was holding in it between Josh and Alden's faces. "Here. For you."

Josh blinked down at it. It looked like a small black box. "What is it?"

Alden reached out and poked it. "Looks dangerous."

"It's a taser," Blanche explained in a tense voice.

As if on cue, both Alden and Josh went, "Whoooooa!" and reared backwards, away from the taser. Alden fell to one side of the couch; Josh fell back on the other. His head hit the armrest. It made everything in his skull shudder and wobble, like a figurine on an off-balance shelf. He closed his eyes and went, "Oh God."

"Bee, maybe this isn't the best time," Marcus said.

Josh kept his eyes closed. It seemed wise. "You have a nickname of a nickname? Wow."

"Look, he needs something to protect himself with. A taser is optimal—"

"Is that even legal?" Dylan asked. His voice was getting loud in that way it did when he was upset.

"Yes. Tasers are legal in South Dakota," Blanche replied. "It is also the perfect weapon for a pretty useless person."

"Wow," Dylan said.

"Savage," Alden chirped.

"Ruuuuuuude," Josh moaned. "I have saved Adrian, like, twice by now. I should get points for that."

"Look," and suddenly there was a slender and cool hand grabbing at his hand. The hand forced a palm-sized rectangular object into his hand and curled fingers around his. Another hand reached out and rearranged his fingers and grip. "Okay," Blanche said. "All you have to do is turn on this switch," and their thumbs found the switch and together flicked it on, "and then push it into the other person."

Josh kept his eyes closed but curled his fingers tighter around the taser. "Do that again," he requested.

Blanche's hands went through the motion of turning off the taser, turning on the taser, and then a forward push. "Did you get that?"

"Flick, wait a second, then forward push. Got it."

"Right." Her thumb flicked the taser off again. "Just remember to keep it turned off if you're not using it. And if you hold it against a person for too long, you could actually kill them, so be careful, alright?"

"Alright," Josh agreed quietly. He folded his fingers around the taser and pulled it into his chest, over his heart. He said, "Thanks, Blanche. Can I go to sleep now?"

A third long sigh through her nose. "Yeah. Sure."

"Not in my bed, you're not," Dylan butted in. A larger, warmer hand grabbed Josh's free one. "C'mon, man. Up and at 'em."

Josh forced his eyes open to see Dylan looking down at him. With a groan, he forced his body up into a sitting position and then, with Dylan pulling on his arm, up on his feet. Dylan then dropped his hand, and put his hands on Josh's back, steering him down the hall. "Alright, let's go. I think Cross is still sleeping anyways."

Dylan steered him towards Marcus' bedroom and opened the door quietly. The room inside was dark and Josh could hear Adrian's soft snores. He stumbled towards the bed, waited for Dylan to turn the blankets down, and then crawled underneath. Dylan tucked him in in soft motions, then whispered, "I'll check on ya' in about half an hour, okay man?"

Josh grunted. The walk here had worn him out again, and his head was still foggy and thick. Everything hurt and everything was scary and he was going to miss Christmas.

"'Kay. Night, man," Dylan whispered again. A few seconds later, the door closed, and Adrian made a sound in his sleep. Something knocked into Josh's foot -- he guessed it was Adrian's foot -- and then, still hugging the taser to his chest, he fell into the darkness.

Dylan woke him up the first time. It was a couple of strong shakes, a whispered, "Josh! Wake up, man!" and then another couple of shakes.

Josh moaned weakly and swatted at the voice's general direction. His hand was caught by another hand and then, "Hey, hey, shh… I just wanna make sure you're alive."

"I'm alive," Josh slurred.

"Okay. Okay." Dylan's voice sounded weird. "You're alive."

"I'm sleeping," Josh mumbled, already curling back into the darkness.

"Okay, Josh. You're sleeping."

Then Alden:

"Josh? Joshua?" There were hands on his arm, and they shook and shook and shook, like a dryer rumbling back and forth.

"I'm 'wake, Immawake," Josh mumbled.

"Oh, thank God. Okay, um, Dylan said to check your pupils…" and then the hands were on his face and forcing him to turn.

He blinked eyes open and looked at Alden's face. "You have a nice face," he informed her.

She bit her lip. "Okay, sweetie. So do you."

"Yeah, yeah, yeah," he mumbled before he slipped back into the darkness.

Third time:

"Josh? Joshua? You must awaken."

Josh forced his eyes open and squinted at Hannah. "You."

She smiled -- it wasn't her sunrise smile, but it was a smile nonetheless. "Me. How is your head?"

"Hurts," Josh mumbled. "You look like a song."

Her face made a weird expression. "A song?"

"Mmhmm..." Josh turned more on his side. "You're just like an angel. Your skin makes me cry..."

Her face went a lovely shade of pink. "Oh. Um-"

"Float like a feather..." he mumbled. "In a beau'ful world... You're so... special..."

"Sleep, Josh," she whispered, passing a hand over his hair. It was soft and gentle, just like her. "Go to sleep."

"I wish I was special..."

Fourth:

"You got a concussion?"

That was Adrian's voice. Josh curled into a tighter ball and groaned, "Go away..."

"An actual concussion." Adrian's voice was tired, like it hurt to speak. "I've learned about those."

"Good for you," Josh grumbled, reaching for his pillow.

"What's in your hand?" Adrian asked. "A box?"

"It's a taser." He shoved his face deeper into the pillow.

"A taser? You have a taser?"

"I'm useless," Josh explained, shifting to get more comfortable.

"So they gave you a taser?"

"Yeah..."

"Are they stupid?"

And Josh would have laughed, but he was already practically asleep.

And finally:

"Hey, weirdo. You hungry?"

Josh peeled back his eyelids just enough to glare at Blanche. "No."

She leaned in, seemed to examine his eyes, and then rocked back on her heels. She shrugged. "Okay. I'll put your portion in the fridge for later, 'kay?"

Josh closed his eyes again. "'Kay."

He listened to her walk away and the squeak of a door opening. Then: "Hey. I'm glad you're not dead."

"Whoooo..." Josh droned, trying to gather enough enthusiasm to sound sincere. He fell asleep instead.

When Josh woke up for real, he was aware of two things. The first was that his head was pounding, but not unbearably so. The second was that he really needed to piss.

He opened his eyes and became aware of a few other things: he was still in bed, and there was a weight beside him -- Adrian softly snored and shifted a little. The room was dark around him, and his stomach was paining in that please-feed-me-I'm-dying kind of way. Slowly, he reached out a hand for his phone on the nightstand -- someone had plugged it in for him. The screen glowed softly, and he peered at the time. 2:12. Man, was his sleep schedule whacked now.

He groaned and forced himself up on his elbows. Bathroom. He needed to get to the bathroom. His mouth felt like something had died in there -- he should probably grab some water, too. He rolled himself out of bed and realized he was still in his jeans, socks, and shirt. At least his socks had protected him from the cold of the floor; however, he felt clammy all over, as if he'd been sweating in his sleep. He shuddered, gross, and stumbled his way to the door. He opened it as slowly as he could so he didn't disturb Adrian, and then inched out into the hallway before heading for the bathroom.

He relieved himself and as he ducked his head under the tap to gulp cool water down, the ache in his head became more persistent. He pulled his head out of the stream of water and closed his eyes, feeling his pulse drum on the inside of his eyelids. Man, but a concussion was a bitch.

He turned the tap off and made his way back to the door. He had kept the lights off, the shimmer of the moonlight through the small upper window giving enough light for him to comfortably move with his night-adjusted vision. Opening the door, he stood in the doorway for a moment and stared down the hall of a house he had no place in. He thought, oddly, of his home back in Rockford, and the night-light that illuminated the main hall at night; the same night-light his mother had picked for him when he was a child. The memory made something in his chest throb, and between that and his headache, he closed his eyes and breathed for a moment, gathering his strength.

Which, of course, was when all the lights in the house

came on.

"Aw, fuuuuuck," Josh groaned, covering his face with his hands and curling into the doorframe. The brightness made his head spasm in pain, and he squeezed his eyes tight as if that could block out the blinding light. Instead, it made his head swim, and he leaned against the doorframe until he thought he could bear to open his eyes. He squinted, fought back the bile rising in the back of his throat, and frowned at Adrian peering from the doorframe of the bedroom.

"You okay?" he asked, his voice groggy in that just-woke-up way.

Josh blinked away the water in his eyes and nodded jerkily. "Yeah. I'm, uh. I'm fine. Shit," he gasped as another wave of pain shuddered through his head. "Just. My head."

There were footsteps, and then a very gentle hand cupped the side of his head. "Are you able to walk?" Adrian asked.

Josh closed his eyes and breathed. "Yeah. I think so."

"Because something is going on," Adrian continued, voice gruff but gentle. "And I need you to be awake enough to stay safe."

Josh stood for a moment and took inventory of himself. "I can't move fast, but I can move," he decided finally.

"Good enough." The hand left his head and clapped his shoulder. "C'mon. I wanna check on the kitchen."

"The kitchen?" Josh followed him, trying to keep his steps smooth. From another room, he could hear groaning that sounded a lot like Dylan when he first woke up from a nap. Aw man, that guy was sleeping on the couch -- the lights must be killer in there.

"Was it just the lights that came on, or did anything else turn on?" Adrian wondered, walking into the kitchen. "Like… the stove. Or oven," he added, stalking over to the appliances in question, and spinning dials off.

Josh blinked at him and said, "Would, uh. Would that have hurt us?"

Adrian glanced at him. "Don't know. Depends on how clean their oven is or if someone got near to it. Either way, it's a hazard we don't have time to deal with. Now, c'mon." And he walked back over to Josh, hooked his fingers into Josh's shirtsleeve, and steered him back into the hallway and towards the living room.

Inside the living room, Dylan was pulling aside the curtain to look out the window in the pyjama pants and undershirt he normally slept in.

"Get away from the window!" Adrian snapped

Dylan released the curtain and turned, a scowl on his drowsy face. "They know something's up," he snapped. "It's two o'clock and all the lights are on; what the hell is going on!" he finished in a raised voice.

It made Josh wince and he pressed a hand against his forehead. "Dude," he gasped. "Inside voices please."

"No time for that," came another voice. Josh opened his eyes and looked up towards the top of the stairs where a similarly dressed TJ stood. He pressed his hands against the railing of the stairs, eyes darting between them all, and then hopped up and over the railing, dropping the several feet to the main landing. Josh inhaled sharply -- dude, what the actual hell?! -- but he landed on his feet softly and simply.

Josh breathed. "He's a cat."

TJ spared him a glance and a quirk of a smile, and then turned to Adrian with a serious expression. "We gotta get the normals to a safe place."

"What do you suggest?" Adrian asked. "Do you wanna hide them in the basement or--"

Which is just when the smoke detectors started blaring.

The sound went straight through Josh like a sharp weapon -- through his brain and out the other side. He swore and bent over, hands covering his ears and eyes pressed closed. Throughout the house, shouts and cries sounded like a weird rollcall and the smoke detectors rang on and on and on.

Concussions were a bitch.

"What the hell is going on?" he heard Dylan shout.

"They're psyching us out, man!" TJ shouted back.

There were hands on Josh's shoulders, and he was slowly pushed back until his back pressed against the wall. "Stay there," Adrian ordered; and Josh opened his eyes enough to see Adrian's worried, stressed face before he darted back down the hall.

TJ was glaring in the direction of the other hall towards the front door, and Dylan was casting worried glances upstairs. Josh wished he could just think (dude, just think, you need to think), but his head was ringing from the detectors and the lights.

Suddenly there was the sound of a gun going off -- bang! -- and an abrupt scream. Dylan and Josh locked eyes, and there was an instant understanding. Alden. That was Alden's scream.

Dylan's eyes ran up and down Josh's body quickly, in that distant but calculating way he had when he was taking inventory of injuries. Josh had seen him do it a dozen times before when he visited Dylan at his soccer practices or when they overheard someone complaining about pain. Josh pushed himself off the wall, but before he could make himself step forward, Dylan was already heading for the stairs with his hand reaching for the railing.

Bang!

Josh's head swung around -- and the world went black for a second before his vision cleared -- because that gunshot was coming from the front door. Another shot rang out.

"Shit," TJ said, voice calm. "Someone get Erik down here. Now."

A hand grabbed Josh's shoulder -- and oh my God, it was the Woman, it was totally the Woman -- but no. It was Adrian, and he was pushing the taser into Josh's chest. He gave Josh a quick nod and then bolted, brushing past him and heading for the front door with TJ right on his heels.

Bang! echoed from upstairs, and another series of female shouts followed. Josh turned to see Dylan almost at the top of the stairs, moving as fast as he could.

Josh exhaled a slow, long breath, focused his mind, and pushed himself off the wall. The stairs. He had to go upstairs and check on the girls and find Erik and--

Another bang and then all the lights and detectors went out with a quiet shhhm. Josh stopped in the middle of the living room and looked around slowly. The entire house was still, like that moment in a movie before shit hit the fan. Nothing was moving, and he couldn't see where

Dylan was.

"Dill?" he called, his voice wavering.

"TJ, I need light now!" Adrian called out.

"They're not working, Cross!"

Thud! from upstairs, an aborted scream, and suddenly a loud series of running footsteps from upstairs. "Dill?" Josh called again, a bit firmer as his eyes slowly began to adjust to the dark; and then suddenly a man charged onto the upstairs landing, seemed to hit something, and then slammed into the stair railing before tumbling over it, landing in a muted crash a few feet away from a frozen Josh.

"Holy shit," he gasped as the crumpled figure shuddered, groaned, and then collapsed into a pile on the floor.

"Oy!"

Josh's head snapped up and he stared at a dark figure at the top of the stairs. His eyes were finally adjusted enough to make out Marcus, hands planted on the stair railing and face set. "Romero!" he shouted, seemingly ignoring everyone else. "Where the hell are you?"

Bang! Crash!

"Shit!" TJ yelped.

Josh turned to the front door and stumbled backwards as TJ and Adrian ran back into the living room. TJ kept moving straight for the stairs, while Adrian slowed enough to look at Josh and snap, "Hide!" before following on TJ's heels.

Josh moved backwards until his back hit the wall, his right hand pressing against the frame of the open hallway just as a lean figure stalked into the living room. Her hair was tied back, and her hands flexed at her sides.

The Woman. Oh hell, Josh thought as he slid around the frame and tried to duck back into the hall.

TJ was already moving up the stairs, and then movement caught Josh's eye at the top of the stairs. He watched as another female figure stepped up to Marcus's side, raised an arm, and flicked on a flashlight.

The beam of light shone right on the Woman's face, and she hissed and raised a clawed hand to cover her face. At the base of the stairs, Adrian turned on his heel, raised his hands, and pulled the newly formed shadows of the Woman's form up out of the ground and around her legs. She looked down, face twisted up in a scowl, and snapped, "Not these damn things again!"

And then Josh felt the weight of the taser in his hand and remembered that Adrian had passed it to him. He looked into the living room: the crumbled form of what looked like that Angry Dude from the mall; the trapped Woman half bent over and scratching at the shadows clinging to her legs; Adrian posed and focused at the base of the stairs; TJ tripping over Dylan's curled up form on the stairs and saying, "C'mon, man, you gotta move;" and Blanche and Marcus straight and tall at the top of the stairs, the former holding that flashlight steady and the latter looking back into the upstairs rooms.

It would have been a perfect picture if he hadn't been living in it.

He felt the weight of the taser in his hand, pushed aside the constant ache of his skull, and pushed forward. His thumb found the switch and slid it into the on position while he moved forward, going around the side of the Woman. She twisted and squirmed as she clawed at the shadows sticking to her legs and didn't even notice Josh stepping up and pushing the humming taser into the small of her back.

Instantly she gasped and pulled away. Josh followed, keeping the taser in contact with her body as she shuddered and made a small scream and then fell limp, held up by the shadows.

Josh pulled the taser away and flicked it off, blinking as Adrian exhaled and slowly released the shadows, lowering the Woman in a controlled fall. He felt a rushing in his ears, similar to the way he felt the first time he'd knocked the Woman into unconsciousness. He said, "Oh my God. That worked. Blanche, that actually--"

"Down, Josh!" she snapped; and because Josh was a stupid, disobedient human, he turned around instead.

The Man in the Vest stood in the doorway, a gun held up and aimed right at Josh. He didn't say anything, just dropped his eyes and the gun down a couple of feet. As he pulled the trigger, Josh felt the cold touch of shadows wrap around his chest and pull.

Bang! went the gun, and Josh stumbled backwards as the shadows pulled him away. The bullet hit the floor with a crack of wood splintering, and Josh watched as the flashlight beam moved and shone right in the Man in the Vest's face. He hissed in a very similar manner to the Woman, and as the shadows helped steady Josh, he heard Blanche say, "Just shoot his knee out."

As the shadows melted off of Josh -- and wasn't that a strange way to describe it when they were cold and clammy, not warm and silky -- he turned back to the stairwell and the figures on it and watched as a third form joined Blanche and Marcus, raise their arm -- no, not their arm, his arm, it was Erik -- and aim right at the Man in the Vest. Josh turned his head to see the man straighten and say, very calmly, "Lumiere."

Josh had a split second to think, Wait, isn't that a candlestick? before all the lights turned back on with a buzz of blinding white.

Josh closed his eyes tight as he gasped out a shout; behind him he heard similar cries of pain and alarm. He bent his head low and wished that this back-and-forth of light and dark would stop, just please stop, his head couldn't take it anymore. His entire skull was throbbing and aching, and he was afraid to open his eyes because he knew the light would make the pain sharp and cutting. But then he heard a satisfied grunt, and he peeked his eyes open and looked at the ground long enough to see his own shadow being pulled away from where it met his feet, swirled around his body, and then out towards the front door.

It was a strange feeling, watching his shadow move; even though he knew, technically, that it wasn't a part of him whatsoever, there was still a certain amount of possession he felt over it. The shadow was formed by him; therefore, it was a part of him. Now, it was under Adrian's control which meant, kind of, that it was a part of him. He blinked against the light and sharp pain and circling thoughts, and turned his head to follow his shadow's path as it travelled across the floor, meeting with another shadow, and then slinking up a pair of pressed pants. It slid up and up to the waistline and then past that, coating a dark green vest and expensive gray shirt.

He raised his head and stared at the Man in the Vest who was covered from collarbone to feet in smoky gray shadows. The Man in the Vest looked back at Josh, eyes intent but expression rather calm and calculating. He didn't seem upset at all.

Behind and high above them, Hannah's voice suddenly broke through with, "Erik! Erik, come!"

Josh didn't have to turn to know that Erik had gone after that voice; he could hear the footsteps, and what little he knew of Erik told him he responded to Hannah's cries the same way Josh ran when Lilly called him. Besides, for reasons he couldn't understand, he couldn't take his eyes away from the Man in the Vest's.

And then Adrian gasped out a sound of surprise and pain, and the shadows wrapped around the Man in the Vest slipped slightly. The man's lips quirked up before Josh turned around to see the Angry Dude with one hand wrapped around Adrian's ankle and shakily trying to get up on his other hand and knees.

"Uh, guys!" Josh called.

Movement on the stairs caught his eye and he looked up in time to see TJ, two-thirds of the way up the stairs, plant his hands on the bannister, inhale sharply, and then flip himself over the bannister. With a strange sense of distance, Josh watched as TJ fell through the air and landed, feet first, right on the Angry Dude's back. He winced as the Angry Dude's breath left his body in a whoosh and he collapsed again under TJ's weight.

On Josh's other side, the Man in the Vest mildly grunted, "Ouch."

For a split second, Josh didn't know whether he wanted to laugh because of him or hate him. Possibly both. Could you appreciate someone's comedic timing even while thinking they were a psychopath?

But – and Josh wasn't sure how – the Angry Dude managed to twist himself around (to be fair, he was almost twice as big as TJ), and swipe at TJ with a paw of a hand. TJ slapped it aside, but suddenly the two of them were caught in a fight of swinging hands and bony elbows and grunts of pain.

"Move, Bee," Marcus snapped as he stormed down the stairs. At the base, Adrian was sweating and trembling a little, but he fisted his hands and set his shoulders.

Behind him, Josh heard the Man in the Vest grunt again and say, "Mmm… No. I don't think so."

By now Marcus was on the main floor, and he held his palm out like he was trying to get someone to stop, and there was a shimmer in the air between TJ and the Angry Dude. The Angry Dude started growling and punched that shimmer once, twice, three times while TJ scrambled off of him, warding off the kicking legs.

Adrian hissed out a breath of pain and readjusted his footing. Josh turned to see the Man in the Vest twisting and squirming against the shadows. Josh exhaled and stepped backwards, back towards the hall, and then back again, and again, and again--

Which is when all the lights went out again.

"Shit!" Adrian gasped as the shadows disappeared. Above, Blanche swore and scrambled with the flashlight. The Man in the Vest rolled his shoulders, raised his arm, and said, "Enough," just as he aimed the gun at the still-wrestling pile that was TJ, the Angry Dude, and now Marcus. TJ was trying to hold the Angry Dude's legs while Marcus and the Angry Dude were fighting with air shimmers and wildly moving fists. Suddenly there was light on the pile, and a mass of shadows, and just as the gun went off, Adrian raised his hands and Marcus raised his head, and in the same instance, there was a shimmer in the air and shadows rising from the ground, and the bullet pinged away as if it was nothing.

Then the Woman, still on the ground in the middle of all this mess, groaned a deep groan and shuddered up onto her hands, and Josh said, "Oh my God, why won't you die?" Even though he didn't actually want her to die, he just wanted her to leave them alone; why couldn't she just leave them all alone--

Suddenly there was something grabbing him by the back of the shirt, a hand clutching the back of his right hand, and he looked down just in time to see the taser in his hand spark to light as the hand holding his hand pushed towards his chest and the hand on his shirt pushed him forward.

Then there was shuddering, sharp, blinding pain and he couldn't breathe, and fire was in all of his veins, burning and shuddering and spreading out in blinding light--

Until, suddenly, there was nothing.

Chapter Twelve: Of Dreaming, Driving, and Dividing

"Ughhhhhh..."

He couldn't move. Actually, he couldn't feel his body. He knew, objectively, that he had one, the same way he knew he was wearing his Iron Man boxers. But he couldn't feel his limbs or his digits or the heavy weight of gravity pushing down on his rather average body.

He just... was.

"What happened?" he breathed, opening his eyes. At least, he thought he opened his eyes. Nothing changed when he did. Everything around him was dark, the same darkness that lived behind your eyelids.

"Well, Josh. This is called shock."

Tori. That was Tori's voice. How the hell was Tori--

"Actually, this is your body dealing with shock," her voice continued. "But whatever. Same difference."

"I think I got tasered," Josh said.

"Yep. Whoever was messing with the lights got you good."

Josh blinked. The darkness didn't change; did he even blink or did he just think that he blinked? "So, there's a fourth person? I didn't even see them..."

Something tapped his forehead -- bom, bom, bom.

"C'mon, Josh. Who do you think was messing with the lights?"

"Oh. Right." He felt betrayed somehow, which didn't even make sense. "I wonder who it was."

"It could honestly be anyone and we may never know because, let's face it, Josh, you're not a good detective."

Josh frowned. "Aren't you supposed to be making me feel better?"

"Am I? I mean, I don't know. I'm not actually Tori. I'm just your brain's version of Tori." She paused. "I hope I'm safe wherever I am."

Josh sighed a long, slow sigh. "This is a pretty sad dream sequence, Tori."

"You're a pretty sad guy, Josh." Another pause. "Plus, no offence, but you're basically the sidekick in this story. There's no grand epiphany for you."

"I am the Sam to Adrian's Frodo," he concluded. "Hey! Wait. Sam gets a happy ending!"

"If you survive Mount Doom, sure. But honestly, are you even past the first book?"

"Hell if I know." A thought occurred to him. "Oh my God. Alden and Dylan are Merry and Pippin."

"Enough with the metaphor!" Tori snapped. "You need to wake up!"

Josh wasn't sure if his eyes were open or not, but either way, what did it matter? There was only darkness: still, utter darkness. "How? I can't feel my body. I can't see anything. I can't even see you."

Tori was silent. There was nothing for a long time. No weight, no heartbeat, no light, no movement. He was all alone in a sea he couldn't see.

"Tori? Am I dead?"

"No," she said. "But you're not good."

Josh hummed. The silence and the darkness were easier when one was gone -- the talking helped a lot. "I had a dream that I was three hundred pounds. And though I was very heavy, I floated 'til I couldn't see the ground," he sung softly.

"Calling for help, Brian Wilson?" Tori asked. Her voice was kind in a way he hadn't heard from her in a while.

"Yeah," he admitted. "I just… I hope they're okay. Those people mean business."

"Alden's pretty wimpy too," Tori said. "And Dylan's only human."

Josh frowned. "You're not helping very much."

"I'm just saying that I don't think Adrian should be your main concern right now."

"Who said he was?"

"I can read your mind, Josh. Especially since I'm basically a product of your mind right now. I know exactly what you're thinking."

He made a face. She was right; Alden and Dylan were a lot more fragile than Adrian. But neither of them had been targeted like he had been, except for a bit of stalking. Josh had seen the aftermath of an altercation -- he'd been involved in altercations even!

"Aren't you glad I taught you that word?" Tori asked.

"You're the best English tutor I ever had," he answered honestly. "And I can't believe I got tased with my own taser." Like, how lame could a dude be?

"To be honest, Josh, he seems more trouble than he's worth. I mean, you could die."

Josh was silent for a minute. "Yeah. I know." But who else was going to help the guy? He didn't exactly make it easy to be friends, even though he was obviously aching for friendship. Plus, he was Josh's final photography project; if Josh got an A in his course, he kind of owed Adrian big time.

"I don't get it," Tori said. "Why stick around?"

Because he liked Adrian. He'd liked him the moment he'd seen him touching that tombstone with the kind of gentle respect he hoped others looked at his mother's tombstone with.

"Because we're the same. I am he is, you are he is, you are me and we are both together," he sang softly. Everyone loved a good Beatles song, even Tori.

"I don't think those are the right words."

"Maybe not. But trying to figure out the real ones make my head hurt."

"Your head is hurting?"

That's when he felt it: a vibration. The whole world was vibrating with the hum of an engine.

"Tori? You still there?"

"Yeah." But her voice was softer, like she was moving away.

Josh reached for her -- he couldn't feel his arm, and he didn't know where she was, or if she even was, but he still lurched towards her with a sudden desperation. "Don't go."

"Shhh," she soothed. The vibrations grew louder, a humming in the air and a shudder in his body. "Shh," she repeated. "It's okay, Josh. You're waking up."

"Wait, I'm not ready to—"

The vibrations got louder, turning into rumbling, and then, just as he became aware of his world lightening up -- as if someone had turned a light on in another part of the house -- he understood that he was moving. He was in motion and there were voices around him, and there was music playing, and he had a body again.

He had a body and his head throbbed.

"Uggghhhh," he groaned, pushing his aching head into whatever he was resting against. It had mass and resisted his push, and it went taut when he rolled his forehead into it. He inhaled, felt his chest shudder in pain, and exhaled in a rush. "Gawwwwd," he moaned, squeezing his eyes tight.

"Hey. Hey, you're okay."

There was a large hand gingerly brushing his head then, touching down like an unsteady landing, lifting up again, and then settling softly. It covered the curve of his scalp and secured it, as if his head was a precious thing. It made the ache bearable, made the throbbing something he could breathe through.

"Take your time," Adrian said. "You've been out for a while."

Josh kept his eyes closed and focused on breathing for several seconds. When he felt he could do that, he considered the rest of the world: the hum of the car, the forward motion of the vehicle, the thrum of a baseline from the radio, and the slight motions of Adrian's breathing.

He realized: "I'm on your lap."

"It's fine, Deering," Adrian said. "You were unconscious, and we didn't want your head rattling around."

That... was logical, but still: "You don't like touching."

"Shh," Adrian said; and it sounded like Tori (but it hadn't really been Tori, had it?), and his fingers curled and uncurled around his head like it was trying to comfort him but didn't know how. "Don't worry about it."

Josh sighed and pushed back into the leg he was resting against. It wasn't worth the battle and he hurt too much to argue anyways. Instead, he just breathed through the pain, and waited as his body filled back in.

But if he was lying on Adrian and the car was moving, that meant that someone was driving the car.

"Alden?"

"Wrong girl, creeper."

Josh opened his eyes and shifted his gaze over to see Blanche in the driver's seat. All he could see was her profile, and her long, white-blonde hair tied back in a messy ponytail. She looked tired, her eyes tight and weary. When he glanced at her hands on the steering wheel, her knuckles were even paler than the rest of her.

"Where's Alden?" he clarified.

Adrian's fingers flexed on his head again. "She's in Cory. Dylan and Marcus are with her. Everyone's okay, Josh."

"Seriously though, man, we're all good." That sounded like TJ, and Josh moved his eyes to see TJ's shoulder and some of his profile in the passenger's seat. "You got the worst beating of us all."

Josh blinked and stared into the space between the two. "I got tased."

"Yeah. Never saw that coming," Adrian said, his voice tight. Josh glanced over just in time to see Blanche's fingers flex on the steering wheel.

"How did we get out?" he asked, watching the tension in Blanche's right arm.

"Your friend, Alden, she called the police." There was a kind of pride or satisfaction in TJ's voice. "The sirens came a-rolling in, and the four of them scattered."

Josh blinked and then rolled his neck to look up at Adrian. His face was gray, there was stubble on his jaw, and it looked like his hair had dried in a weird way. "Why do we never think of calling the police?"

Adrian glanced down at him. "You don't because you're an idiot. I don't because powers and police don't mix."

Josh thought about that for a little bit. "Yeah, okay. That sounds right." He closed his eyes and breathed for a moment. "But everyone is okay? Hannah and Erik are too?"

"Everyone's fine," Blanche said. "We split up and are en route to a safe house."

Josh opened his eyes and looked up at Adrian. "Why are we in this car?" he whispered.

Adrian glanced back down at him. "Because I could barely walk and you were barely breathing. I don't think anyone was in the right mindset to argue."

Josh blinked. "Yeah. Okay. That's fair."

"Hey, dude." Josh turned his head to see TJ twisted right around in his seat, a phone in his hand and a grin on his face. "So, like, apparently Alden started to cry when he told her you were awake. You two dating or what?"

Aw, Alden. Please don't cry. Wait, did that mean Dylan cried too? "Alden and me are soulmates. She's the

Pikachu to my Ash. Dating her would be like dating my camera."

Blanche actually let go of the steering wheel with one hand to wave it dismissively in the air. "She's into that other one, anyways. The cute one -- Declan?"

Josh frowned. "The cute one?"

"His name is Dylan," Adrian corrected.

"What do you mean, the cute one?" Josh repeated. When Blanche merely returned her hand to the steering wheel, he forced an elbow underneath him and pushed himself off of Adrian's lap. The world suddenly started to spin, and his stomach gave a violent lurch. "Oh shit," he blurted.

The hand came off the steering wheel again. "I swear to God, if you vomit in this car, I will kick your ass so hard your future girlfriends will wonder why there's an imprint of a heel in your butt."

Josh slowly and unsteadily blinked at her, even while he felt Adrian's hands on his shoulders to steady him. "Dude. That's kind of hot."

TJ was grinning. "That was totally hot. Babe, you are a goddess."

Blanche exhaled slowly through her nose -- her shoulders rose and fell with the motion. "Shut. Up. I'm trying to concentrate. Cross, I thought you said you were handling him."

"Handling me?" Josh repeated. That was insulting.

"I'm handling him fine," Adrian retorted. One of his hands moved to Josh's back. "How nauseous are you; scale from one to ten?"

Josh blinked and placed a hand on his stomach. "Uh...

Four? Mmmguessing four."

"That would be the concussion talking." The hand rubbed in circles; it was rather soothing and reminded Josh of his mother. Which was odd, considering it was Adrian's hand. "I think your car is safe from vomit," Adrian continued, pitching his voice towards Blanche. "It was just the change in altitude throwing him off."

"I literally just sat up."

"You've been unconscious for hours," Adrian said. "And you've had a really rough twenty-four hours. You're allowed to be weak."

Josh frowned. Just because it was true didn't mean he had to like it. But he inhaled a long breath to steady himself, and then pushed himself into an upright sitting position. His head spun for a second and his stomach rolled, but he focused on breathing and holding everything in place. The nausea passed after a few seconds and his head settled back into an almost tolerable ache. "Ugh. I suck."

"Nah, man," TJ said, twisting around in his seat to grin back at Josh. "You're alive. That's, like, awesome."

Josh blinked at him. Well… he guessed TJ was right. He still sucked though; he was the only one who got knocked out. "Sure, man," he said instead, not wanting to argue.

"We should be there in about fifteen minutes," Blanche announced. "Unless I need to make another detour…"

Josh glanced over at Adrian. "Detour?" he whispered.

"She's trying to make sure we aren't being followed," Adrian answered. "Everyone is taking a different, convoluted route. We've been driving for over an hour now, and we left last."

Josh blinked. "Is all this necessary?"

"Yes," Blanche said. Her tone was very matter of fact, but Josh caught a glimpse of her white knuckles curled around the steering wheel. Something twisted up inside of him: she was stressed out and scared and still trying to lead them all into safety.

"Okay," he said. He leaned back into his seat and closed his eyes. The hum of the car wasn't really helping his headache, but wasn't really hurting it either, and the world outside was that weird shade of light that happened when the sun was getting ready to rise. That wasn't really helping his headache either (although, to be honest, he was pretty sure everything was going to hurt his head at this point), and the darkness was kind of comforting. Kind of like a giant blanket. Especially since he knew that he wasn't trapped inside of it.

A large and almost clammy hand landed on his: "C'mon, Deering. Seatbelt." Then a presence passed in front of him and grabbed something by his left shoulder. The belt came across his torso and then, after a couple of seconds, clicked into place. It settled against him, tying him to the real world.

"Thanks," Josh said, keeping his eyes closed.

"Wow," TJ said, his voice giddy and distant. "That was amazing. Do you think Marcellus would put my seatbelt on for me?"

"No," Blanche said, voice taut.

"You sure? I think he might."

"Why don't you ask him then?"

"Well, maybe I will." A pause. "I will. I'm texting him

right now."

"You do that."

"So, like, how badly did they wreck the house?" Josh asked -- because all he could think of was the gunshots and the crashing and Alden's screams.

There was silence for a long moment. "Well, I don't think we're going back there; how's that?" TJ finally said.

Josh opened his eyes about halfway. "Are you, like, gonna need to pay for repairs?"

TJ twisted around in his seat again and gave Josh a grin. "Oh, no worries, man. We got home insurance."

Josh blinked. "Dude. That's, like, totally adult of you."

TJ's grin grew, and he shrugged a shoulder. "Man, what can I say? We're, like, totally mature here."

Blanche 'psshed'. "Oh please. You eat Lucky Charms for breakfast." Her eyes darted up and met Josh's through the rear-view mirror. "That's Erik's doing," she explained. "He and Hannah have been on their own for almost a decade; he had to grow up really fast." Her eyes focused back on the road in front of them. "They've been a huge help this last year," she said quietly.

Josh stared at the back of her head for a long moment. For all her harsh words and brittle edges, there was something about her, something deep inside her, that was soft and scared. He thought of the first time he'd seen her: standing in the cemetery with her hair blowing back like a cape and her soft-looking hoodie and too-large necklace. He looked at her now, with her hair tied back in a loose ponytail and her swollen knuckles and compressed lips. He wanted to reach out and touch her shoulder, tell her that it was okay, that she could relax and breathe a little; but it would have been a lie. He didn't know what was coming next, but he knew that they hadn't reached the end yet.

His phone buzzed in his pocket. He blinked once, then twice, and stared down at where it sat in his jeans' pocket, vibrating over and over again. "What the hell?" he said, pulling it out. It shook in his hand, 'Unknown Caller' lighting up the screen.

Something in his gut tightened. "I have a bad feeling about this."

"Me too," Adrian said, pressing his shoulder against Josh's. They stared down at the phone as it clicked over to voicemail. A few seconds later, the phone started buzzing again, rocking with that same 'Unknown Caller'.

Josh glanced over at Adrian. "I don't wanna answer it," he admitted, voice soft.

Adrian was completely focused on the phone, lips pressed into a thin line. "Me neither."

"Uh, babe?" TJ's voice broke through, drawing Josh's attention half away from the buzzing phone. "Marcellus hasn't answered me back."

"It's been literally three minutes," Adrian said, not looking up from the phone.

"Nah, man. When me and Marcus are talking, we're talking. There's never a wait time. And, like… He had been texting something. And then he stopped."

Josh's phone went to voicemail again, and then, a few seconds later, started buzzing again.

"Aid," he said, not really sure what he wanted to say, but needing to say something.

There was a pause and then: "Shit." Adrian's hand reached out and he scrolled his thumb over the answer button and then pressed the speaker button. "Hello?" he snapped -- which would be totally rude if it was a wrong number or something.

"Well, it's about time," the Woman drawled; and Josh's heart stopped in his chest. "I didn't think we hit you that hard."

Josh heard Adrian inhale sharply through his teeth and then: "How the hell did you get this number?"

"Hmm," the Woman hummed. "That's a very good question; how did we get this number, Sarge?"

There was a pause on the other side of the phone, but not a silent pause. There were noises, like overhearing music playing through someone else's headphones: there but indistinguishable. Josh looked at Adrian -- who was the Woman talking to? -- and he looked back, his expression tight.

"That's right," the Woman's voice returned. "We took it out of your friend's contact list."

Josh suddenly couldn't breathe. Which friend? Alden? Dylan? Maybe even Tori?

"You do realize that we have your number now, right?" Blanche called over her shoulder. Josh raised his head to see that she was still driving down the road, and what he could see of her face in the rear-view mirror was focused. TJ was turned halfway in his seat, eyes glued to the phone still in Josh's palm. "You handled this like the amateurs you are," Blanche finished, voice hard.

The Woman hummed again, the sound a little staticky over the phone line. "You're assuming that I have a problem with you having this number; I don't." She paused for a moment, and Josh finally noticed that his hands were shaking. "It's come to my... attention... that we may be having a miscommunication." There was a weird twist in her voice, one Josh didn't understand. "So, we're gonna try something else."

"Like what?" Adrian snapped.

"You're going to meet us by the airport," the Woman said. "There's a hotel across the way – The Falcon's Roost – and at the reception desk say you're there to speak to the doctor. And then we're going to have a conversation. No harm, no foul."

"Bullshit," Josh blurted -- and maybe it would have been brave if his voice didn't crack halfway through the word.

"You're right," the Woman said -- and Josh could almost hear the shrug in her voice. "You have no way of knowing if we're lying. But you're still going to come."

"Why do you say that?" Adrian asked.

A heavy sigh crackled over the phone. "Sooooo boring," the Woman said. "Alright." There was silence for a moment and then, as if the phone was pulled away from her: "Say hi."

"Hey, man," Dylan said, his voice shaky.

Josh watched as Adrian closed his eyes in resignation, as TJ hissed out a curse through his teeth, and how Blanche's figure shuddered in her seat. As for himself, he was pretty sure his blood wasn't flowing through his body anymore and hadn't been since Adrian had answered the damn phone. "Hey, dude," he replied weakly. "You guys okay?"

"Uh. Well. Me and Alden are mostly okay," Dylan answered. "I think they've sprained Alden's wrist, though -- not that she'll let me check it--" and that was the voice Dylan used when he wanted to punch something.

"She's fine," the Woman's distant voice said dismissively. "Now watch your tone."

"What about Marcus?" Adrian asked; and, God, was Josh glad that one of them was thinking.

"Uh." There was a very telling pause, and Josh looked up to see TJ's face lose most of its colour. "He's alive."

TJ exhaled a loud, relieved breath and sagged forward.

"He's, uh. Just not really, uh. Conscious. Right now. And the car is kind of, um. Not in the best shape? I mean, we left it in the ditch, so."

"The ditch?" Josh blurted.

"Yeah. They kind of... drove us off the road. So, you know, you don't have to meet us at this hotel if you don't want to--"

"But you want to," the Woman snapped, her voice clear. It was pretty obvious she had taken the phone back. "The Falcon's Roost. Next to the airport. See you soon." And then she hung up.

"What a bitch," TJ breathed.

Josh stared at his phone screen and willed himself to stop shaking. He needed to get himself together. He had to do something. He had to do—

"I think I'm gonna be sick," he croaked, as his stomach rolled.

Blanche swore, and suddenly the car was swerving over to the side of the road. The sideways motion made

Josh's head spin and his stomach lurch. It came to a sudden stop, and then the locks clicked. "Cross, get him out of this car."

Adrian reached over, plucked the phone out of Josh's hand and then unbuckled his seatbelt in quick, assured motions. He reached over, opened the car door, and said, "C'mon, Josh, head outside. In-between your knees, that's it, and breathe. Okay? Just breathe."

Josh followed directions, head between his knees, fingers curled into the car seat, and eyes closed tight. He focused on breathing and keeping everything down, but bile rose in his throat and he coughed weakly, spitting it out and feeling some dribble down his chin. The whole world was spinning and then it wasn't, but everything in him ached.

"God," he moaned. "We're dead. We're so dead."

There was a hand on his back, rubbing slow circles over his shirt. "Not yet, Deering," Adrian whispered. "We're not dead yet."

"We gotta go, babe," he heard TJ say in the car behind them. "We can't leave them."

"I know that," she answered. "I know that, I-- fuck!" she shouted suddenly. There was a sudden smacking sound of flesh against object. "Hannah. Call Hannah. We need to know— what if they got--"

Josh coughed again, and the most pathetic looking vomit he'd ever seen spat out of his mouth. He wiped at his mouth and chin with a shaky hand.

"Right, okay, right. I'll do that, you just. Just breathe, okay, Bee?" TJ said behind them.

"This is all my fault," Josh whispered, swallowing

down the sour taste in his mouth.

The hand on his back paused. "How the hell is this your fault?" Adrian asked, his voice quiet.

"I should have done something. If I wasn't so useless, maybe they'd be okay and safe with their families; why the hell did I make them come with us?"

"Because they were in danger, Josh. They were being stalked. They were at risk."

"But maybe we could have led them away from them. Maybe we could have kept them safe, maybe we could have--"

"Maybe I could have ignored you when you asked for help with your project," Adrian interrupted. "Maybe we all could have gone to different universities. Look, there's no point in looking in the past. Do you blame me for all this?"

Josh raised his head and shook it. "No, no, of course not--"

"Then why the hell are you blaming yourself?"

"Because. Because..." Josh looked at his limp hands and the puddle of bile and saliva soaking into the gravel between his feet. He didn't even have anything in his stomach to throw up, that's how pathetic he was. "Because I'm safe and they're not," he whispered.

"Seriously?" Adrian's hand squeezed in that space where Josh's neck met his shoulder. "Josh. You have a concussion, you've been unconscious for almost five hours, you're almost as pale as me, and your pupils are still two different sizes."

Josh raised his head and twisted it to look back at Adrian. He blinked at him. "They are?"

Adrian nodded seriously back at him. "You look like you belong in a hospital on an IV drip. You are not safe. You're hurt and we're about to drive into a trap. None of this is your fault. None of this is anybody's fault except for those people hunting us. So, if you're gonna beat up anybody, let's try to beat up them before we attack ourselves, okay?"

Josh couldn't help it; he started to grin. "Dude. You totally just gave me a pep talk."

Adrian rolled his eyes. "Yeah. Well. You've given me enough. Guess it's time to return the favour or something."

"Or something," Josh agreed, still grinning. He wiped his mouth off with the back of his hand and made a face. "God. Anybody have gum or something?"

"I wasn't gonna say it, but yeah. Your breath reeks."

The laugh bubbled out without warning. "Screw you, Cross."

"She's not answering," TJ said; and whatever okayness Josh had been feeling broke like ice underneath his feet. Both him and Adrian turned to see TJ holding a cellphone in his hand and looking at Blanche with a serious expression. "And we both know that Erik'll be driving--"

"So he definitely won't answer," Blanche finished with a sigh. She pressed her forehead against the steering wheel and breathed.

Afraid of what all that sounded like, Josh asked, "Um. Are Hannah and Erik… okay?"

TJ looked over at him. "Don't know. They won't answer." He looked at his phone and sighed. "That could mean they can't come to the phone or… they just don't wanna answer."

Josh glanced at Adrian whose face was pinched. "Is, uh. Is that something they do, uh. Often?"

TJ was silent for a long moment before he tucked his phone away in his pocket. "They were alone for a long time before they joined us. Sometimes they forget to coordinate with us, and sometimes..."

"We've split up before," Blanche said, her voice subdued. "They've always come back though. Just... on their own schedule. When it's safe to."

Which implied that whatever they were about to do wasn't safe. Josh looked at Adrian again, who looked back at him. Josh inhaled and then exhaled. "So. What now?" he said, looking back at Blanche.

She breathed for another moment, not answering. TJ reached out a hand and laid it against the back of her neck, thumb gently stroking her skin. It was a surprisingly tender moment, and for a flash, watching Blanche's shoulders relax, Josh understood: they really did care about each other.

"We're gonna go to that hotel," TJ answered for her.

Blanche nodded slowly, then lifted her head off the steering wheel. "First things first though; we need to cover our tracks." She reached out a hand and turned the car back on, the engine rumbling around them.

Josh frowned but pulled himself back into the car. He slammed his door shut and said, "But? They already know we're coming? Why do we need to cover our tracks?"

"Because they might not be the only ones after us," Blanche said, her voice firm. "Now put on your seatbelts."

They found Alden's car, Cory, upside down in a ditch fifteen minutes later. The windshield was smashed in, and the two side-windows Josh could see from the road were badly cracked with the spider web pattern of the almost-broken. There were dents and one of the wheels was half-off, wobbling slightly back and forth like an unsteady teeter-totter.

The very sight of it was so vivid that two contrasting urges rose inside of Josh: the need to photograph it, and the lurch of his stomach. He turned away from it to cough up the bile that urged up his throat. It made his throat burn and he spat out what he could from his mouth. "God," he groaned. "That hurts."

"You need to eat something," Adrian said from behind him.

"I don't think I could keep it down," Josh admitted, wiping his mouth with the back of his hand.

"Keep talking, ladies," Blanche said, her voice carrying easily. Josh turned to see her slide down the side of the ditch with a large container in her hand. She stopped beside the car and rolled her shoulders. "Stand back!" she called, before she started spraying the car with some kind of liquid from the canister.

It only took a second for Josh to recognize the smell and his stomach dropped. "Dude! Is that gas?!"

"Yup," TJ said, his voice oddly satisfied. He stood near the trunk of the car, hands crossed over his chest, watching Blanche with a fondly proud expression on his face.

Josh gaped. "You carry a container of gas in the back of your car?" he cried.

"You never know when you're gonna need it!" Blanche called back, moving around to spray the entire car.

Josh just watched her, completely out of words. Finally, after a few seconds, he turned to TJ. "Dude, what the hell does a goddess like that see in you?"

TJ glanced at Josh, a grin on his lips. "I'm a good cook," he replied.

Josh blinked at that and then turned to Adrian who simply shrugged, his hands tucked deep in his coat pockets. Josh scowled at him, and then turned back to Blanche, who had gotten most of the car covered by now.

"Maybe I should take lessons?" he voiced out loud.

"It's a good skill to have," TJ encouraged. "Totally worth the money."

Josh simply nodded, and the three of them watched as Blanche finished hosing down the car. She then stepped over to the rear of the car and pulled something out of her jacket pocket, before fiddling with the license plate.

Josh squinted. "What is she doing?"

"Removing the plates," Adrian answered. "Don't want people knowing whose car this was."

That made Josh stomach twist again and his chest feel empty, like it was missing the weight of a camera. He wondered where'd it gotten to; had it been totally trashed in the chaos of the house destruction? How the hell was he going to afford another one?

She hefted the container up in her arms and then climbed back out of the ditch; Josh offered her a hand. She took it with a grateful grunt, and he pulled her out. She shook her head, her hair falling even more out of her ponytail, and then passed TJ the canister. He took it and opened the trunk before placing it carefully back in there. Once the trunk was closed, she turned to face Cory, her hands on her hips. "Alright," she said. "Who wants the honours?"

Josh waited for a moment, and then said, "I kind of feel like, since I'm Alden's friend, I should take the blame." He felt their eyes on him and then admitted, "Also, I kinda really hate this car."

Blanche grinned at him, her pale eyes glinting, and passed him a Zippo lighter. "Go at it, creeper. Let's light this thing up."

Josh accepted the lighter (did she keep one of these just for possibilities like this?), flicked it on (it took a couple of tries, but then, almost everything he did did), and, inhaling sharply, flung the lit lighter at the car.

It landed, miraculously, right in the center of the underbelly. After a brief pause of Oh no I messed it up, there was a muted whoosh and the whole car was engulfed in flames.

"Shit!" he yelped, taking a step back. TJ burst out into a laugh and Blanche threw her head back and cackled at the sky like a triumphant witch.

"You hear that, hunters!" she shouted. "We're gonna take you down!"

"Fuck yeah!" TJ shouted right on her heels.

Josh looked at them, then at Cory, burning right before their eyes, and then to Adrian, who was watching the whole scene with a small smile on his face. Josh swallowed and said, "Alden is gonna murder me."

Adrian glanced over at him and his smile spread. He shrugged. "Eh. Maybe the Woman'll take you down first." His eyes shone with something that read like hope.

Chapter Thirteen:
Of Hotels, Hunters, and Honesty

Honestly, the weirdest thing about The Falcon's Roost was its super odd name. It looked very similar to every other hotel Josh had ever seen -- a few storeys tall, fairly large windows, big glass doors, and a decently maintained parking lot. The most interesting part of the exterior was the design of the name: Falcon's Roost was in some kind of capital letter cursive with a circle behind it, the upper curve looking like a sun peeking over the horizon of letters, and the lower curve looking like the edge of a bowl or nest.

Josh stood outside Blanche's car, the door still open in case something happened and he had to jump back inside suddenly. "Dude. Where did they come up with the name?"

"It's obviously some kind of code name," TJ answered, shutting his door behind him. He squinted up at the sign with a suspicious expression. "Like, 'c'mon, man, this is a great hideout' kind of code."

Blanche passed by Josh and he caught her very dramatic eyeroll. "Good grief," she muttered as she moved towards the trunk of the car.

Josh turned and watched as she and Adrian pulled a

couple of bags out of the trunk. She grabbed a purse and a bag while Adrian was bent in half and seemingly rustling through the bags. Blanche moved away from the trunk and passed the bookbag to TJ, who took it and pulled it across his back without a word.

Adrian straightened and turned towards Josh. "Here."

In his hands was Josh's camera.

Josh's mouth dropped open slightly. He'd packed it when they'd started this road trip just – dude, was it really just two days ago? – but he'd been so busy with running for his life that he'd forgotten about it. And here it was, obviously packed just in case Josh needed it. He reached for it, his chest suddenly full, and as he cradled it close, he blurted out: "Dude."

"I don't really know," Adrian said, as if he had to explain himself. "It's just… this whole thing started because of that camera. Seems like it's something you should have."

"Dude."

"I mean. Don't break it. It looks expensive, and I know you're kind of attached, so… Be careful, okay?"

Josh looked up at Adrian and tried to make his mouth work. "Dude," was all he managed to say.

Adrian grinned a small grin and then held out a granola bar. "This too. Just in case."

Josh took it, checked the flavour (mmm, smores), and then tucked it into his coat pocket for a later time. He unzipped his coat halfway, pulled the strap of his camera over his head, and settled the camera against his chest before he pulled the zipper back up a few inches. The weight of it against his chest made something steady inside of him, as if he'd been given a piece of armour or a key to something he needed to unlock. He looked at Adrian, who was shoving something in his own coat pockets, and said quietly, "Thanks, dude."

Adrian glanced up at him. "You really need a better vocabulary." And then he reached up and shut the trunk door.

"You guys ready?" Blanche asked, drawing their attention. She looked crisp and cool, her hair neatly redone in a ponytail and her winter coat white and pristine.

Adrian gave her a nod. "We're ready."

She gave a nod back. "Alright." Then she clicked a button on her key fob and the car double beeped as the doors locked.

It suddenly struck Josh as hilarious -- as if whatever they were about to walk into was going to be okay because she locked the doors of her car, as if what they were about to do was normal, as if they weren't about to die -- but he was obviously the only one who thought so, because Blanche turned on her heel and headed straight for those big glass doors. TJ followed right after her, and Adrian sent one more glance towards Josh before walking behind TJ. Josh inhaled slowly, felt his camera rise with his breath…

…and raised the camera to his eye, flicked the shutter open, and took in the sight of the three walking towards a totally normal hotel and their possible destruction. He took it quick, not bothering with focus or framing – it was enough just to have it, to know that they were here and they were brave – before he settled it against his chest again and followed Adrian across the parking lot and through the glass doors.

The Falcon's Roost had a fairly typical hotel lobby. There were a couple of small tables to the right of the main doors half-covered with pamphlets, maps, and coffee sweetener packages. On the left of the main doors was a corner couch and a couple of loveseats turned to face the decently sized flat screen TV, which was tuned into the weather channel. Straight in front of them was that very long main desk that almost every hotel had, and a couple of young women standing behind it. They both wore black blouses with gold name tags and professional smiles.

Blanche was already at the desk when Josh finally stopped looking around, TJ at her elbow. Adrian was looking at the TV, eyes narrowed as if he actually cared about the high air pressure moving across the east coast of North America.

"--here to see the doctor," Blanche was saying, her words clear. Josh turned to focus on her, and kind of gaped at her nerve. She was honestly the bravest person he'd ever met, and there was something incredibly magnetic about that; as if, by being around her, he was absorbing some of her courage and could be a hero himself.

The woman Blanche was speaking to glanced at the other woman curiously. The former had curly dark hair forced into submission and looked to be around their age, while the other woman had straight hair with professionally done highlights. She was the one who looked back at Blanche and said coolly, "The doctor isn't currently taking walk-ins."

Josh glanced towards Adrian, who was moving towards the front desk. He followed as Blanche answered, "I think you'll find we have an appointment."

"A reservation, if you will," TJ added, leaning forward. All three women paused and looked at him; Josh could only imagine that Blanche's expression matched the desk-girls' confused expressions. TJ straightened: "'Cause... it's a hotel? You make reservations at a hotel and appointments... at... the doctor's..." he trailed off before falling silent.

Josh reached his side and he patted TJ consolingly on the shoulder. He got it, man. Girls were scary.

The desk-girls exchanged another look and then the highlighted one said, "If you'll excuse me for a moment." She stepped off to the side and picked up a phone.

The woman with dark hair glanced at the four of them and smiled -- it was more awkward than Josh figured her public smile normally was, but he gave her mad props for trying. He sent her a smile as thanks for her efforts, and she blinked at him before her smile strengthened and became more real. It was a very good smile, and she was pretty cute--

Adrian elbowed him discreetly in the side. "She's working at the hunters' hideout," he hissed lowly. "That means she's on their side."

Oh. Well, if that was true, that meant she was a bad guy. But she seemed pretty normal for a bad guy... "Maybe she only works here part-time?" Josh whispered back. "Maybe she doesn't know them?"

Adrian frowned at him. "Seriously? Seriously?"

"Whaaaaat?" Josh shrugged, his palms facing the ceiling. "It's possible!"

The woman with highlights hung up the phone with a little click and turned to face them. Her eyes fell on each of them in turn, and when they reached Josh, he felt himself straighten. Her lips twitched, and then settled again. "If you'll follow me," she said, stepping out from behind the desk and heading towards the elevator near the TV.

Blanche, TJ, and Adrian followed immediately, but Josh took another look at the girl still at the front desk, whose eyebrows had scrunched towards her forehead slightly. Something swelled inside him, like a feeling he knew as truth, and he reached out with one hand to touch the desk between them. She looked down at it and then back up at him, eyes wide and hazel. She had freckles sprinkled across her nose and cheekbones, little stars of dark brown against her lighter brown skin.

Quietly, he said, "They're not very nice people. You may want to look for better employment."

Her mouth dropped open a little. "I don't--" she started, but then--

"Josh!" Adrian called from the other side of the room.

Josh didn't start; he knew it was coming. Instead, he just smiled at the girl, glanced down at her nametag, and then stopped. He had planned on being suave about knowing her name, say something kind of cool and heroic like James Bond or something, and instead he blurted, "Oh my God, that is the coolest name ever; how do you pronounce it?"

"Josh!" Adrian snapped again.

"Sorry, sorry," Josh babbled; he kind of mentally stumbled when Mariatu smiled that real smile at him, with her cheeks flushing slightly and her eyes warm. "No, but seriously," he stressed, leaning towards her. "Please, be careful." And then he jogged off, grimacing at the glares on the highlighted woman and Blanche's faces, TJ's amused grin, and Adrian's embarrassed scowl. He scooted into the elevator, sliding in by Adrian's side and repeated, "Sorry, sorry, let's go."

The highlighted woman -- whose name tag, Josh finally saw, read Holly -- huffed a small breath, and pressed the 4 button. After a second, the elevator doors slid closed and the five of them waited in silence as they travelled up.

Josh felt Adrian's glare, even if he couldn't see it. He waited it out for a moment, watching as the light above the doors moved from M to 2, and then yielded and glanced over. Adrian was clearly waiting for this, because he immediately mouthed, 'Seriously?'

Josh shrugged, just like he had before. 'What?' he mouthed back. 'She's not evil.'

Adrian held his glare for another few seconds and then closed his eyes slowly, as if he couldn't handle Josh's face any longer.

Josh would have been insulted except, well, he couldn't really blame Adrian. They were going into a trap for sure, and Adrian was probably going to have to do some exhausting shadow stuff, and he was probably dreading the whole thing; but it wasn't Josh's fault that there was clearly an innocent in the lobby! He had to warn her. It was his civic duty or something.

The lights above the door turned from 2 to 3, and Josh watched as TJ rolled his shoulders and exhaled. Holly glanced at her nails, frowning at them -- did she not like the colour? They looked fine to Josh -- and Blanche fingered the strap of her purse. Josh glanced back at Adrian and saw that he was doing some deep breathing -- probably shouldn't disturb him -- so he looked back at the doors and the lights above them. Before his eyes, the light flickered from 3 to 4 and the doors beeped before sliding open.

Holly led the way with a, "Follow me, please." Blanche followed with TJ right on her heels, and Josh waited until Adrian's shoulder brushed his before he moved forward too. The five turned left and went down a hallway: Holly in the lead, Blanche and TJ the second line, and Adrian and Josh bringing up the rear.

There were far fewer doors than Josh was expecting in this hallway; usually hotels had rows of rooms, but they had only passed one the entire time. It really made Josh question whether this was even a hotel, which is why he asked, "What part of the hotel is this?"

Holly turned her head -- not enough to look at Josh, but enough to acknowledge him. "This is where we accommodate professionals. We have a collection of four conference rooms and two suites that we pride ourselves on."

Oh. Josh looked over at Adrian, who was frowning at the back of Holly's head. He was still frowning when she stopped at a door, knocked twice, and then slid down a card key that seemingly appeared out of nowhere. No, seriously, Josh had no idea where she had been holding it.

The lock on the door beeped once, and then a small circular light blinked green, and the door clicked. Holly reached for the doorknob and turned it, swinging the door open. She stopped in the doorway, her body blocking Josh's view of the inside. "I have the walk-in's here, doctor," she called.

"Oh!" a voice said from inside. "Excellent! Please, let them in."

Holly turned about as she opened the door. "After you," she gestured with an open palm.

Kudos to Blanche: she walked right in there without hesitation. TJ gave Holly a nod before he followed his girlfriend, and Josh heard Adrian's slow exhale before he moved forward as well. Josh touched the camera still hanging around his neck, resting on the solid machinery for a second, grounding himself, before he stepped inside as well.

It was a conference room. There was a large, rectangular table in the centre and a flat screen TV on the opposite wall of the doorway. There must have been ten chairs perfectly spaced around the table, each with comfortable backs and swivel legs. There were two sets of windows on Josh's right, with a floral armchair between them.

Sitting in that armchair was the Woman, her legs bent so her feet nestled in the seat with her, her fingers toying with the curtain that covered half of one of the windows. She peered out of that window, her hair falling over her face like her own curtain. For a second, she looked like a small child waiting for her parents to come home, and something inside Josh's chest lurched towards her before the ache in his head took over and reminded him: Oh yeah; she's evil.

At the head of the table, if the four of them were at the foot (which is what it felt like to Josh), was a man with a shock of red hair -- like, he was a serious ginger -- and large glasses. He had on a polo shirt and his hands were curled around something. At his immediate side, on Josh's left, was the Man in the Vest, who lounged casually in his chair, twisting back and forth slightly. Directly across from him was a broad-shouldered man with short, slightly curled hair, a simple, black t-shirt, and a bright tattoo that wound up his neck. From this distance, Josh couldn't make out what it was of, but it looked... slinky, whatever it was.

A couple of chairs down from the Man in the Vest was the woman from the mall. Even as Josh jolted with surprise -- it was the woman with the green dress who had been staring at him right before that crazy GameShop incident -- something inside him went, Oh. Her. Of course it was her.

In the chair closest to the door, slumped down with a large scowl and arms crossed over his chest, was Marcus. He raised his head as they entered the room, and his shoulders fell slightly. "Hey. You came," he said.

"Dude," TJ sighed, and Josh watched as everything in his body kind of fell, as if something heavy had just dropped off of him. "Of course we came." He stepped forward, up to Marcus' side, and the two of them exchanged a series of hand gestures, the kind of secret handshakes only best friends had.

Josh looked back at the ginger watching them all from the other end of the table and squared his shoulders. Blanche was just watching Marcus and TJ reunite with a twist of a smile, and Adrian's eyes kept darting between the Man in the Vest and the Woman. Someone had to do something, something probably stupid, and it might as well be him.

"So!" he called, taking a single step forward. Everyone's eyes turned to him, including the Woman's, and he gulped. He focused on the ginger, made sure to lock eyes with him. "You must be the Final Boss."

He meant it. Here they were, walking right into a trap; obviously the man at the head of the table, surrounded by at least three of the people who were hunting them (and where was the Angry Dude from the mall and house, anyways? He wasn't dead, was he?) must be giving them orders. Therefore: the Final Boss.

The ginger brightened, his hands going flat on the table. With that smile, and the glint in his eyes that Josh could recognize even from this distance, he looked suddenly young. Like, Erik's age, or maybe a little older – definitely not as old as Josh thought supervillains should be.

"Well, actually," the man said. It was in the voice that had welcomed them inside earlier.

He was interrupted with a heavy scoff from the Man with the Tattoo. He rolled his shoulders, spun his chair around to face Josh, and shot him a grin. There was something strangely charming about his face, even if he looked like he had probably spent some time in jail (and Josh could hear Tori hissing about stereotyping people with tattoos, but he figured he could be cut some slack since they were the bad guys). "Kid, don't be stupid. This guy's--" and he gestured at the ginger with a thumb thrown over his shoulder-- "more like the Koopa Kid. You ain't seen nothing yet."

The ginger -- who, Josh guessed, he should name

something else, since the Final Boss was apparently inaccurate, and ginger was just rude -- scowled at the Man with the Tattoo. He looked kind of fierce when he did, like some rodent who had identified prey and was preparing to take it down. "You'll regret that remark," he snapped, voice precise.

"You'll resemble that remark," the Man in the Vest commented, lips twisted and eyes half-closed. He and the Man with the Tattoo met each other's eyes, and they grinned at each other, cruel and mocking.

The ginger/not-Final Boss exhaled a breath that kind of sounded like a growl, and his hands fisted on the table. His rodent-like eyes marked the Man in the Vest as his other target, before he closed them, inhaled and exhaled again, and looked at Josh and his friends.

"Let's start again, hm?" He paused for a moment, but it wasn't so they could answer; Josh could tell. "My name is Dr. McCallum."

Josh blinked, and something settled inside him: ah. A name. He could work with a name. "Oh. You're the doctor we're here to see." He squinted at the doctor a second later. "Wait. What kind of doctor are we talking about here?"

"I have two PhDs," McCallum explained, sitting back in his chair and pulling his hands closer to him. "Biochem and genetic engineering, with a speciality for DNA re-creation." He smiled, as if those words should mean something to Josh.

Josh nodded for a second, trying to make sense of that. "Cool," he said, knowing full well it sounded pretty lame.

"What do you want from us?" Blanche snapped, taking a step forward. Josh watched as TJ and Marcus squared their shoulders, like they'd been waiting for orders. "You've been hunting us for weeks now, hiding in the shadows. Well?" She spread her arms out, open and vulnerable and bold and brave. "You've got us. So what do you want?"

"And where're my friends?" Josh added, suddenly shockingly aware that Alden and Dylan weren't in the room. He figured they were safe -- Marcus would have said something if they weren't -- but the last thing he'd heard was that Marcus was unconscious and Alden had sprained her wrist, and here was Marcus obviously conscious. So where were they?

The Man with the Tattoo glanced across the table at the Man in the Vest and grinned at him. The Green Lady (she had a green shirt on; it worked, okay?) blinked at them all and then yawned, covering her mouth with an elegant hand.

Dr. McCallum nodded, as if they were finally where he wanted them to be. "We want to help you," he said.

There was dead silence across the room, as if no one believed what the doctor was saying.

Josh glanced over at Adrian, who was squinting at Dr. McCallum like he'd gotten something stuck in his eyes and it was hurting him. TJ and Marcus exchanged looks like Dude, is he serious; Oh man, you haven't heard anything yet. Blanche, once again, was the one who took charge with a shifting of her feet, a crossing of her arms over her chest and a blunt: "What the fuck are you talking about?"

The Woman huffed a loud sigh, drawing Josh's attention as she slumped further down in her chair and pulled out a cellphone. Josh blinked as she seemingly tuned out the entire room – and something told him she'd heard whatever was coming before. He looked over to see that the Green Lady had closed her eyes and leaned her head back against the headrest, the Man with the Tattoo had sprawled out in his chair, and the Man in the Vest had grabbed one of the pens in a pile at that end of the table and was doodling something on a piece of paper.

We're not the first people they've hunted, he thought.

"You must understand," Dr. McCallum started, bringing Josh's focus back to him. "The idea that there are powered people," he pointedly looked at Blanche, Adrian, TJ and Marcus, "and that there may have been powered people throughout history could redefine humanity."

And then, like someone dumping water over him, Josh realized that he wasn't a part of this. He was completely outside of this; he shouldn't even be in the room. He should find Alden and Dylan and let these guys with their secrets continue being private. He inched backwards, away from all this crazy, and then stopped.

Adrian had reached over and curled his fingers around the hem of Josh's coat, tugging just enough to be noticeable. His eyes didn't leave Dr. McCallum's direction, but he didn't let go of Josh's coat either.

So Josh stilled, thought for a second, and then shifted to the right just enough so his shoulder brushed Adrian's. And then, with that contact, Adrian's fingers dropped off of Josh's coat and his shoulders relaxed.

"To be perfectly honest," Dr. McCallum continued,

"we're not entirely sure how new this development is. We have records dating back to the Second World War, but very little information on how these people came to be, or what their origins are. Perhaps there has always been a more evolved human and it's only now, with the population rising exponentially, and technology making the world a far more accessible place, that you are becoming visible. Ultimately, while fascinating to try to understand how, the history does not change the present -- which is that your generation has the greatest number of your kind that we have seen.

"These abilities have a wide range of strengths and manifestations – and yet each come with their drawbacks." And with this, Dr. McCallum's lips quirked up slightly. "The more power, the bigger the drawback. Many of your kind are at risk by the very thing that makes them unique. And that's where we come in.

"The people we work with want to understand your abilities. We want to understand where they come from, and how they are passed on. What part of your DNA has evolved to awaken such differences? Is there a way for us to use these abilities to help people?" He gestured with one hand. "Some of your abilities are incredibly useful. Cellular regeneration, physical manipulations of limbs, emotional connection, telepathic abilities… All of these can only help humans become more. But only if we can keep you alive long enough to let you pass on your genetic code."

"Uh, not to interrupt," TJ interrupted. "But I have no idea what you're talking about with these risks."

Dr. McCallum tilted his head to the side, eyeing TJ.

"Not that you're aware of," he said blandly. "You have a very simple ability, however. I am sure you encountered this at your school – Port Haven, correct?"

Josh felt his friends stiffen.

"There are various levels of abilities. The more dynamic the power, the greater the risk." Dr. McCallum's eyes shifted to Marcus. "For instance, how much energy do you expel with your shields?"

Josh watched as Marcus flinched, a shudder that rippled across his muscles. "I don't—"

"I have a hypothesis concerning what, exactly, your shields are comprised of," Dr. McCallum said, one hand reaching for the pen on the table and spinning it between his fingers. "If I'm correct, you could be severely damaging the structural integrity of your own cells." His lips quirked again. "I'm just not entirely sure whether that will result in the liquidation of your body, or merely the violent disintegration of it."

Josh was very aware of his heartbeat thrumming in his chest, and he watched as Marcus went very still. TJ's eyes were wide, and his fingers were curled around Marcus' wrist.

"Another example," Dr. McCallum said, eyes moving towards Josh and Adrian. Josh flinched, pressing his shoulder deeper into Adrian's. "What exactly are you using to form your shadow creations? How often have you come to the brink of unconsciousness for a few small shadow walls? What happens if you don't stop; will you die from exhaustion?"

All Josh could see was the memory of the gray of Adrian's face, the sweat that dropped from his face, the way he could barely walk after, legs crumpling underneath him. He swallowed and chose not to speak.

Dr. McCallum seemed to see all he needed to, though, for his smile grew. "We can help with that," he said softly. "We believe we can stabilize your abilities and teach you how to develop them to their full potential while keeping you safe."

"You believe," Blanche snapped, drawing Josh's attention. His eyes fell to where her hands were curled underneath her arms, fingers so tightly wound that he could see her knuckles from here. "You believe you can help us when we don't even need your help; you're promising protection when the only ones we've needed protection from are you—"

"Unfortunately, most abilities seem to operate from hormonal changes – the fight versus flight response, for instance," Dr. McCallum explained, actually looking sorry. "For us to have a more complete overview of the situation, we need to activate this response."

"And so you chase us," Adrian concluded, voice resigned.

The Man with the Tattoo smirked a small smirk, and the Man in the Vest glanced up before looking back down at his paper.

"And so we chase you," Dr. McCallum agreed. "And believe you me, we're not the only ones who are interested in your kind. Interested parties are rising every day, and many do not have your best interests at heart. They would be more than satisfied to wait for you to destroy yourself and examine whatever is left behind."

"Or kill us themselves," Marcus butted in, voice hard.

Dr. McCallum gave a small shrug of agreement. "A probability, to be sure. Many don't have the moral code that we do here."

Josh couldn't help it – his eyes went straight to the Woman and narrowed in on the smirk playing on her lips. His eyes darted back to the Man with the Tattoo, who seemed to be grinning to himself. Moral code. Moral code my ass, he thought to himself, still feeling his head throb, noticing how Marcus held himself like he was in pain, feeling his chest still ache. And he thought of Dylan and Alden – where the hell were they? – and remembered that Dylan said Alden was hurt and-

He pressed his arm hard against Adrian's, turned his head to the side and hissed, "We've gotta find Alden." And Dylan, he added mentally, but he knew that Adrian would know what he meant.

Adrian's mouth firmed up, and his shoulders straightened back. "Look, this is all fascinating," he said, "but we came here for a reason."

McCallum blinked once and glanced over at the Man in the Vest who tilted his head to the side, eyes still on his paper. "The loud ones," he answered, frowning slightly to himself.

As recognition cleared on McCallum's face, it hit Josh again: We don't matter. Dylan, Alden, and he were just tools, something these guys could use to manipulate the ones who did matter. He swallowed, steeled his courage, and said, "Dude, it sounds like you guys have a lot to talk about, and, like, honestly, it's totally over my head, so if someone could just let me see my friends, I'd be totally cool to, like, wait. While you guys finish."

And it was a lie, it was all a lie: while he was out of his depth, while he knew he wasn't a part of this, Adrian had asked him to stay and so he wanted to stay; he wanted to support Adrian, Blanche, TJ, and Marcus, he wanted them to know that he was on their side, but someone had to check on Alden and Dylan. Adrian understood; he hadn't flinched at Josh's words. The glance that Blanche sent over her shoulder at him told him she got it, too.

McCallum smiled a small smile. "Yes, of course. Your friends. Maybe you could—" and he looked across at the Man with the Tattoo.

The Man with the Tattoo looked back, scoffed once, and then leaned across the table, eyes focusing on the Green Lady. "Oy. Wanna show 'em the way?"

"No," she said simply, her eyes still closed.

Josh watched as a smile twitched at the Man in the Vest's mouth and the Man with the Tattoo rolled his eyes. Something happened, something passed between them – they had known each other for a while – and then the Man in the Vest said, "S'il vous plait?"

She opened her eyes and raised her head. She blinked over at Josh and said, "Oh. You." Her face brightened – for a second, she was somewhat pretty, somewhat child-like, somewhat glowing. "You're funny. Okay."

Josh blinked back at her. "You think I'm funny? Wait. How do you know I'm funny?"

She pushed herself up onto her feet; her jeans were frayed at the edges and what looked like earphone wires poked out of a pocket. "I've been watching you. You're funny. You make things brighter around you. Laughter makes the buzzing move. The wires wake up." She walked over to him, slipping past Blanche without touching her. She stopped right in front of him, too close for a stranger; he couldn't help it, he flinched into Adrian. He pressed back, steadying him.

The Green Lady beamed at him with wild eyes. "See? Funny. Weak and funny. Come on." She moved right past him, shoulder just skimming his; he got a shock from her and shuddered back.

Adrian gave him a gentle shove back. "Go. We'll be okay."

Josh glanced back at him – yeah, but will I? -- and then followed the Green Lady. He stepped into the hallway and she spun on her heel, back down towards where they caught the elevator earlier. He trotted after her; she moved quickly but gracefully, like she was flowing down the hallway.

He felt like he should say something, maybe because he just didn't do well with silence. "So, uh, have you worked with these people for long?"

She looked over her shoulder at him and slowed just enough that he could catch up. "Not long. Not long enough, either."

Josh frowned at that. "So… does that mean you believe what the doctor says? About saving people like you?"

She paused, stopping completely in a smooth motion. Josh, because he was a clumsy human, kind of stumbled like someone who didn't know how to shift gears properly. "Saving… Yes. I suppose they do save some people. Gratitude is a heavy price to pay though." She hummed, her eyes far away.

"Did they save you?" Josh pressed. Honestly, he

should be a detective or a cop for his amazing interrogation skills.

She stared blankly for another moment before she shivered slightly and grinned brightly, turning her head to face him. "They think they did."

She was honestly the most confusing person ever. "You don't agree?"

She hummed a short note and shrugged her shoulders in a fluid motion. "I don't know. I don't know what might have happened. I don't know what's going to happen. Who can say which path is worse?"

"But you chose this path – them – for a reason, right?"

She tilted her head back and forth like a rocking chair. "Yeah, I guess."

"So… why?"

She turned her head to look down the hallway and stared at something he couldn't see. Maybe she was seeing the path unfold before her like the length of the hallway. Maybe she was totally cracked. Josh didn't know, and honestly his head hurt too much to try to figure it out.

She blinked out of it and then giggled. "It looked like fun." And with that, she started walking forward again.

Josh stuttered after her – fun? Hunting people was fun? – and managed to catch up as she practically glided down the hall. After a couple of seconds, she started humming to herself; it wasn't a song he knew enough to name, but it had a happy melody and she smiled as she went.

And then, very suddenly, she stopped. Josh snapped to a stop and finally became aware that they had reached a door almost exactly like the one the others were still in. He glanced back the way they came – while the doctor held the conference room further down the hall, this one was the one closest to the elevator doors. The artist in him twitched at how they didn't mirror each other.

"Here we are!" she sang; and she reached out with one thin hand to the locking mechanism and slid her fingers down over the smooth surface. The machine blinked green, and the lock clicked over.

Josh's mouth dropped open. "Whoa. That's cool."

She turned her head, her hand already curled around the doorknob. "You're funny," she repeated with a headshake. Then she opened the door wide with a twist of her hand and a push forward.

Josh stepped forward, slipping past the Green Lady and into the room. His eyes immediately fell on Alden who was sitting in the large recliner at the head of the table, her legs thrown over one arm and her head tilted back into the plush headrest. Something moved on Josh's right and he turned to see Dylan pushing himself out of a striped armchair, face already brightening.

"Josh!" he blurted, striding forward.

Josh reached out, stumbling forward and arms out, and the two met in what was definitely the closest embrace they'd ever had. Dylan gasped a breath against Josh's shoulder and Josh's arms probably squeezed him too tight; but he was okay, he was breathing, and they were all together again.

"Josh!" Alden squawked, and Josh pulled his head up just enough to see her scramble to get her legs around the chair. Once her feet landed on the floor, she was speed-walking towards him; he peeled one arm off a still-shaking Dylan to welcome her in. She collided with them, one arm slinking around Dylan's waist and the other hugging Josh's. Josh wrapped his own tight around her shoulders and pulled her in, and he felt Dylan shift and slide one arm out from around Josh to wrap around Alden.

For a long moment, the three of them just held on to each other. Josh ducked his head into Alden's hair, she buried her head into his chest, and Dylan kind of knocked his head against Josh's.

A click sounded behind them and Josh raised his head; the door was closed and the Green Lady was nowhere to be seen. Something inside him went Huh, I guess she does have some tact. Then Alden sniffed hard, and he went back to the circle.

He didn't know how long they stood there. Long enough for Dylan's breathing to steady, for Alden's sniffing to stop, and for Josh to feel like he had been given a painkiller. Dylan wiggled free first, slipping arms out and stepping back, head ducked down. As he moved back, Alden moved into his place and hugged Josh completely; he shifted so it was a full hug.

Josh looked over at Dylan and thought that his friend looked very, very tired. There was a dark red splotch on his cheek that promised an excellent bruise. "Hey, man," he said softly.

Dylan exhaled again, and then raised his head. His eyes widened, and he blurted: "Man, you look awful."

Alden's head snapped up. "Oh my God, your eyes!" she gasped, one hand coming up to touch his cheek.

"I'm okay," he said, looking down at her. He looked

back at Dylan and grinned. "Dude, seriously, I'm fine. A little concussed, somewhat nauseous, and my head is, like, seriously killing me, but I'm okay."

Dylan's mouth pressed together, but he didn't argue.

"They told us you woke up in the car; you were out for ages," Alden said, face still scrunched up.

Josh shrugged a shoulder, hating the worry on her face. "Yeah, but I've been awake for, like, I dunno… almost two hours now? So I'm pretty good."

She scowled. "Your pupils are wacked up," she stated bluntly.

"And so's your wrist; what's your point?" he snapped back.

Alden flinched back a little, and the hand fell off Josh's face to curl around her other wrist defensively. Immediately, Josh felt guilt slam into his stomach, and he sighed, closing his eyes. His head thrummed beneath his eyelids. "Sorry," he grumbled. "It's just been…"

"You're a mess," Dylan said. "But so are we, so…" he shrugged, hands slipping into his pockets.

"Yeah, what happened to your face?"

"Josh!" Alden scolded, hitting his upper arm with her elbow.

"That huge dude from the mall," Dylan answered. "Backhanded me when I started 'talking back' to them." He scowled and took one hand out of his pocket to rub at the sore spot on his cheek. "Asshole."

So the Angry Dude was still around somewhere. Good to know. "They're all assholes," Josh said. "Can you believe they're actually trying to tell them that they want to help?"

"Wait, what?" Alden asked, squinting up at him.

"Wait, everyone's here?" Dylan spoke over her, stepping up to him.

"Yeah, dude—well. Most of them." Josh paused. "We can't get a hold of Hannah or Erik, but..." And he thought of those two siblings and how they'd saved them earlier at the mall, and—"But I don't think they've abandoned us."

Alden's hands started tugging at his shirt. "Come on, sit down. You can tell us everything once you sit down—"

"Alden, wait, your wrist—" Josh stammered as she pulled him towards the striped plush chair Dylan had been in minutes before.

"It's fine, it's fine, just sit." She pushed him down and then settled on the floor at his feet, legs curled under her. "Okay, so who all is here?"

"And what's the plan?" Dylan asked, stepping over and then perching on the window ledge. One of his feet settled and tucked under one of Alden's thighs, and Josh frowned at it. Annnnnd now it was official. Welcome Josh, to the world of the Third Wheel.

He let it go for now and gave them the low-down of what had happened – although he did skip over the part where they burned Cory. He did not want to deal with that thunderstorm when it came.

"Wait, they're just talking?" Dylan asked once Josh caught them all up. His face was in that frowny-disbelief expression that he usually wore when his team started sucking in games. "Those bastards have been chasing us for a week, and now they're just talking? Like, what, civilized people?"

Josh nodded. "Yup. The doctor says they needed to understand the limits of their powers, which requires a conflict or something? Something about fight versus flight and research." He shrugged his shoulders. "Apparently they wanna help."

"Bullshit," Dylan snapped.

At Josh's feet, Alden nodded solemnly. "Dylan's right. There's no way they don't mean us any harm. They electrocuted you, Josh."

Josh's head throbbed as if in agreement. "Dude, don't worry. I don't think anyone is really buying it. It's more like, y'know, as long as no one is actively trying to maim anyone, maybe we shouldn't rock the boat?" He looked pointedly at Alden's wrist. "Especially considering how pathetic we all are."

Alden looked down at her wrist and rubbed it gently with her opposite hand, drooping a little, kind of like a flower. Actually, her hair was pretty frizzy and the braids were looking a little rough. His heart ached a bit at the sight; she was usually pretty put together, if not in a makeup way.

"They were still talking when I left, so." He stopped as he had a terrible thought. He closed his eyes for a second and then purposely shrugged it away. "Hopefully they're all still in one piece, right?"

Alden straightened, and Dylan tensed. "Wait, you left them?" Dylan barked.

Josh pulled back. "Uh. Yeah? I had to find you…?"

"Josh!" Alden slapped his leg with her good hand, and then slapped it again. "How could you! Adrian needs you – what the hell are you doing here?" She slapped his leg a third time.

"Um, ow? Please stop bruising me; I have a concussion."

She stopped, hand inches away from hitting him for a fourth time. She seemed indecisive and then a sneaker-clad foot shoved Josh's other leg. "That's your head, moron," Dylan snapped. "And obviously we need to beat some sense into you – we're fine."

Josh glanced between the two of them with their matching scowling faces. "Yeah, but… The car accident… And like… You guys have nothing to do with this."

Dylan rolled his eyes. "Right, like Blanche and them asked to be hunted."

"That's victimizing, Josh," Alden added. "That's not cool."

Josh didn't know what he was feeling. Pride? Gratitude? Bewilderment? "So… you guys want me to… go… back?"

Alden slapped one of his legs and Dylan kicked the other again. "Yes!" they snapped together.

"Okay, okay!" Josh yelped, curling his legs up to his chest to avoid the beatings. "I'll go! Forgive me for caring about you, you crazy monkeys!"

Alden stood up in a rather graceful movement and walked over to the door. She slapped it several times with an open palm, making a loud, echoing wham, wham, wham through the room. "Oy! Anybody out there?"

The door immediately swung open, taking Alden completely by surprise and making her stumble backwards a couple of steps. Dylan immediately got to his feet and started towards her, while Josh was twisted in his chair, staring at the Green Lady.

She was looking at Alden with an almost unfocused expression on her face. "Why so loud?" she asked.

Alden straightened up and narrowed her eyes at the Green Lady just as Dylan reached her side. Josh noticed the way Dylan placed a hand on the small of her back and the way Alden seemed to inhale and draw strength from it.

"Josh needs to go back to the others," Alden announced, as if she was giving the crazy lady orders.

The Green Lady glanced over at Josh and her lips curled. "Visit over already?"

"He's needed more elsewhere," Alden said, which Josh wasn't sure of, but if he wasn't wanted here, then what was he supposed to do?

The Green Lady didn't bother looking at Alden; instead she kept her eyes on Josh. "And what makes you so special?" It wasn't said rudely, not like The Woman would have said it. No, it was almost curious.

Josh shrugged and pressed his hand over his camera, tucking it close to his chest. "I take pretty good photos sometimes."

Something in her eyes illuminated like a spark of light and her expression seemed to settle. "Ah… An artist." She observed him for another few seconds and then blinked – the light was gone. "Alright; this way." She turned like some kind of dancer and walked right through the open door.

Josh scrambled to get to his feet and bolted after her; he blurted out a quick, "I'll be back!" to his friends, and crossed the threshold. As soon as his feet were in the hall, the Green Lady gave the door a push and it clicked shut behind him.

She cocked her head to the side. "Did you want the void or the threesome?"

It wasn't difficult to figure out who was who. "The void. I'd like the void."

Her lips twitched at the edges. "Okay." She turned again – she did a lot of sudden, wide turns – and started gliding down the hall, back the way they'd come before. Josh followed.

"Uh... Why did they split up?" he asked, because while he wasn't surprised that Blanche and her men had stayed together, he was surprised that she would let Adrian go alone.

The Green Lady shrugged. "Dunno. I was waiting at your room; I just saw them leave."

Oh. That made a lot of sense actually. "Right. Okay. Uh... Are they all still okay?"

From what he could see of her face, she was smiling. "Everyone was walking."

...That was a good sign, right?

She led him all the way back to the original conference room, which made something twitch in Josh's stomach. Why would Adrian still be talking to the hunters? But he couldn't hear any voices inside; was the room soundproofed or were they no longer talking? And if they weren't talking, what happened?

She stopped at the door and ran a couple of fingers down the locking mechanism. The light turned green and the door clicked open. She pushed it open with the same hand and looked back at him. "Here you go. Have fun."

Josh stepped a single step into the room and saw Adrian staring out the window with the large floral armchair at his right hip. A quick glance around told Josh that no one else was in the room, which made that twitch in his stomach turn into a rock and then sink.

He stepped further into the room, and immediately she huffed, "Finally," from behind him, and let the door close. It shut right on his ass, bumping him forward a bit. He grunted at the impact – rude! – but instead of complaining, he just watched Adrian, who had his arms crossed tight against his chest and a scowl on his face.

Something was wrong. This wasn't what Josh had been expecting. He didn't know what he'd been expecting – honestly, a large part of him had been pretty sure that the Woman was gonna take him down within minutes of seeing him – but he knew it wasn't this: the team split up and Adrian alone.

Two thoughts struck him in response to those observations: one – divide and conquer. That must have been the hunters' plan; easier to take them all down – and two – but Adrian wasn't alone. He had Josh, as pathetic as he was.

"Aid?" he called, taking another step into the room.

Adrian flinched like he'd been shocked, and then his head snapped around. His face was pale -- not quite gray yet, but definitely not healthy -- and his eyes were dark with bruises underneath. His shoulders slumped as he recognized Josh, and he exhaled. "Oh. It's you."

"Dude, what the hell?" Josh walked farther into the room, keeping his distance from the table – not really sure why he didn't want to touch it, but decidedly not wanting to touch it – and moving towards him. "Where are the others, where are the hunters, what are you doing here?"

Adrian blinked once, then twice, and then turned around to slump back against the window. "He wanted to talk to me about my powers. He said he had ideas or something… And then a couple of them took the other three to another room to discuss their options or something? I don't…" He shook his head and closed his eyes. "He said I was wasting my potential."

Josh paused at the armchair, his hip resting against the arm. "What do you mean?"

Adrian swallowed and slowly sunk down, down, down against the window until he was sitting on the floor. He opened his eyes and stared at the wall across from him. "My potential. He said he'd been looking at my powers for a while, trying to figure out how they worked. And he thinks I can do more."

Josh didn't want to sit in the chair, where The Woman had been sitting just a little while ago, but he also knew he should sit down since his head was beginning to ache again. He compromised: he lowered himself onto the floor, using the chair as a backrest and folding his legs under him. Adrian had his stretched out, and this way they could each keep their space while knowing they weren't alone. "Do you need to talk it out?"

Adrian pressed his lips together and his eyes grew cold. "I don't want to give him the time of day."

"Except that you're staring out a window and overthinking things." Josh sighed and reached up to readjust the strap of his camera. It wasn't crooked, but he needed to do something with his hands. "C'mon, dude. How much do you really understand about your powers? If he made you listen anyways, you might as well get what you can from it."

Adrian didn't say anything for a long time, just breathed in and out. Josh waited for several long seconds and then pulled out his phone. He could totally play Candy Crush while he waited, right? It wasn't rude if he was just giving Adrian space, right?

"What does Google say a shadow is?" Adrian asked suddenly.

Josh blinked once, then twice, then minimized his game. He pulled up an internet browser and googled what's a shadow. He waited and then, "So, it's a dark area formed when light from a light source is blocked."

"Right. Or – and this is what the doctor was saying – another way to think of it is if a shadow is some essence of an object. Since a shadow can only be formed by an object, it must carry a bit of that object in its creation. So: some kind of shadow essence. And my ability to manipulate a shadow is actually me playing with these essences." For the first time in minutes, Adrian glanced over at Josh and met his eyes. "Follow me so far?"

Josh blinked once and tucked his phone back into his coat pocket. "Sure." Why couldn't Adrian just shrug his shoulders and say, 'Cool, shadow powers.' Wouldn't that make everything so much easier?

"Well, if that's the case, then once I've manipulated that essence, I don't really have limitations on how I change them." He paused for a moment. "Well, no. I definitely have limitations, I just haven't even come close to reaching them yet. Anyways, if I can change a shadow into a blanket... Why can't I change it into a hammer?"

Josh frowned, squinting his eyes at him. "Wait, a hammer?"

Adrian nodded. "Yeah. A tool. Why am I always throwing blankets at people—"

"Sometimes you use crazy tentacle arms too," Josh reminded him. "To grab people."

Adrian shrugged a shoulder. "Okay, but they're basically cylindrical blankets."

"I mean... If you wanna think about it... Most things are just different shaped blankets."

Adrian stopped. Something about his expression told Josh that he was in the middle of an epiphany: his eyes were unfocused and far away even as his gray face brightened from some inside light. "Oh," he said quietly. "Oh, that's what he meant."

Josh leaned towards him. "So, like... the doctor wasn't completely crazy?"

Adrian frowned, but not in an angry way. It was thoughtful and soft. "No, he... I think he may be right..."

Josh waited for a few seconds for Adrian to finish that sentence, but when he didn't: "But only about your powers, right? Not about the whole helping them and letting them research you, right?"

Adrian turned to face him fully, a slightly offended expression on his face. "Oh, no. No. They're obviously insane. But, it's like that crazy prof you get who's clearly a bigot, but also knows the best ways to memorize the periodic table – take what you can and screw the rest, right?"

Something warm grew in Josh's chest and it finally overcame the nausea in his stomach. He said, "Yeah, totally. I had one of those last semester."

Adrian smiled a bit and nodded, eyes falling away and looking at the floor. "Different shaped blankets…"

Josh let him be for a solid ten seconds, and then said, "So. Uh. Where did they go?"

Adrian struggled out of his blankness. "Hm?"

"The doctor and the hunters. Where did they go?"

"Uh… I don't… know. He said he'd let me think things over and that he had things to do, and that he'd be back to check on me later."

Josh frowned. "Wait, so he just left you here?"

"I'm pretty sure they locked the door."

Josh squinted at him. "Are you sure? I've always been able to leave a hotel room."

"This isn't a hotel, Josh; it's a bad guy's headquarters."

Josh groaned as he pushed himself up into a standing position. Ugh, his head. "Are you sure it's their headquarters? I mean, really? They had receptionists."

Adrian got to his feet as well, scowling again. "Deering, just because you think a girl is cute doesn't mean that she's not a bad guy—"

"Dude, I told you, she's not ev—"

At which point, suddenly and extremely loudly, an alarm shrilled through the room.

Chapter Fourteen: Of Fencing, Fighting, and Fingerprints

The sound vibrated through Josh's skull, sending whatever relief he had been feeling right out the window – he was right back to the car and the pounding and the bright light behind his eyes. Immediately, his hands flew to his ears and his eyes screwed shut, trying to block out what he could. He bent over in half, trying to get some kind of cover as the alarm rang on and on and on and on…

"Josh!" Adrian was saying. "Josh, it's just the fire alarm; you need to breathe!"

Another fire alarm. All he'd been hearing for the past day were fire alarms – if it wasn't for the concussion, maybe he'd be desensitized by now. As it was, Josh just inhaled and exhaled several times and finally gasped out, "Why?"

"I don't know," Adrian answered, because Adrian understood. "Something must have happened outside this room. Since we didn't hear anything, it either happened far away or the room is soundproofed. Either way, we've got to get out of here first."

"Right," Josh breathed. "Right, okay." He forced his eyes open and focused on Adrian's worried face. "So, we'll leave."

Adrian made a face – it looked like a strange mix of relief and exasperation. "Josh, the door is locked."

"You checked it?"

"I don't need to check it – it's their headquarters; the door is obviously locked!"

Josh stared at him. "Dude, my head hurts too much for this. Look, we need to get out of here, right?"

Adrian made a face but nodded.

Josh gestured towards the door. "Plan A." Then he gestured towards the windows with his other hand. "Plan B." He dropped his hands to his sides. "Honestly, I don't think we'll survive jumping out the windows; super soldiers we are not."

Adrian glared at him for a few moments – the alarm blared and blared and blared. Finally, he huffed once, almost inaudibly over the fire alarm, and stalked over towards the door. Josh followed him, giving him space, and watched as he reached out for the door handle. He turned the handle and gave it a pull.

Nothing happened. The alarm kept blaring.

"What if you pushed it?" Josh asked.

Adrian shot him the dirtiest look he'd sent yet – and he'd sent Josh some doozies. "That's not how this door opens."

Josh shrugged his shoulders, then winced, closing his eyes. Man, his head. "Just… try it anyways, man. Please."

Adrian didn't answer, and for a moment there was only the ringing of the alarm. Then there was a huff and something that sounded like a shove. "Nothing, Josh. The door swings inside, and it's locked."

Josh breathed. He hadn't known until today that it was possible to feel nauseous from a headache. "Then you've gotta unlock it, Aid."

"With what key, Josh?"

"With a shadow key." Josh forced his eyes open and stared at Adrian meaningfully. "You're gonna make a shadow key."

Adrian's mouth dropped open a little. "You've gotta be kidding me."

Josh gave a very loose shrug. The alarm's constant blaring was really messing with his everything. "I thought we just agreed that you could make different shaped shadow blankets. Now's the perfect time to try it."

"The perfect— Deering!" Adrian snapped. "Are you listening to yourself? This isn't the movies; I don't know how to pick a lock – and weren't these key-card doors anyways; how do you even pick a key-card door?!"

He was babbling. Josh squinted at him. He'd never heard Adrian babble before. "Dude, are you panicking?"

Adrian pressed his lips together for one second, a stark comparison to his wide eyes, and then: "I swear to God, if you say 'dude' one more time, I'm gonna punch you."

Josh leaned back slightly. "Oh my God, you're panicking."

Adrian clenched his fists. "No, I'm not. I just don't understand why you're so damn fixated on these shadows blankets and this stupid door!"

Josh squinted at him again. It didn't help his head at all, but it didn't hurt it either. "Aid. We both agree we have to leave this room. This stupid door is our only way out. I have a concussion, a camera, and a crappy cell phone.

You have health, powers, and a brand-new epiphany. One of us is the hero in this scenario, and one of us is the comedic sidekick. Guess which one gets to open this stupid door?"

Adrian breathed for several long seconds. He inhaled for a long time, held it, and then exhaled. He closed his eyes and did it again. Josh let him; the alarm rang on, Adrian breathed, and Josh continued to be grateful that he hadn't eaten that granola bar Adrian had offered him, because he probably would have thrown it up right now.

"I still have no idea how to pick a lock," Adrian finally said, voice very tight. Good, he had himself under control.

"Maybe you could, like… just shove the shadows in and hope for the best?"

Adrian closed his eyes and rubbed his forehead with one hand. There was a small part of Josh that felt bad that Adrian had seemingly developed a headache, but the rest of him kind of felt like maybe he had a better idea of how Josh had been feeling for literally hours. "Dirty joke aside," Adrian answered – and wow, Josh must be totally out of it if he'd missed that one – "what if it makes the doorknob explode?"

"Well, then it'd be totally awesome." Josh curled his hands together at his chest and then splayed them out in jazz hands. "Boom!"

Adrian stared at him for several long seconds. "I hate you," he droned, but then turned towards the door. He squinted at the door handle, and then cast a look at Josh's feet. "Scooch over a bit, would ya'?"

Josh shuffled over back towards the windows, where the late morning sun was still shining through. Almost immediately, Adrian made a tugging motion with his hand, and Josh's shadow rose into the air like a snake.

Josh frowned at it. "That's new."

Adrian didn't answer; instead he guided the shadow into the small hole inside the door handle. He squinted at it, and then tilted his head to the side, kind of like a curious dog. "Honestly, Deering, I have no idea what I'm doing here. How do you even pick a lock?"

"Dunno, man. Isn't something supposed to click or something?"

"How am I supposed to hear clicking over this alarm?" But even as he spoke, Adrian crouched down and put his ear next to the lock. He was silent for several seconds and then, "Deering, what the hell am I looking for?"

"Dude, I dunno." Josh watched this go on for a couple more seconds, a single, finger-like shadow twisting inside a lock, and then: "Is it just me, or does this somehow seem suuuuuper sexual?"

Adrian flinched violently. "Josh, I swear to God—" and then he stopped. He pulled his head back, squinted at the door handle, and then reached up and turned it, pulling it towards them.

The door glided open with ease.

Josh's jaw dropped open. "Dude. You did it. You actually did it."

Adrian was just staring at the door. "Yeah. I did."

"You opened the door." Josh stared at it for another moment and then: "Should we, like… leave?"

"Oh, yeah, yeah," Adrian blurted, pushing himself up on his feet. He strode through the door, Josh scrambling at his heels.

The hall was empty, which was the only good thing as the alarm was sounding just as loudly out here as it had been in the room and was also accompanied by emergency lights flashing in strategic places where the wall met the ceiling. Josh squinted at a certain one a few feet away from them and understood that those lights would be super useful if it was dark out, but since it was late morning, they were mostly just epilepsy-inducing. Like, they seriously made his head spin if he looked at them too long.

"Ugh," he grunted, closing his eyes and turning his head away. That was a dumb move, Josh. Don't stare at the weird, flashing lights.

"Alright, Josh, which way?"

"Huh?" he mumbled, lifting his head and peeling his eyes open. Adrian was looking down to their right as if something was going to magically appear at the end of the hallway. A giant sign maybe? Who knew.

"Dylan and Alden: which way?" Adrian clarified, his voice hard.

Josh pressed his eyes closed for a moment, trying to focus. "Uh, left; this way." He turned back towards the elevators, back the way the Green Lady had taken him, back to where Alden and Dylan were waiting for them. He started moving with Adrian right at his side. "What about the others?" he asked.

"They seem to be pretty self-sufficient," Adrian answered – and the man was right. Who was leaning on whom for help anyways? "Besides, they're probably the ones that set off the alarm in the first place."

Josh thought about that for a second: "Huh. You're right."

"Why are you so surpri-" and Adrian stopped; mid-word, mid-step.

And Josh fumbled to a halt too because there right in front of them, halfway down the hall that stretched to the other conference rooms, was the Angry Dude.

He stood there, hands already in fists at his sides, glaring at them from many feet away. He rolled his shoulders and spoke.

Josh couldn't hear him over the sound of the alarm. "What?" he shouted back.

The Angry Dude frowned – Josh could tell even from here – and called back, his voice louder. Josh made out something like, 'worth… trouble… no?'

Josh raised his hands and waved in the space around his ears. The alarm blared on and on and on. "Dude! I can't — the alarm, y'know?" He made an exaggerated shrug. "Sorry!" he shouted.

"You are the biggest asshole I've ever met," Adrian said, and he almost sounded proud.

"I dunno, man," Josh said as the Angry Dude huffed and started stomping towards them. "I think I'm pissing him off even more."

"Yeah, you're pretty good at that," Adrian agreed, already spreading his hands at his sides.

By now, the Angry Dude was stepping into the clearing where the elevators were. "I said!" he shouted, his voice deep and furious. "That you guys aren't worth the trouble!"

"Hey!" Josh called back, cupping his hands around his mouth. "I heard that! Keep going, you're doing great!"

"Asshole," Adrian repeated, his voice admiring. Josh squinted as a shadow seemed to start growing from behind the man stalking towards them.

The Angry Dude let out some strangled growl/yell of rage – the kind of sound a very stressed retail worker makes as soon as they've entered the Employees Only room to look for something a pretentious customer has demanded they search for the week before Christmas – and then grabbed a very large potted plant and lifted it over his head.

"Whoops," Josh said, taking a step back.

"Nah," Adrian said calmly. "We're good."

And even as the man made as if he was going to heave the pot and plant at them, the shadow slithered across the floor and wrapped its way tight around the man's left calf.

"Aw yeah!" Josh shouted, clapping his hands together once.

The Angry Dude looked down at the shadow tightening around his leg, inhaled a deep breath, and then shouted: "El!"

And then: the lights shut off and the alarm went silent.

Something inside Josh – mostly his crazy, spinning head – sighed with utter relief, even as Adrian spat, "Shit," because apparently his shadow had mostly been comprised of artificial lights, not natural – c'mon, dude, live a little greener.

The Angry Dude grinned a kind of psychotic grin

(it reminded Josh of the Woman's smile, honestly. Like, predatory), centered the potted plant in his arms, and then chucked it.

As it sailed through the air at them, Josh was suddenly reminded of those Youtube videos Alden had shown him of big, burly men tossing tree stumps. It seemed a lot less ridiculous now that something was soaring through the air towards him, quickly getting larger and larger and—

"Move!" Adrian shouted, and suddenly there were hands shoving Josh to the left, and he slammed sideways against the wall, squashing his left arm and knocking his throbbing skull, and then a smash! as the potted plant crashed into the floor just inches away from where he and Adrian had been standing. The ceramic pot shattered, and Josh yelped as his lower legs were bombarded with shards of pottery and dirt littered the floor and his shoes. From the corner of his eye, he watched the small palm-like tree sway once, twice, and then topple sideways, landing with a soft oof right in front of Adrian's legs.

Josh stared at it. Adrian stared at it. Then Adrian inhaled a long, slow breath and raised a hand, curling his fingers into weird, weird motions. Slowly, a wisp of shadow caused by the sun's beams through the windows of the elevator lobby hitting the tree rose out of the ground, like a snake out of a snake-charmer's basket. Josh heard a curse and then heavy footsteps, and he looked up to see the Angry Dude stalking towards them.

His heart clenched in his chest even as his head gave another unpleasant throb. "Uh, Aid?"

"Give me a minute, Deering."

A distraction. Oh, God, Adrian wanted Josh to distract

the Angry Dude. Josh put a hand to his chest, trying to steady himself, when his palm fell on his camera. It was solid underneath his hand, real and comforting. He remembered then what it was that started all this mess – or at least what dragged him into this mess. A photography project and a creepy ol' muse. A creepy ol' muse who had helped him out and was now asking for help himself.

Josh's fingers curled around the camera, feeling the familiar buttons he knew better than he knew his own face. Sliding some mechanisms and clicking on a button, thumbing the cap off the lens in an easy flick, he called, "Hey, asshole."

And just as the Angry Dude's head snapped over in his direction, in a move that gave him the self-given nickname of The Flash, Josh raised his camera and snapped a picture of the man's face with his flash turned all the way up.

The first flash snapped into the man's eyes and as he yelped and raised his hands up, Josh kept snapping. He used one hand to steady himself against the wall as the other arm stretched out and snapped picture after picture of the Angry Dude's face twisted into blind agony.

"Ha," Adrian huffed beside him, and Josh glanced over to see Adrian's hand close around the handle of a very long, very thin shadow sword. The tip dipped down slightly, like the blade was too heavy for itself.

Josh was so shocked he actually stopped clicking. "Dude. What the hell?"

"Shut up, Deering, and let me riposte." Adrian settled himself into some kind of defensive position? Maybe? Josh didn't know, but it wasn't a normal standing position, that was for sure. He took a deep breath and then, as the Angry Dude shook off the last of the flash and raised his head, Adrian jolted forward and stabbed the man in the chest.

"Whoa!" Josh blurted, pressing himself against the wall, clutching his camera like an old lady might clutch her pearls.

The Angry Dude let out a hiss of pained breath, and when Adrian pulled the blade away, the black shadow glinted in the sun's light. Josh glanced over and saw a pinprick of blood staining the Angry Dude's shirt.

"Whoa," Josh repeated, a little more reverently.

The man glared at Adrian under surprisingly well-groomed eyebrows. Actually, now that they were so close to him with pretty decent lighting, it was obvious that the Angry Dude was not a slob. He seemed to care about his appearance at least a little, since his hair wasn't overgrown and his beard, although full, was shaped.

Josh's chest lurched the same way it had upon seeing the Woman stare out the window, the same way it twisted at the Man in the Vest and the Man with the Tattoo's knowing and fond smiles at each other, the way it ached at seeing the Green Lady's unfocused eyes. It took him a second to understand it, but then: empathy? Was he feeling a connection to these people that had hunted him and his friends across state lines? Why? Why couldn't they just be evil?

"I fucking hate fencing," the Angry Dude said with a groan, rolling his shoulders.

Josh squinted at him. "Wait. That sounds like you get fenced a lot."

Adrian looked at him sideways. "Please stop talking to the bad guy."

The Angry Dude ignored Adrian and stood up straight. His shadow went sideways, and his shoulders were broad. "Every second person that went to that damn Port Haven school fences. Didn't they have any other sports?"

Adrian frowned at him. "It was supposed to teach us precision and patience."

The man scowled. "You can learn that with baseball too! I mean: who fences anymore?"

Adrian's frown grew. "I do." And then he took a quick step forward and stabbed the man again.

"Ow!" the man spat, stumbling back a step. "Stop that!"

"You just threw a fucking tree at us!" Josh yelped, suddenly feeling the need to come to their defense. "That's totally worth a couple of stabs! At least!"

"Probably three," Adrian agreed, and then stepped forward and stabbed the man in his left bicep.

The man hissed out a breath, braced himself, and then squinted at them. "Do that again. I dare you."

Adrian narrowed his eyes, and something moving from behind the Angry Dude caught Josh's eye. "Alright," Adrian said. "I accept." And then he darted forward, making to stab him again.

This time the Angry Dude caught the sword in his hand, curling fingers over the blade. Josh winced – wouldn't that cut into your palm, dude? – but the guy just glared at Adrian and yanked him towards him.

A couple of things happened at once: Adrian stumbled forward; the shadow sword kind of melted like ice cream over a cone; that thing that caught Josh's eye moments before slid quickly across the floor; and the Angry Dude made as if to headbutt Adrian.

(Which was super rude. What were they, cavemen?)

But thankfully, the sword melting made his grip loosen and his sudden lack of possession of anything Adrian made him falter. Which was all Adrian needed to catch his footing, and direct the shadow zooming across the floor up over the Angry Dude's back and wrapped around his face.

Josh inhaled sharply as Adrian did some weird flick of his wrist and suddenly the shadow blanket around the man's head kind of solidified and tightened. Josh watched as the man tried to get his fingers under the shadow and yank it off, but he couldn't seem to get a grip. He began to tug and scratch at it, the whole time his chest heaving for breath as angry, muted sounds escaped from the shadow covering.

Josh felt sick to his stomach as this went on, as the Angry Dude struggled and pulled and panted, and Adrian watched with straight back and careful eyes. After a very long time – seconds? A minute? Josh didn't know; too long – the man fell to his knees and his hands seemed clumsy and heavy, slapping at the shadow more than anything.

Josh took a step forward and grabbed Adrian's sleeve. "Aid. Aid, let him go."

"Not yet," Adrian said very carefully, eyes very focused. The hair around his temples was dark with moisture, and Josh realized with a jolt that Adrian was using his powers as they spoke.

Slowly – oh God, it took forever! – the man fell on the

floor, limp and still.

"Oh my God, you killed him," Josh breathed.

Adrian tilted his head to the side. "Not quite." And then he waved his hand and the shadows slipped off the man's face, like Adrian was pulling the covers off of a bed. Beneath them, the man's face was still and calm – and huh. He was pretty normal looking once he wasn't so angry.

Josh waited until he saw the man's chest rise and fall once, twice, three times.

"Dude," he breathed. "That was dark."

Adrian sent him a very sardonic look. He curled his hand, almost like he was gathering something up, and the shadows still lingering around the man's body lifted off the ground and hovered in the air like some kind of soccer ball. He reached for it, and the moment the tips of his fingers touched the floating shadow ball, they melted into a kind of snake that slid over his fingers, down his hand, and curling around his wrist like a punk, Velcro bracelet left over from middle school.

Josh blinked at him. "What the hell?"

Adrian was just looking at the bracelet, twisting his arm to examine all parts of it. "It's all just differently shaped blankets," he misquoted, his voice soft. "It's much… easier, now that I'm not fighting it."

"That seems like a common theme in hero quests," Josh said, because he really didn't know what to say.

Adrian looked up from admiring his own work, his arm falling to his side. "I'm not a superhero," he snapped. He looked down, made a face, and then took an exaggerated step over the Angry Dude. Or. Sleeping dude now.

Josh rolled his eyes. "You're totally a superhero." Instead of following Adrian's lead, he inched around the man on the floor, keeping his back pressed against the wall. "You're basically Luke Skywalker."

When Josh looked up, safe on the other side of the man, Adrian was scowling at him. "Seriously? Skywalker?"

Josh nodded. "Yeah, definitely. Dylan is C3PO and Alden is R2." He started walking down the hall, towards their friends.

Adrian kept pace like Josh knew he would. "And who are you in this crazy scenario? Princess Leia?"

Josh stopped halfway through the lobby, his heart throbbing in his chest, and looked straight at Adrian. "You seriously think I'm cool enough to be Princess Leia? Really?"

Adrian's shoulders inched towards his ears and he pointedly did not meet Josh's eyes and kept walking, striding past him. "Sure, why not?" His voice was determinedly casual – which meant he wasn't feeling casual at all.

Josh stumbled forward, catching up. "Dude! That's the nicest thing I've ever heard! She's totally badass!" He thought about that for a second. "Wait, you think I'm badass?"

Adrian shrugged his shoulders, eyes straight. "I mean. You did tase the Woman. And knock her out with a bookbag."

"Huh." Josh thought about that for a second and then grinned. "I'm a badass." Then he stopped, because: "Dude, it's this door."

Adrian paused, having walked a little bit past the door. He turned slowly, casually, his eyes narrowed. "You're a pretty awful guide."

Josh shrugged. "Concussion!" he reminded him as cheerfully as he could manage.

Adrian paused at the door, frowned at him, sighed a little sigh, and then stared at the lock. He looked at it for a few seconds and then said, "Two things."

"Okay."

"First: I'm pretty sure this is gonna be a trap."

Josh thought about that for a moment. "I mean. Yeah. Probably. But like… Dylan needs to destroy his brother at video games, so… We kind of need to save them."

"Oh, I know. I just want it to be known that we're walking into a trap." He shot a side-eye at Josh. "Since, you know: concussion."

Josh nodded. "Consider it known."

Adrian nodded back. "Okay, second thing: Is this another key card lock?"

"Uh… I think so?"

Adrian sent him another dirty, dry look (which sounded like something Josh had totally heard someone on TV order as a drink: a dry, dirty… something), and said, "That lady unlocked it for you earlier, didn't she?"

"Yeah, but she just like—" and Josh ran his fingers over the little black box in the same way that Green Lady had. "And then: beep!"

Adrian's forehead wrinkled. "You mean it was fingerprinted?"

"No, no, no, dude. She's got electricity powers." Josh pointed at the ceiling. "She's the light flicker."

Adrian's shoulders – which had been up by his ears – relaxed. "Oh. Okay. Then…" and he focused back on the lockbox, and the shadow punk bracelet slid off his wrist and flowed over the back of his hand as he reached out and touched the box. The shadow slipped down, flattening as it went, kind of like a key card.

Josh waited a second, feeling something in his chest swell. "Dude, I just want you to know that I'm like crazy proud of how much you've grown. You're barely even sweating!"

Adrian exhaled very slowly through his nose even as the box bleeped green. He straightened up, reached for the door handle, and said, "Get ready."

He swung open the door and kind of half stepped in, half stepped aside so Josh could join him. And even though Josh was pretty useless, he still appreciated that, for the moment at least, he wasn't the sidekick.

He stepped up to join Adrian, and then paused.

Because the Woman was filing her nails.

She was sitting in one of the big spinny desk chairs, slightly to the right of the end of the long conference table. Behind her, back in the armchair, was Alden whose head shot up at the sound of the door opening. At her feet Dylan was kneeling and wrapping Alden's wrist, his expression worried and pissed.

"Josh!" Alden yelped, trying to stand.

"Don't," the Woman said without even lifting her head.

Alden stopped, halfway standing, her left wrist still clasped in Dylan's hands. She stared at the Woman's casual position and slowly settled back in the chair.

Dylan watched her entire action and then looked at Josh without saying a word.

Josh tried to smile at them, but his eyes kept going towards the Woman. Her nails were extended, long and pointy and black, and her legs were flung over the arm of the chair, swinging idly. He felt himself frown at her, because here she was being effortlessly cool and evil, and all they really wanted to do was go home safe.

"Sorry for interrupting," Adrian drawled, and Josh couldn't help the huff that escaped his mouth.

The Woman sighed a long sigh and examined her nails. "Honestly, this whole thing is such a shitstorm," she said as if she really didn't care. "I don't even know what that man is thinking. You guys obviously aren't ready for recruitment." She shrugged a single shoulder. "Time to move on."

Josh squinted at her. "This is seriously the weirdest monologue I've ever heard."

She looked up at him and her lips quirked up in a half-smirk. "C'mon, boys. There's nothing really villainous here." She turned, letting her legs drop off the arm of the chair and land on the floor. "I just like hurting people. It gives me some kind of hormone or pheromone rush." She shrugged again, resting her arms on the chair's arms and swinging slightly back and forth. "I don't really know which; the doctor thinks it's all very fascinating. Like my body is rewarding me for using my ability. Some kind of evolution thing." She rolled her eyes and then pushed herself up onto her feet. "All I know is that it feels good to hurt people." And her smile grew wider. "So, guess what they hired me to do?"

Adrian stared straight at her, his expression the kind that Josh would have titled: Determination IV. "Do you like getting hurt too? Because if not, this might be unpleasant for you."

Josh turned and stared at him, actually wondering if he'd heard him correctly. "Unpleasant? Seriously?"

Adrian eyed him quickly and then focused on the Woman again. "What?"

Josh couldn't stop his head from shaking. "We really need to work on your trash talk."

"Let's not," the Woman said; and she hooked her foot around one of the legs of the chair and did some weird sideswipe so that the chair went sliding and spinning right at Josh.

Josh did the only sensible thing: he yelped and flung himself to the side. Even as he did so, a voice in his head that kind of sounded like both Tori and Adrian whispered, God, you're such a drama queen.

He landed poorly in a crumbled pile a couple of feet away from the door (ow. Seriously: concussion), and the door slammed half into its frame and half into the wall.

"Josh!" Alden yelped.

"Shut up," the Woman growled – and then there was the sound of action happening.

Josh groaned and rolled away from the door, mostly just wanting to get away from Adrian so he didn't have to worry about him. By the time he'd gotten to one knee and one foot, head raised, he could see Adrian had turned his wrist shadow into some kind of small shield jutting out of his arm and using it to block the Woman's swipes, slowly trying to direct the two of them away from Josh.

Josh turned his head. There was Dylan's jacket on a chair between him and the conference table. He saw Dylan standing up, one hand curled around Alden's arm, and Alden half-standing from the chair, both of their expressions a mix of horror and awe. Right, Josh thought. They've never seen Adrian's powers like this. Which was all well and good, but right now Adrian needed help.

He locked eyes with Alden and raised his hands in a couple of quick movements: Up, up, get up, girl. She seemed to get it, because she got up on her feet. A quick glance at the floor: not enough shadows yet. He gestured to the left, directing them that way, long, slow sweeps of his hand. Slowly, careful, don't draw attention.

It worked; the two of them inched along the window. Josh stopped watching them, keeping an eye on the floor, measuring shadows. As soon as they were long enough (at least, he hoped they were long enough) he held up a hand to stop them. He got to his feet, stepped over to the spinny chair that had tried to kill him, not taking his eyes off of the fight – swipe, block, swipe, block, swipe against Adrian's torso, wince, step back – pointed with his other hand at the shadows, and then cried, "How's that, Aid?"

Maybe it was a stupid move, but he figured the risk was worth it. And it was, because Adrian glanced over quickly, but the Woman turned her whole head in Josh's direction. Then, as both pairs of eyes followed the path Josh was pointing towards, Josh grabbed the chair's arm and hurled the whole chair at the Woman, sending it spinning across the floor.

He didn't really think it was going to work, so when it missed its target by several inches, separating the Woman and Adrian rather than hitting her, he wasn't surprised or upset. Because it had done its purpose: it had distracted her.

She stepped nimbly away from the chair, shooting it a dirty look at it slid past her and banged into the table behind her. She snapped her head towards Josh and said, "Are you serious?"

Josh shrugged, wide and loose. He took a step to the left, keeping his eyes on the Woman. "I mean, worth a shot, right?"

She sneered. "I swear, you're the most pathetic—"

Josh took another step and reached out a hand.

"—waste of a—What are you doing?"

Josh paused, his hand on Dylan's jacket. "What?"

She took a step towards him. "What the hell do you think you're gonna do with that? Hit me with it?"

I mean, you guys took my taser, so… "Uh. Yeah. That was pretty much the plan," Josh admitted, fingers curling in the fabric.

She blinked at him, arms loose at her sides and mouth slightly open. "Did you actually think that was going to work?"

"Not really," Josh admitted.

"Then wh-?"

Which is when Adrian, who this entire time had been gathering Dylan and Alden's shadow, stepped behind her and beaned her with a shadow bookbag.

The Woman gasped, lurching forward in pain. She stumbled, caught her footing – and Josh pulled the jacket to his side, already striding forward – and turned, glaring at Adrian, hands outstretched. "I swear—"

Josh whipped the jacket at the back of her head – it was denim; he would never again mock Dylan's layered dressing style.

The Woman gasped, tilted like an unstable sandcastle, and Adrian hit her again with the bookbag. Then Josh hit her with the jacket: back and forth, one side with the bookbag, other side with the jacket, until she fell backwards, legs crumpling beneath her.

"I hate—" she gasped, which is when Adrian hit her again, and again, and again, and finally, as she fell to a slump on the ground, again.

They waited, both weapons still ready, as the Woman lay motionless. Josh counted to twenty before he said, "Is she…?"

Adrian's voice was low and shaky. "I think so. Should I hit her again?"

"Maybe once more to be sure," Josh agreed.

Fwam! The bookbag came down on her head and then shattered like a black icicle, with the pieces of shadow sliding down her head, neck, and shoulders like running water.

Adrian fell to his knees beside her, panting. Josh looked over at him, and God, his face was gray and the hair around his temples and forehead was wet. "That would have been so much easier with the taser," Adrian gasped.

Josh relaxed, panting back at him. "I was thinking the same thing! We're, like, the same person."

Adrian looked up wearily, still bent over his knees trying to catch his breath. Then, in a very dry, deadpan voice: "Sure, dude. We've, like, totally bonded."

And Josh couldn't help it: between the adrenaline, the fear, the aching head, and heavy chest, he burst out into giggles as his legs collapsed underneath him.

Chapter Fifteen:
Of Threats, Terror, and Taking Off

"Um." Alden's voice broke through Josh's giggles. He looked up from where he sat on the floor to see her and Dylan standing right where he told to them to stay. "Are you guys okay?"

Josh couldn't help it; his eyes fell to their body language. Dylan had one arm wrapped around Alden's shoulders, tugging her into his side, and she had curled herself into him. Great. Just great.

"Don't tell me you guys had a moment," he groaned. "Please, please don't tell me you guys have made out while I've been thrown into walls. 'Cause, like. That would be totally unfair."

Dylan's face immediately went blood red while Alden relaxed, scoffing and rolling her eyes. "Unfair? You know what's unfair, Joshua? Watching you be unconscious for multiple hours. Now that is unfair."

Josh thought about that for a serious second before: "Isn't it more unfair for the person that's actually unconscious?"

"No," Alden finished, her voice curt as she strode across the room. She stepped over the Woman without any fear before dropping to her knees and wrapping her arms around his neck. "Thank God you're okay," she whispered, pressing her face into his shoulder.

Pretty much everything in Josh's body hurt, but he still had enough energy to wrap an arm around her and return her hug. "Thank God you're okay," he countered. He hid his face in her hair for a few seconds, breathing in her mostly okay self. They would be okay. He could almost believe it now.

"Man, Cross, you look awful."

Josh raised his head to see Dylan clapping a hand onto Adrian's shoulder; thankfully, it didn't look like a hard clap, but it still made Adrian sway a little.

Adrian huffed a breath. "It's been a really long day," he admitted.

Dylan nodded. "Think we can get out of here?"

"Adrian figured out how to make keys now," Josh said, grinning with whatever energy he had left. "So we should be okay."

Alden's head popped up; her face creased with a frown. "Josh! Seriously? We can just frisk her!" She waved at the Woman's still form.

Josh froze. Maybe it was pathetic of him, but he super didn't want to touch her. She had hurt him enough already; what if she jumped up like a zombie?

Dylan must have seen the fear on his face, because he cracked a smile back at him before stepping over to the Woman, kneeling down, and digging through her jacket pockets.

"Dude, be care—" but Dylan raised a key card between two fingers, getting back onto his feet. Oh. She really was out. Cool.

"C'mon," Dylan said. "Let's go." He held out a hand for Alden, and she took it, accepting the pull up to her feet, and then threaded their fingers together.

It was disgustingly cute. Josh felt his head throb and stomach roll at the sight. "I might actually hate you guys," he said.

"Bite me," Alden said, scrunching her nose at him.

The two of them walked over to the door hand in hand. Josh looked over at Adrian, who by now was also sitting on his butt staring at their friends. Josh huffed out a laugh and said, "Yeah, Aid, let's go. No big deal."

Adrian sent him a sardonic look of, Can you believe them? He heaved a big, heavy breath before forcing himself up to his feet. It took a few seconds and he looked pretty unsteady, but he was standing. Which is more than Josh could say.

He exhaled a long breath, gathered his strength, and pushed his feet underneath him and then the rest of his body up. Soon he was on his feet too, swaying a little. A few seconds later, Adrian had grabbed his elbow and held him still. "We could pretend we're in a three-legged race?" he offered in a low voice.

Josh chuckled a little. "Yeah, dude. That sounds good." And with that, they slung their arms over each other's shoulders, and stumbled over to the door that Dylan had already opened.

Alden was glancing down the hall, kind of like a careful watchdog, while Dylan held the door open for them. "You guys actually look terrible," he said, frowning at them with sincere concern. "Maybe I should—"

"I don't think a first aid kit can solve exhaustion," Josh

said. He clapped Dylan on the shoulder as they passed him. "But thanks, man."

Alden pointed back the way they came. "Elevators, right?"

"Yup," Josh said.

Alden led the way, which was actually really stupid, but Josh and Adrian were kind of useless right now anyways. From here, the form of that Angry Dude was still lying flat on the floor and quite visible. Alden paused, looking over her shoulder and said, "Uh... Are we sure he's out?"

Josh nodded, because what else was there to say?

"It's been a long day," Adrian repeated as they passed her. Josh wasn't sure what use they'd be, but Adrian probably felt better leading the way. Once they stepped into the lobby, Adrian stumbled to a stop, almost bringing him and Josh to the ground.

Not that Josh blamed him, because leaning across the way next to the elevators was a very tired looking Marcus. At his side, body ready for trouble and eyes sharp was TJ, while Blanche was frowning at the up/down buttons for the elevator.

TJ exhaled loudly and said, "Oh thank God, you're okay."

Marcus opened his eyes while Blanche spun around. She gasped out, "There you are;" while Marcus said, "Hey, guys," before closing his eyes again.

Josh frowned at Blanche. "I thought you found things; whaddya mean, 'There you are'? Haven't you been looking for us?"

Her mouth opened a little, and then, amazingly, she

flushed red. "I mean… Kind of?"

"Kind of?!" Josh repeated.

"Wow," Alden said from behind him. "I feel loved."

TJ shrugged a big shrug. "We knew you guys would be okay."

"Dude!" Josh gasped, straightening up, accidentally almost shrugging Adrian's arm off his shoulders. "That's such bullshit! There's three special yous, and only one special us! How is that fair?"

"Hey!" TJ scowled, pushing himself off the wall. "We just had to deal with some psycho lady with freaky electricity powers; she was shocking us with televisions!"

Josh pointed at the Angry Dude still lying several feet down the hall. "Aid had to take down him and that sadistic woman with the nails! That's two against one!"

At this point, the elevator beeped and opened its doors. Blanche sighed and gestured towards it. "Maybe we can continue this inside?"

TJ growled an angry breath but pulled one of Marcus' arms over his shoulders and led him inside the elevator. Adrian and Josh stumbled inside with Alden and Dylan right on their heels. Blanche slipped inside last and faced the doors, finger reaching for the M button and then the CLOSE button.

As the doors slid shut and the elevator stuttered to a start, a part of Josh started feeling kind of bad. They'd all had bad days; he really shouldn't be getting mad because theirs had been slightly worse than theirs. Besides, trying to get out of here was probably gonna be a group effort and they really couldn't afford division at this point in the game.

"Sorry," he said, frowning at the floor. "Concussion. It kinda makes me grumpy."

TJ exhaled a long breath. "Yeah, I'm sorry, too. We should have looked for you harder. We, uh. We're not used to having a bigger crew yet. It's been the three of us for awhile now."

"S'cool," Josh said. "We weren't really looking for you guys either."

Adrian rolled his shoulders, slipping his arm off Josh's shoulders and out from under Josh's arm. For a second, Josh felt sad; why'd he have to do that? "Now that we've all made up," he said, "how awful do you think it's gonna be down there?"

Oh. Because he was preparing for battle and needed to focus with some personal space. Made sense.

"Like a seven," Blanche said. "I think we've already took out their hard hitters. I have literally no idea what the other three can do."

"Bet'cha Hannah would know," Marcus mumbled.

Josh frowned and swayed a little back into Adrian. For once, the guy didn't shrug him off. You're a good man, Adrian Cross. "Where'd they go, anyways?"

"Who knows?" TJ answered, shrugging the shoulder that wasn't holding up Marcus. "They've been their own team even longer than we have. Sometimes they just… forget about us."

On Josh's other side, Alden sighed a big sigh. "Can I just say that you guys are terrible at teamwork? Like, you guys would all fail if this was a class and there was an exam."

Adrian glanced over at Josh, and Josh caught it and

basically read his mind: There is a class, and this is an exam, and you'd better hope we don't fail.

Josh reached out and squeezed Adrian's shoulder… and then hung on because it was rather difficult to stand on his own. Which is when the elevator 'beeped!' and the doors opened with a soft 'whoosh.'

There was quiet for a few seconds before Blanche set her shoulders, whispered, "Okay," and then stepped forward.

"God, she's ballsy," Josh muttered. Even as the words slipped out of his mouth, he thought, I didn't mean to say that.

Alden shot him a very disgusted look. "God, that's sexist," she countered before she stepped forward right on Blanche's heels.

Dylan followed, kind of in a hurry, which Josh respected because Alden was in that kind of a mood where she was just argumentative which was just dangerous. TJ helped Marcus limp out of the elevator behind them, and Adrian looked over at Josh.

Josh said, "I'm cool, dude. We got this."

Adrian frowned. "Can you even stand?"

"Sure," Josh said, leaning even further into Adrian. "Forward, march!" He waved a hand before him like he was encouraging them forward, but it was much limper than he meant for it to be.

Adrian seemed to take this all in for a second, sighed a bit, moved one of his feet forward to stop the elevator doors from closing on them, and then wrapped his arm back around Josh's shoulders and steadied him before stepping out. The elevator doors had closed behind them before they'd taken ten steps. But ten steps into the main lobby was enough to make Josh's breath catch in his throat.

The cute girl – Mariatu – was still standing behind the reception desk, but her body language screamed severe discomfort from the way her hand played with the collar of her shirt, her eyes focused on a corner Josh couldn't really see all that well, and her limbs were poised as if she was ready to move suddenly if the situation required it. Blanche, TJ, and Marcus had stopped at the small tables and chair near the door, glaring at the edge of the TV and corner of a loveseat that Josh could see. It was actually a very inconveniently designed hotel lobby in that a good quarter of it was cut off by a half-wall that shut off the elevators and a washroom from the rest of it. Alden and Dylan were standing, eyes wide, between the three 'special' people and the Emergency Exit (God, but those red letters shone just enough to hurt Josh's eyes) on the wall opposite Josh and Adrian. They were staring at the same corner as the other three were.

Josh swallowed and looked at Adrian, who was surveying the room too. Adrian glanced over at him quickly, gathered his breath, and then walked them over to the edge of the corner of that half-wall, where he stopped.

Because, sitting in one of the loveseats with a remote in his hand and frowning at the flat-screen TV, was Dr. McCallum. He looked exactly the same as he did in that conference room – definitely not like he'd engaged in any kind of fight. In fact, when Josh took a second look, he realized that there was a phone pressed up against Dr. McCallum's ear. In the corner couch beside him were the

Man with the Tattoo and the Man in the Vest. The Man with the Tattoo sat facing Josh's friends, an amused smile on his face, with one arm stretched out across the back of the couch, one ankle resting against the other knee as if everything was super casual. The Man in the Vest sat near the corner of the couch, facing the TV but not actually paying any attention to it. Instead he was frowning softly at the notebook in his lap – his legs were crossed – and fiddling with a pen in one hand. There wasn't any attention paid to Josh and his friends, if you excused the Man with the Tattoo's eyes; but he didn't look like he was in any hurry to stop them.

Josh took this all in, inhaled slowly, then turned his head to whisper into Adrian's ear, "Why aren't we leaving?"

"'Cause we're waiting for your friends," the Man with the Tattoo answered.

Josh jumped in place; he could have sworn he whispered that.

The Man with the Tattoo's amused smile shifted into a smirk as his eyes glanced over towards Josh and Adrian. As they locked with Josh's, he suddenly felt like he couldn't move – he shouldn't move – and he wasn't even sure he was breathing. Then the man blinked, the paralysis slipped away like Adrian's shadows, and the man said, "You're not that hard to figure out, kid. Take a breather; he's gonna be a bit."

Josh stared at him, then turned to his friends who were all staring at the man as if he was a tiger or something crazy like that. Josh looked over towards the doors that opened to the outside world, and said, "No, seriously, why aren't we leaving?"

Which is when Dr. McCallum pulled his phone away from his ear, smashed an angry finger against the screen – Josh watched as the Man with the Tattoo leaned towards the Man in the Vest and mutter something to him – then sat back into the loveseat, turning a glare at something behind Josh and Adrian. "Who allowed a gun into this building?"

Josh turned his head, wondering if he was snapping at Mariatu (because not cool, man), but instead noticed Holly standing next to an Employee's Only door behind the desk. She looked shaken for the first time since they'd met (admittedly, Josh hadn't spent a lot of time with her), and she said, "I-I'm very sorry, sir, but there aren't any guns—"

Which is when, of course, the Emergency Exit door slammed open and Erik stepped out, a gun aimed right at Dr. McCallum's head.

The Man with the Tattoo's eyes shifted to Dr. McCallum. "Told you he was the dangerous one."

When the door had slammed open, Alden had squeaked and curled into Dylan, who had pushed her behind him. Beside them, TJ and Marcus seemed to brighten and strengthen right up, while Blanche's body posture seemed to lose some of its tenseness.

"Give me one good reason I shouldn't shoot you right now," Erik said, his eyes trained on Dr. McCallum.

Behind him, Hannah's head peeked out, and a hand rested on Erik's shoulder. Seeing Hannah was okay – there wasn't a single mark on her face – Josh felt a knot that he didn't know he was carrying loosen inside of him.

She seemed to whisper something in Erik's ear because his eyes darted between the three men on the couches.

Dr. McCallum relaxed into the cushions, his expression easing. "Because right now you're potential. Kill me and you're a liability."

Erik's aim didn't waver, but several feet away from him, Blanche turned back to face the doctor. "Explain," she snapped.

The doctor sighed a heavy sigh; Josh couldn't believe he didn't seem concerned about the gun aimed at his head. "It's like I told you: we want to help you. Your powers are not only incredible but incredibly dangerous. Every single person we have found has had difficulty managing their powers, often to the point of damaging themselves or people they care about."

Adrian flinched; it was a motion that shuddered through Josh seeing as they were still leaning on each other for support.

"All we want is a chance to work with you; a mutually beneficial arrangement where we help you explore and stabilize your abilities, and in doing so, better understand humanity." Dr. McCallum spread his hands and shrugged, something close to a smile on his face. "It's all very simple."

Again, Hannah leaned in to whisper something in Erik's ear; he flinched at whatever she said, but still kept his focus on the doctor. "You have large claims for those who attack and hurt others." Erik made a small gesture with the gun that somehow managed to encompass everyone who wasn't part of the bad guys. Josh wished he knew how to do something like that. "From the looks of it, you take very little mind to those in your care."

A scoff from the couch caught Josh's attention again: the Man with the Tattoo was practically grinning, even as he leaned forward with both feet on the ground and elbows on his knees. The Man in the Vest looked amused himself.

Meanwhile, Dr. McCallum sighed a heavy sigh. "As I have explained to your friends, in order to fully understand the scope of your abilities, the flight versus fight—"

"Ja, I got that," Erik interrupted, which caused the doctor to glare at him. "I just think it's stupid to damage potential recruitments. What kind of loyalty are you trying to gain?" He shook his head. "Recruitment by fear only works if you can maintain the threat. We," and he made that gesture with the gun again, "are stronger than you. The threat is minimal. In fact," and he raised the gun a little more, shifting it slightly, "I can shoot you right now and the threat is gone."

"You think we're all there is?" Dr. McCallum retorted. "We're merely a small group; a room in a manor, if you will. Hurting us will put a target on your backs—"

"Uh, you may not have noticed," TJ interrupted, drawing everyone's eyes, "but we've kind of taken down three of your guys. If 'hurting you'," and Josh could hear the quotation marks in his voice and suddenly felt a splash of laughter and pride, "puts a target on our backs, then..." He shrugged too, fairly easily since Marcus was no longer leaning on him. "Seems to me that target is already there."

"They won't stop watching you," the Man in the Vest said quite suddenly. Josh looked over at him, the way he leaned back in his seat with his notebook closed on his lap. "Once you are in their sights, they will never take their eyes off of you." He shrugged; unlike the doctor and TJ, it was a smooth, elegant motion, like something a dancer might do. "Perhaps you are used to that, however; perhaps it's something you can handle in your day-to-day lives." His eyes hardened. "Perhaps not."

"We're not the only ones watching you," Dr McCallum added. There was a difference between their tones – while the Man in the Vest seemed rather indifferent, the doctor seemed sincere and encouraging, almost like he wanted to help them. "There are others with resources to find you, and they won't take you quietly. They'll kidnap and torture and take whatever information they can from you, and then toss you aside once they're done. But we genuinely are trying to make the world a better—"

"Fuck you," Adrian snapped.

Josh couldn't help it; he breathed out a laugh and a smile, because God, was he ever proud of Adrian. Someone had to say it; and that it was Adrian? Even better. Like the hero's final stand of defiance or something.

Dr. McCallum was scowling and glaring, and he bit off, "Look—"

"If you don't wanna join us, you don't have to," the Man with the Tattoo said, cutting the doctor off. He exhaled, settling back on the couch. "But we weren't kidding when we said they won't ever stop watching. They'll watch and wait until the moment is right, and then they'll sweep in and take you anyways. You can run and argue all you want, but the fact is: different is dangerous, and danger? Has consequences." He shook his head. "If they don't get you, someone else will. Or…" He exhaled, glanced over at the Man in the Vest, and then back at them, eyes sweeping over the group. Josh felt something knot in his gut again. "They'll go after your families. And then they'll get you."

There was quiet for several seconds, and Josh watched as Blanche, TJ, and Marcus exchanged glances and silent words, as Erik slowly lowered the gun a few inches, Hannah whispering quickly in his ear. Josh could still feel Adrian leaning against him even as he leaned back, and he could feel the tension in his body.

And then Josh caught the eye of Dylan. He watched as Dylan looked around, glanced back at Alden, inhaled, and then said, "For once, I'm gonna go with what Josh said. We're leaving." And then, with one hand curled around Alden's good wrist, he started for the main doors.

Dr. McCallum nodded, twisted slightly in the loveseat he sat in, and pressed a couple of buttons on the remote he still held. "That's fine. Admittedly, you're not our main concern, Dylan Christopher Bohyer-Hart."

Dylan paused where he was, maybe ten steps away from the main doors, and Alden's head snapped back to look at the doctor. Something she saw made her gasp, and Josh wished he knew what made her go so pale.

"…son of Michael Bohyer and Elizabeth Hart, brother to Kyle and Megan." Dr. McCallum paused, tilting his head to the side; it looked like he was watching something on the TV at Josh's shoulder. Josh tried to angle his body to look at the screen without pushing Adrian away; it wasn't exactly working. Maybe if he'd taken yoga or something, he'd be flexible enough to move in desperate situations like right now.

"And I would get a doctor to take a look at that wrist, Alden Elizabeth Gwinn, daughter of Samuel and Caitlyn Gwinn," Dr. McCallum continued. He paused before adding, "I am sorry about that, but sometimes accidents happen."

Alden stared at the TV screen for another few moments; God, Josh wished he could see what was on it. She swallowed once, then straightened her shoulders. "Let's go, Dylan. I wanna go."

Dylan, who had been watching the TV screen too, kind of shuddered, readjusted his grip on her wrist. "Right." He looked over at Josh, eyes questioning and a little scared, and then he turned back to the door and kept walking.

Josh glanced over at Adrian. "Are we leaving?" he asked quietly.

Adrian looked back, set his jaw, and said, "We sure are." And with some teamwork, an elbow here and a shoulder there, they readjusted themselves and stepped forward to follow Dylan and Josh. A couple of steps towards the doors put them at an angle where Josh could look over his shoulder to see the TV screen.

And then he stumbled, because right there was the same photo that had been at his dad's desk for the last decade: his mother leaning against a beautiful weeping willow tree with a toddler Lilly on her lap who was laughing as an elementary school Josh tickled her and their father held one of their mother's feet in his lap, a gentle smile on his face.

It was a strange sensation, as if the world had dropped and Josh was left on an island. He could hear the others whispering, could even hear Adrian saying, "Oh… Oh hell;" but it wasn't really registering. All Josh could really think of was Lilly. What if they find Lilly?

"How odd that your parents neglected to give you a middle name, Joshua Deering," the doctor was musing. He wasn't even bothering to look at him, that bastard! "Although, I'm sure Bridget was able to convince Alexander that it wasn't a big deal. Or, perhaps they couldn't come to an agreement on what name would work; either way, they seemed to come to a consensus for your little sister, Lillian Grace, didn't they?"

Josh inhaled slowly, very slowly. Then, as the screen changed to a newer picture, one taken just last year at Josh's high school graduation, with him in that awful gown and cap, Lilly hugging his waist and cackling with glee, his dad with a proud hand on his shoulder, and Jennifer gently touching his other arm, he felt something steel inside him. He knew what it was; he'd felt it what seemed like weeks ago (but it was only days ago, wasn't it?) when he'd first met the Woman: that determined, I'm probably gonna die, so I might as well go down belligerent, feeling.

"Your stepmother seems appropriate, however," the doctor was saying. "Strange that she kept her name though…"

"Keep walking," Josh said fairly loudly. He gave Adrian a shove with the arm he had slung over his shoulders and took a hard step forward. "Just keep moving, dude. They're just blowhards."

"They're not exactly the strongest people around," Dr. McCallum mused. He didn't even flinch at Josh's excellent burn. "Wouldn't even take much to scare them."

Adrian wasn't moving, so Josh gave him another shove. "Dude, move. We can't do anything here and my head is killing me, so move."

"Not like your family, Adrian Dominic Cross," Dr. McCallum said; and Adrian planted his feet and stopped like a stubborn animal. Josh stumbled again, almost losing his footing.

"That's enough," Adrian whispered, and there was something about his voice that made a shiver run through Josh's chest.

"Large family, isn't it? We're still trying to understand why it is that some evolutions run through a family, and others appear seemingly randomly. There must be a common thread though; perhaps your niece or nephew will turn out to be like you…"

Even as Josh was thinking, Oh man, that's just mean, Adrian had inhaled deeply, body tense and growing tenser. The shiver in his chest spread until it almost felt like there was a cold wave washing over his entire torso, not entirely unlike being covered in one of Adrian's shadow blankets.

"Aid, c'mon," Josh whispered. "Just ignore him." He could see something moving in the corner of his eye, could hear whispers like overhearing someone's too-loud music through their earbuds, but he focused on Adrian's darkening face and almost terrifying eyes.

"Either way, it'd be prudent to keep an eye on them," Dr. McCallum said. "And if they do present early in life, not unlike yourself, well… Children see the truth more clearly than adults—"

"I said enough!" Adrian shouted; and he spread his

arms, basically throwing Josh off of him, and the world changed.

It was far too fast for Josh to completely understand what was happening: the lights went out with the immediate suddenness of a power outage without the zoom that accompanied it, shadows burst out of the corners of the room like the tentacles of some kraken sea creature, and gasps sounded before being cut off with strange gurgles. The whole thing took a couple of seconds, and a room that had previously been filled with life, and the quiet noises that no one really noticed, was silenced.

Josh, sprawled out next to Adrian, elbows having hit the floor – the scrape of friction and jolting of surface against surface made him gasp – and, legs limp and akimbo, closed his eyes to take a moment to breathe through the dizziness of the sudden change in position. Cursing this concussion (would he be useless forever?), he opened his eyes and his jaw dropped.

The room was filled with shadows. Everything was dark and shifting as if the room was alive. From where Josh was sitting, he had a clear view to the front door -- or what used to be the doors. Instead, the wall and doors were coated in rippling darkness, and Dylan and Alden – who must have been just about to pass through the doors – were wrapped in shadowy tentacles past their noses. All Josh could see were their terrified eyes, foreheads, and hair; and he could see their eyes going glassy and their skin paling right before his eyes.

He twisted towards Adrian. All he could see were his legs, so his eyes focused on the background figures of Blanche, TJ, Marcus, Erik, and Hannah. They were wrapped and coated just like Dylan and Alden. He blinked hard, focused back on Adrian's legs, and followed the line of his body up until he reached his face, a face that was gray and twisted in pain and anger and grief, and two arms outstretched on either side, limbs shaking and fingers curled.

For a brief second, he noticed that there was roughly a four-foot radius of shadow-free land around Adrian. A couple of inches away from Josh's right fingers, the shadows shivered and rolled like waves on a pond.

"Aid," he croaked. He struggled to sit up with his head spinning and sharp pain spiking at the back of his head. Once up, however, he reached out with a hand and gripped Adrian's pant leg. "Aid, let them go."

Adrian snarled. "No." His eyes were focused on whatever was behind Josh; Josh realized, remembering the layout of the room, that was where the doctor and those two men had been.

He tugged harder, terrified at what Adrian might do. "Aid, you're suffocating them; let them go."

"Not. Yet," Adrian bit out, eyes narrowing in concentration.

"Aid, it's not just them, it's everyone! Aid, you're choking them all."

That seemed to catch his attention; his eyes glanced down to Josh for a quick second before raising and focusing again.

But it was enough to spark hope in Josh's chest. "Aid, you're killing Blanche."

Adrian blinked, eyes becoming unfocused.

"Adrian, you're killing Hannah and Alden." Josh had

sat up and scooched over enough to grab at Adrian's shirt and was now tugging hard at it. "You're not a murderer, Aid, you're a hero; let them go."

Another second of Adrian wavering – Josh could feel him swaying slightly – and then he relaxed his fingers. He watched, not closely but enough to notice, the shadows slipping off Blanche's face and a chorus of deep breaths, followed by a range of panting and gasps. The room was still dark, however, and the floor and walls still quivered with power.

"Okay, okay, okay," Josh chanted, shifting so he could support Adrian instead of trying to pull him over. "Good, that's good." He could hear a guy gasping, What the fuck? and a girl going, Oh my God, oh my God, oh my God... He ignored them. He stared at Adrian and said, "Thank you for not killing them."

"Uh huh," Adrian grunted.

"Okay, step two." Josh thought as quickly as his aching head would let him. "Let everyone but them go." He knew that Adrian would know who 'them' were; he couldn't seem to take his eyes off of them anyways. "Pull the shadows off our friends."

Adrian's mouth opened slightly, and Josh waited for a few seconds until Adrian gasped, "I can't."

"You can't," he repeated.

Adrian shook his head. "I can't. I can't... focus."

"Okay... Then let everyone go."

"No." It was immediate and firm.

Josh frowned. "Aid, I don't think they're gonna go anywhere. You almost suffocated them."

"Doesn't matter."

Josh fell back onto his butt, trying to think of something. They had to go, and the bad guys had to stay here. That was literally all they needed to do. But if Adrian couldn't tell the difference between friend and foe right now…

"Aid?" He was thinking so, so hard right now.

"Josh?"

"Can you tell the difference between living and… not?" This was the craziest idea he'd ever had; this was so stupid—

"Uh…" And Adrian tilted his head to one side, frowned a little, then said, "Yeeeeees. I think…" And then his face creased, flinching away from a blow Josh couldn't see. "I can't—"

"Breathe," Josh instructed. "I need you to breathe—and I need everyone else to shut up!" he snapped, projecting his voice for a second. He focused back on Adrian. "I need you to focus on the living things."

"I can't—"

"Find Blanche," Josh said. "Find her crazy necklace; you know, that huge pendant thing."

Adrian closed his eyes and swayed. Josh grabbed him, moving a knee onto his foot as if that could steady the foundation. "Got it," he breathed.

"Good. Can we take the shadows off of her? Just, like…" Josh made a face at himself. "Let them fall off."

Quiet, the slight swaying of Adrian, and then, "Oh thank God." Josh took his eyes off of Adrian and peered around long enough to see Blanche on her hands and knees and free of shadows.

The hope that had been struggling in Josh's chest suddenly flared to life. "Dude! That was awesome! Okay, let's try Marcus..."

And slowly, gently, with shadows still quivering all around them, Josh coached Adrian through releasing each one of their friends: Marcus, then Erik (because Blanche had asked for him next), who quickly opened up a bookbag that Josh hadn't noticed before and jogged over to the couch. Josh wasn't quite sure what he was doing over there with Blanche, but voices that he hadn't been paying attention to were quieted. As they did that, Josh talked Adrian through TJ's release, Hannah's, Alden's, and finally Dylan's. With each person, the shadows in the room became a little lighter, a little stiller, and life noises returned like a hum of animation; Adrian grew grayer and the swaying grew worse.

When all their friends were freed, Josh looked behind him where Blanche, Erik, and Hannah were watching the three men. "Are they, uh—"

"They're contained," Blanche said, looking up at Josh. She looked off to the side, back towards the reception desk. "What do you wanna do with them?"

Josh looked in that direction, too. Both women were contained in tentacles, but while Holly was glaring at them, Mariatu had tear streaks on her cheeks and a scared frown. He said, "Can we contain Holly, but let Mariatu go?" He paused for a moment, then called over, "Did I pronounce that right?"

She breathed out a shaky laugh, but it did get a watery smile from her. "Yeah, that's right."

Blanche said, "You sure?"

Josh twisted around the other way and said, "Hannah? What do you think?"

Hannah turned to look at the two women, closed her eyes for a second, then said, "Josh is right. Mariatu is not a danger to us." She opened her eyes and looked over at Josh, smiling. "Good job."

He felt a flush crawling up his cheeks and turned back to Adrian before he did something stupid. "Alright, Aid. Just a few more."

Each person took a little longer. Once the women were freed, Adrian's legs almost gave out on him, and Josh had to scramble to his feet and hold him up. Slowly, he coached Adrian through releasing the doctor, the Man in the Vest, and the Man with the Tattoo; a quick look over there saw that all three were blindfolded, muzzled, and tied up. He squinted at them; what exactly did their new friends keep in their bags? And why?

"Okay, Aid. Now the room. Just… let go."

And Adrian exhaled a long, heavy sigh and closed his eyes. As the room lightened, the shadows fading like the sun was chasing them away, Adrian slumped forward in Josh's arms, body totally limp. Josh yelped at the sudden deadweight in his arms and, while he didn't manage to stop them both from hitting the ground, he did manage to control their fall so it wasn't painful.

He sat there for a few seconds, breathing through the headache, then said, "Okay. Can we go now?"

Epilogue:
Of Appetizers, Aftermaths, and Auld Lang Syne

"You're weak," Josh teased, shoving another mini cupcake in his mouth. Mmm, chocolate.

"Am not!" Lilly snapped, scowling with vanilla icing at the corner of her mouth. "You're just a cheater." She poked his right bicep, right where the scratches from the Woman were finally almost healed.

"Ow," Josh whined, shying away from her. "What makes me a cheater?"

Lilly rolled her eyes in a very dramatic fashion. Ahhh, twelve-year-olds. "Everyone knows that teenage boys have two stomachs." At these last two words, she poked him in the arm again: boop boop.

"Aw, Lilly, that's not fair. I can't help biology."

She poked him again – it didn't really hurt, but it was the principle of the matter – then reached for another mini cupcake. She grabbed vanilla again, leaving him the last chocolate one. She had her moments, he guessed.

"Jerk," she grumbled.

"Squirt," he retorted, reaching out and tugging at her braid.

There was a grumbling chuckle then, and they both turned to see an older gentleman – fifties? Sixties? How did anyone judge ages anyways? – in a very fine suit smiling at them. "Sorry, sorry," he apologized. "You two were just reminding me of my kids when they were your age."

Lilly brushed a hand down her dress, glanced down like some demure princess that she was not, and asked, "Were they as cute as us, too?"

Josh rolled his eyes as the gentleman released a few hearty ho ho ho's like a true grandpa. "I like to think so," he finally answered. He tipped a glass full of something that looked like wine at them, sent another smile their way, then said, "Happy New Year."

"Happy New Year," they chorused back.

Once upon a time, back when it was just Josh and his parents – and even those couple of years when Lilly was a baby – New Year's Eve was a small thing. Josh remembered it being them and sometimes a couple of Mom or Dad's friends, usually at someone's house who had a dog and other kids around Josh's age, and the whole thing was really chill. But when Josh turned fifteen, his dad had been promoted to manager of some bank, and suddenly New Year's Eve became a Big Deal, and Josh and Lilly had to dress nicely, and Josh had to babysit his sister because there weren't a lot of offspring around, and there was alcohol they weren't allowed to drink, and big talk about money and politics that Josh didn't care about, and a lot of questions about Josh's future plans. While it wasn't Josh's favourite holiday anymore, every year it got a little bit better as Lilly got older and more fun to hang out with.

Also, the food was always solid. While the big supper was usually a little too fancy for his and Lilly's liking, the appetizers (or hors d'oeuvres as the fancy people called them) were A+. Which was why in the last two years Josh and Lilly had created the game: Who Can Eat the Most Appetizers?

(Spoiler alert: it was Josh.)

However, this year Lilly was giving him a run for his money. Josh attributed this to two things: one, Lilly was finally entering puberty which everyone knew required all the calories; and two, Josh was still recovering from the events of two weeks ago (well, thirteen days, but semantics, semantics).

Josh still wasn't quite sure how it happened, but everything had turned out okay and no one was in trouble with any of their parents. This was, of course, partly because they were all adults by now (even if none of them felt like it), so their parents couldn't exactly ground them. But that hadn't stopped the lectures. Or concern. Or worried swats over the head and on their arms.

Erik had driven a freaked-out Dylan and Alden, an exhausted Josh, and an unconscious Adrian to Regional Health Rapid City Hospital where he left them in the Emergency Department before taking off to meet up with the others – Josh never did find out where. Thanks to school and parental units, all of them had some kind of health insurance, and were whisked inside to be diagnosed with a badly sprained wrist, a couple of bruised ribs—

("Wait, you've been walking around with bruised ribs all this time?!" Alden had shrieked.

"Apparently," Dylan had drawled, one hand on his chest.)

--a cut arm, chest, and head that required stitches as well as a mild-moderate concussion—

("What does that mean?" Josh had asked.

The doctor had looked uncomfortable. "Well, you're basically right on the line between the two," he'd answered.

"Cool," Josh had said, closing his eyes and wondering why he had to be so weird.)

--and an odd case of exhaustion and dehydration. Alden had been released that night, Dylan and Josh the next morning, and Adrian allowed to go once he finally woke up about six o'clock that night – almost thirty hours after the whole crazy shadow thing went down.

Amazingly enough, there was an airport in Rapid City, which made things much easier when it came to flying to their respective holiday abodes. Alden had gone to her very large family, Dylan in another direction to his smaller family—

("Dammit, I forgot to buy Kyle his game," he had groaned before stomping off to security.)

--Josh to his small family, and Adrian… back to school.

("You're not going home?" Josh had asked, standing in the security line (their flights were within an hour of each other's, so they'd gone through together).

Adrian had raised an eyebrow. "What home?" he'd asked; and Josh thought it was supposed to be a joke, but it didn't hit like a joke; just like a terribly sad fact. Adrian must have read it on his face, because he'd softened and said, "I haven't had a real home for years."

Which… hadn't helped at all.

"What about your family?" he'd asked.

That had gotten a double eyebrow raise. "After all

that? You seriously think I'm gonna visit my family after all that?"

Josh had swallowed, and said, "Well, maybe you can come home with me—"

"I'm not a stray, Josh. I'll be fine."

Adrian's words had registered then: "Wait. You think they'll go after us this soon? Like, our families? Maybe I shouldn't go—"

"Josh." Adrian's voice had been firm, and he'd placed a hand on Josh's shoulder. "You'll be fine. I'm the catch; you're just the bait."

It was weird feeling both reassured and offended. "Hey! I'm just as much a catch as you are!"

Adrian had smirked a small smirk and said, "Sure, Deering."

Before Josh had been able to defend himself, an airport security guy had said, "Boarding pass and ID, please.")

In between all of this had also been the creation of the story they'd have to tell everyone. Maybe they wouldn't have needed a story… except there was the whole hospital and destroyed car as evidence that something went down.

("You set Cory on fire?!" Alden had shouted at him.

"Okay, in fairness," Josh started, trying to defend himself, "Blanche was the one who told me to—"

"Oh, because we should all listen to weird special girls, right?" Alden had snapped. "No! No, we do not!")

But because none of them were particularly good liars, they stuck with something as close to the truth as possible. So, the official line was that they had lost control when they'd hit a patch of ice and ended up in the ditch.

This explained most of their injuries—

("I, uh, walked into a tree trying to get a good photo?" Josh had improvised when asked about his arm.)

--and the car. They'd been in South Dakota because they had friends that needed help moving since their home was about to be repossessed by the bank when they ran out of money thanks to a house party gone out of control.

("Why didn't you just tell me that in the first place?" Josh's dad had asked.

Josh had shrugged uncomfortably. "We, uh. We weren't really sure what exactly we were walking into. They were, uh, kind of embarrassed about the whole thing."

His dad had narrowed his eyes at him in, like, perfect suspicious father mode until Jennifer had stepped in and welcomed Josh home. She was pretty okay for a stepmom.)

So now everything was as okay as it was going to be, and the holidays had gone well, and Lilly was back to being normal instead of really worried about him, and in five days, Josh would be back to university fighting for drawer space with Dylan.

And that was okay. He was looking forward to the new year. He was looking forward to a quiet semester. Probably. Hopefully.

"Ooooh!" Lilly grabbed his left arm suddenly. "I think I see a cheese dip bread bowl."

"Oh! Where?" Josh stood up on his toes, trying to peer over people's heads.

"Guess," she shot back, and then bolted, sneaking and

slipping past people with the grace of an eel.

Josh was kind of proud while also being annoyed. He loved cheese dip bread bowls. He really wanted to find it, see how much was left.

Which was when his phone started buzzing in his pocket.

Josh wasn't a hundred percent sure how, but he'd gotten both Blanche's and Hannah's numbers. He didn't remember asking for them or passing them his phone, but he blamed the concussion for that. He'd also, through superior Facebook skills, managed to find Mariatu on social media. He'd checked in on her a couple of times to make sure she was okay and that she had cleared out of bad guy land. It turned out she was originally from New Orleans and was totally okay with finding a different hotel to work at, especially since she was doing a degree online. She'd heard of this one motel in Elba, Wisconsin that was looking for help and was going to give them a try, and Josh had said he was willing to be a character reference if need be.

Anyways, Josh stayed pretty on top of his phone these days, especially since he never knew who might be contacting him or for what purpose. But as he slipped his phone out of his pocket, he checked the screen and grinned before he'd even accepted the call. "Dude!" he said happily. "Give me a few; I've gotta find a quiet place."

"'Kay," Adrian said back, seemingly calm. This was good. Adrian deserved some peace and quiet.

Josh wound his way through the crowd, giving his dad a nod and Jennifer a smile when he caught their eye, until he reached the stairs. No one was allowed to go upstairs –

there was only so much floorspace his dad was willing to rent out for a party – but that just meant you could climb up several steps and then settle down for a bit of quiet. He did so, sitting just a couple of steps from the top where a large red ribbon closed off the upper floor.

"'Kay, I'm ready."

Adrian chuckled from the other side of the phone. "You didn't have to go to so much trouble. I was only calling to say Happy New Year."

"Little early for that, man," Josh retorted. "Besides," he said, looking over the crowd of people, "I needed a break. There are way too many people here."

"Thought you were just gonna hang with your sister."

"I am, mostly. But you can't ignore everyone, y'know?" Josh sighed, feeling a wave of peace wash over him. "I've got a pretty good view here 'least."

"Yeah, it's a pretty clear night here too."

Josh laughed. "Nah, man. I'm still inside. I just meant, y'know, when you look over a crowd and see all the different people and you feel above and outside it, but not in a bad way, y'know?"

"...You're wishing you had your camera, huh."

That was another thing: because his dad was basically the host, he didn't want his son hiding behind a camera. That first year, when Josh was fourteen, he'd been allowed to run around and take pictures of everyone with his brand new Nikon, and he'd felt important and like he was actually a part of something. But then came the promotion, and the fancy getups, and now they had professionals take the photographs for the bank's calendar or whatever it was.

But one day Josh would be a professional, and then *he* could be the event photographer, and his dad might actually be proud of him for being himself.

"Kind of." He shrugged. "Not really. I just... I guess there's something really comforting about going through hell and then seeing that the world hasn't really changed. Life keeps going for everyone else, which means it'll keep going for you, too."

There was silence for a few seconds and then: "Kind of like looking up at a night sky and realizing that the world is just a small bit of a huge universe, and whatever you're going through is nothing when you compare it to everything else." Adrian didn't sound glum though; he sounded like he was at peace. "Everything is going to be okay because up there are the same stars as there were thousands of years ago, and they've seen it all and are still shining despite it all."

Josh grinned, not able to help himself. "Well, don't we sound like two dumbass romantics."

Adrian laughed. "Yeah, basically." He was quiet again, and then: "But I do mean it, Josh. Happy New Year. I hope the next year is a lot better than this one."

"Aw, it wasn't so bad," Josh argued, rubbing at the slightly sore scratches on his chest. "I got into the photography program—"

"Bravo," Adrian said dryly but probably sincerely.

"Thanks," Josh said. "And we both made some new friends. And kept our old ones. No one I cared about died—"

"Interesting qualifier," Adrian mused.

"And my dad is finally off my case about trying Business!" Josh finished triumphantly. Mostly because Josh had fulfilled his end of the bargain, but Josh was willing to take what he could get. "So, I dunno. I think we kicked ass."

Adrian hummed. "Sure, Deering. We kicked ass."

"So. Yeah. Happy New Year, Aid." Josh smiled down at the mass of people, finding Lilly by another table full of food.

"See ya' in a few days, Josh."

"You too, dude." And Josh waited to hear the click of Adrian hanging up before he hung up too. He sat there, exhaling slowly, and watched the people, smiled at the lights strung out along the walls and ceiling, and hummed along to the music playing. Then he huffed out a breath.

"Dammit, Aid. Now I want my camera."

Author's Note

Josh and Adrian both started existing for me back in 2011: Josh worked at a small tourist trap where he coaxed ceramic figurines into behaving themselves as they sat stoically on the shelves, and Adrian hesitantly stepped in with a sword on his hip and a tragic prophesy on his shoulders.

Years later, Josh keeps the majority of his conversations with inanimate objects to himself, and Adrian's only history with swords is a fencing class he reluctantly attended (and only because it was too good of a detail from *Infinity* for me to pass it by). What's remarkable to me is how much of the characters have stayed true to that original concept I developed so long ago, and how much they've grown up, rather as if they have matured along with me.

Joshua Deering is nineteen because that's how old I was when I first imagined him and honestly, he has stayed fairly close to that first impression. He is still an artist struggling to find his place in a too-practical world, aching from the loss of his mother, and putting a grin on to hide his uncertainties. Adrian is twenty-three, because that's how old I was when I first started writing *Exposure*. In hindsight, part of the reason I could never get their story quite right was because I couldn't see what Adrian was – besides being something different. While the Engen-verse gave me a credible reason for Adrian's "other-ness", it was only personal experience that gave me the ability to do Adrian's character justice. If some of Josh's quirks are similar to the jokes I often make, if the songs he hums are the songs I love, then many of Adrian's contemplations and quiet determination are lessons and thoughts that only living can teach you.

Back in 2015, the creator of the Engen-verse asked me to write a story set in his universe (a compliment that I didn't understand back then but do now). I said I couldn't write a horror story; Matthew LeDrew told me to write a happy ending instead. So, to all of you, I offer you a happy ending – or, perhaps more accurately, a hopefully possibility. This is a story where the heroes are good because they choose to help one another. All of them have reasons not to reach out, reasons to hide and go at life alone -- and it would likely be a lot less risky. But instead they each make a conscious decision – actually, they keep making the decision over and over again – to care for another person even though it will cost them.

This is in no means a simple thing to do: it's something I aim for personally but often fall short of. But I believe that if we keep choosing to reach out and help, to offer a listening ear and a ready heart, we can make this world a better place by being here. And that's all I really wanted to express with this story…

…along with some bad jokes, a bit of laughter, and some hope. Because I think we could all use those too.

Special thanks to Matthew and Ellen for inviting me to be a part of Engen – both the company and the universe. I don't think any of us were expecting the result of befriending me in that English class, but I think it's turned out okay. Thank you Matthew Daniels for editing – you taught me about smoke detectors, how to properly set a car afire, and that it's about time I get over my fear of the "Track Changes" feature. Shout out to Terri for being my first reader and the big push I needed to finish this thing – thank you for loving my people as much as I do. And also to Keana, who is the reason Josh and Adrian exist at all (it's a long story, KK; ask me in person sometime), and encouraging me to write all these years.

God bless you all,
Erin Vance

ENGEN TIMELINE

With over twenty novels spread over three different series by many different authors, the Engen Universe of titles is growing every day and into genres we couldn't have imagined! From the original ten book *Black Womb* thriller series, its crime novel sequel series *Xander Drew,* our flagship adventure title *Infinity,* or single-novels like *Jacobi Street* or *light|dark,* there's something in the Engen Universe for everyone with more books by more authors on the way soon!

...But how do the events relate to one another, chronologically? While some astute readers have guessed at the potential timeline (some accurately, some not), we're going to finally set the question of the Engen Timeline to rest.

Turn the page for an up-to-date guide of the ever-widening world of Engen, featuring the works of Erin Vance, Ali House, Ellen Curtis, Andrea Hackett, Sarah Thompson, Jay Paulin, and Matthew LeDrew!

In the 10 Years Prior Black September

"Reptilia" by Matthew LeDrew
published in *light | dark* & *Collected Short Fiction*
"Reptilian" by Paul Carberry
published in *Undead Rebirth.*
Danger descends on a small secluded town in the form of a deadly virus with fantastic and terrible side-effects. Can a small group of doctors escape alive?

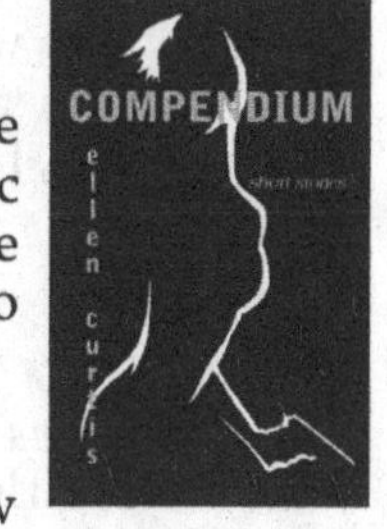

Compendium by Ellen Curtis
Three short stories forming the basis for the Engen Universe's ties to suspense, genetic engeneering, and the supernatural. Features the stories "The Tourniquet Revival," "Falling into Fire" and "At Midnight, the Dawn."

"The Theogony" by Matt LeDrew
published in *light | dark.*
A tale of young Theo Flaherty of the *Infinity* series and his time admitted against his will to the Black Springs hospital, where he learns to paint, and seeks out his father.

Black September

"Revving Engen" by Matthew LeDrew
published in *light | dark.*
A direct lead-in to both *Infinity* and *Black Womb,* Tasha travels to Coral Beach, Maine on a hot tip about a recently discovered young man with incredible abilities.

Infinity by Ellen Curtis & Matthew LeDrew
Faced with a destiny he's uncertain of, the enigmatic Victor must bring together four unique people with very special abilities… or face the tasks ahead alone. Guaranteed to excite!

Black Womb by Matthew LeDrew
Fifteen years ago, something happened in Coral Beach, Maine that resulted in the present death of a seventeen-year-old boy. Now four high-school students must try to solve the mystery… before the killer picks them off.

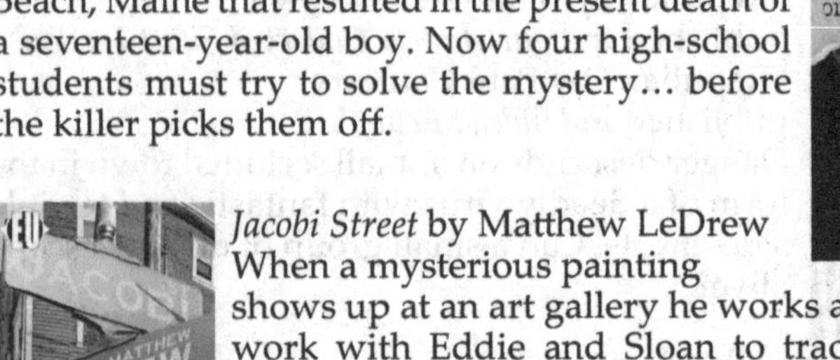

Jacobi Street by Matthew LeDrew
When a mysterious painting shows up at an art gallery he works at, Bob must work with Eddie and Sloan to track down its sinister origins and convince the people living on Jacobi Street of them, before its too late!

Transformations in Pain by Matthew LeDrew
When two girls are assaulted, the residents of Coral Beach must put their shared tragedies behind them and stop the man responsible, as well as unlock the secrets behind the true nature of the Womb…

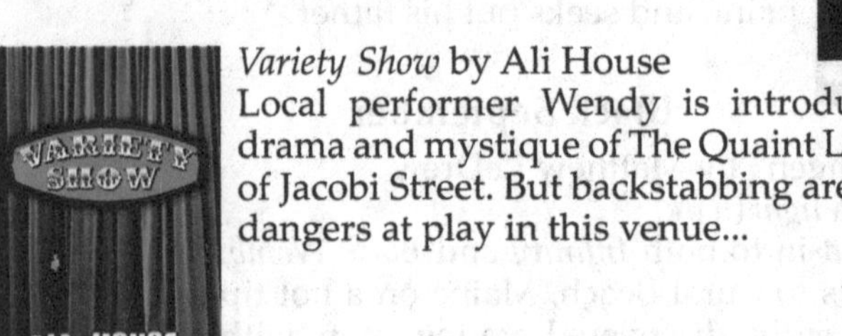

Variety Show by Ali House
Local performer Wendy is introduced to the drama and mystique of The Quaint Little Theatre of Jacobi Street. But backstabbing aren't the only dangers at play in this venue...

Smoke and Mirrors by Matthew LeDrew
The approaching trial of Genblade brings closure to the people of Coral Beach, until people start showing up dead in the same manner they did when he was at large.

"The Inevitable" by Ali House
published in *The Lightbulb Forest*
A young woman must contend with the emergence of a frightening new power alongside the emotional high of a first date.

The Tourniquet Reprisal by Curtis & LeDrew
A man lives in Atlanta, Georgia that people don't talk about, but everyone knows he's there. He arrived a year ago and turned a gaggle of uneducated youth into something new, something to fear.

Roulette by Matthew LeDrew
As the teen suicide rate in Coral Beach starts to climb astronomically fast, Xander travels to Los Angeles to fight his most terrifying adversary yet… and learns that the only thing worse than looking for release… is finding it.

Year One: November

Exodus of Angels by Curtis & LeDrew
Victor's enigmatic past is illuminated when Jaycee accompanies him to visit a new friend in the paliative care ward of the Black Springs hospital, where Theo also happens to be searching for a cure for Leigh.

The Irony of Glass by Matthew Daniels
published in *Undead Rebirth* and *Interstitches.*
Abby and Chad track down a man with the ability to project his emotional state to a remote town, and struggle to escape.

Ghosts of the Past by Matthew LeDrew
Coral Beach faces its most awesome threat when one of Engen's past mistakes is unleashed upon the unsuspecting populous. Friends and enemies unite to fight a common enemy… but will even that be enough?

Touch Your Nose by Matt LeDrew
Simon Monk must infiltrate the San Fransico branch of Shane Industries, a massive company with deep ties to the Engen Universe. Where do his true loyalties lie? And can he get out without causing harm?

Ignorance is Bliss by Matthew LeDrew
After being set through the ringer one too many times, Xander decides that his life with Julie needs a little more attention… which is bad news because a new villain has come to town with his sights set on Adam Genblade.

"Gristle While You Work" by Jay Paulin &
"Scarlett" by Andrea Hackett
published in *light | dark*.

"A Night to Forget" by Kelly Rose &
"New Employment" by Sam Bauer
published in *Undead Rebirth*.

Becoming by Matthew LeDrew
For months Xander Drew has been doing his level best to keep the streets of Coral Beach clean, which means it's time for the forces of darkness to strike back… all at once.

Inner Child by Matthew LeDrew
Julie is hospitalized with life-threatening wounds to both body and soul. But the real threat comes from the hospital walls themselves, as a demonic presence makes itself known to Xander and his friends.

"Comfortably Numb" by Ellen Curtis
published in *Undead Rebirth*.
Xander and Cathy spend an evening hunting the remnants of Coral Beach's gangs when Xander begins to lose control of the Black Womb, threatening their secret.

End of Year One

Gang War by Matthew LeDrew
The Tees, a homicidal gang of evil men, has finally been taken down by Xander Drew. But his victory is short lived, as retired Tees are mysteriously killed. With a town of suspects, anyone can be the culprit… including one of their own.

Chains by Matthew LeDrew
Sociopath Derek Smith has been freed from prison and is praying on the weak; and none are weaker than August Styles: a pregnant girl with Down Syndrome who has run away from home.

"Omega" by Ellen Curtis
published in *light | dark*.
A sinister division of Engen begins a series of experiments on pregnant women in a fashion eerily similar to those that created the original Black Womb project.

The Long Road by Matthew LeDrew
Xander meets the American people — and realizes that the world is harsh and wicked, but can also be soft and gentle, even loving. Xander Drew comes of age on the road, and sets his new direction.

Year Two

Cinders by Matthew LeDrew
Detective Horton enters a violent and dangerous world he didn't know existed beneath the veneer of order and structure that he has based his entire deductive method around.

Sinister Intent by Matthew LeDrew
One of the killers Detective Horton could not catch has resurfaced: a serial killer who flaunts his sinister intent in front of the Los Angeles Police Department, making it so that no one is safe.

Faith by Matthew LeDrew
Xander's mysterious and troublesome past returns to haunt him on the streets of Los Angeles; a place where even more people can get caught in the crossfire of the games of death and deceit that makes up his life.

Flickers in the Night by Matthew LeDrew
Lisa Rowdan is hunted by her haunting -- and powerful -- ex-boyfriend Ryan through a lonely city street. Can she escape him?

One of over twenty great sprine-tingling short stories!

Garden of the 8th Circle by Curtis & LeDrew
Victor brings Chad, Abby, and Alice into a dangerous conflict a decade in the making, fighting an out of control cult for the fate of a young soul. Meanwhile, Theo investigates a mysterious event in Los Angeles.

Family Values by Matthew LeDrew
Xander and his new friends Crowley, Lisa, and Tim investigate a series of kidnappings and murders that stretch back decades, all of which have the same similar twist: victims being found after years of being missing.

The Rats of Refraction by Curtis & LeDrew
When Abby and Alice's secret lives are discovered, they must defend their home and way of life with everything they have against the forces of Circe, a shadow agency that will stop at nothing to abduct people with supernatural abilities.

Fate's Shadow by Matthew LeDrew
When one of Xander's old cases comes up for trial, Megan Greene returns with it. The former friends are led into conflict regarding her client's innocence. However, they put their difference aside when they both become targets of the vigilante known as Shiro Gilbert.

First Aid by Matthew LeDrew
Xander takes his feud with mob boss Stephen Fields to the streets, and his attracts the attention of the *Infinity* team. Before the arrive, he'll have pushed the mob boss into an all out gang war, the likes of which the city will never recover from.

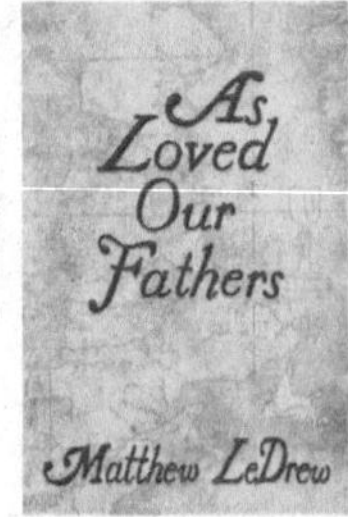

As Loved Our Fathers by Matthew LeDrew

Jona's plans come into view as he travels to the island of Newfoundland in search of a mystical item: the Holy Grail.

Gone by Curtis & LeDrew
Chad's sister has gone missing, resulting in him upending heaven and hell to get her back. His quest embroils him back into the dangerous world he'd hoped to escape, and unlocks the terrible secrets Jona has been investigating.

Moments by Matthew LeDrew
The Shane murders have been happening for months, dogging Xander at every turn. They've been happening for longer than even he knows, stretching back to the Black September. He's taken down Fields. He's taken down Murdock. Now the stage is set for this part of the story to also end.

Exposure by Erin Vance
Joshua Deering just wanted was to pass his final photography project. But that's not what happened. But hindsight is 20/20, and now creepy cemetery guy Adrian, Josh, and Josh's two friends are being stalked by nameless, violent strangers.

"The Port 13 Motel" by Erin Vance &
"Living Light" by Sam Bauer
published in *Undead Rebirth.*

The unlikely return of both Kemp and a cannibalistic serial killer to the Engen Universe.

The Future

"Remers" by Sarah Thompson
published in *light | dark*.
In the not-too-distant future of the Engen Universe, young athletes are the targets of a scouting program to create the next stage of super soldier with cybernetic enhancements.

Timeline I - V by Matthew LeDrew
published in *Undead Rebirth & Collected Shorts*
Faced with the death of his wife, Mikhail breaks the laws of time and space to find a way to save her, only to discover that her fate was sealed in the distant past...

ABOUT THE AUTHOR

Erin Vance is an editor and award-winning, best-selling author from Newfoundland, Canada.

In 2007 she won the Newfoundland & Labrador Arts and Letters competition with her short story "Something White." Since 2016, she has co-helmed the bestselling *From the Rock* series through seven volumes.

Her poem, *Rough Draft*, is featured in the Nelson Literacy 7 Homegrown (Newfoundland Edition).

She is creative, spiritual, and loves reading, writing, and anything to do with words. She currently serves as Editor-In-Chief of Engen Books.

Exposure is her first novel.

www.ingramcontent.com/pod-product-compliance
Lightning Source LLC
Chambersburg PA
CBHW011421010726
47494CB00011B/2441

* 9 7 8 1 9 8 9 4 7 3 8 2 5 *